JUDGMENT ON DELTCHEV

Eric Ambler was born in 1909 in London (where he lives now). Between 1936 and 1940 he wrote six classic novels – including *The Mask of Dimitrios*, which many consider his masterpiece – then spent six years in the British Army, followed by several years writing and producing feature films.

Since 1951 he has written fifteen more highly-acclaimed books of which two (*Passage of Arms* and *The Levanter*) have won the coveted Gold Dagger of the Crime Writers' Association. Eric Ambler's autobiography, *Here Lies Eric Ambler*, was published by Fontana in 1986.

ERIC AMBLER

Judgment on Deltchev

FONTANA/Collins

First published by Hodder and Stoughton Ltd in 1951
First issued in Fontana Paperbacks 1966
Fifth impression February 1989

Copyright © Eric Ambler 1951

Made and printed in Great Britain by
William Collins Sons & Co. Ltd, Glasgow

TO F. WITH THANKS

'Many things in your good people cause me disgust, and
verily, not their evil. I would that they had a madness
by which they had succumbed, like this pale criminal!'
NIETZSCHE: *Thus Spake Zarathustra*

*The characters in this book are entirely imaginary
and bear no relation to any living person*

Chapter 1

Where treason to the state is defined simply as opposition to the government in power the political leader convicted of it will not necessarily lose credit with the people. Indeed, if he is respected or loved by them, his death at the hands of a tyrannical government may serve to give his life a dignity it did not before possess. In that event his enemies may in the end be faced not by the memory of a fallible human being but by a myth, more formidable than the real man could ever have been, and much less vulnerable. His trial, therefore, is no formality but a ceremony of preparation and precaution. He must be discredited and destroyed as a man so that he may safely be dealt with as a criminal. Sometimes, he is induced to confess abjectly to the crimes of which he is accused; but, unless he has himself been a member of the party which now seeks to destroy him, such confessions are not always believed by the people; and when, for example, he is the leader of an unliquidated opposition party it is better to observe outwardly the old legal forms, to bring witnesses, produce evidence and let him try to defend himself.

So it was with Nikolai Petkov in Bulgaria, with Julius Maniu and Ion Mihalache in Rumania and with many other liberals in Eastern Europe. Petkov they hanged. Maniu and Mihalache were condemned to a solitary confinement for life. When Yordan Deltchev's trial took place the pattern for such occasions had been already set.

The charges against him were of 'treason and the preparation of a terrorist plot to assassinate the head of the state.' The trial began before a People's Court on the eleventh of June. He was described in the indictment as 'president of the Agrarian Socialist Party and formerly a member of the Provisional Government of National Unity.' In fact, he had been head of that government and also its Foreign Minister. He was still the leader of the only effective opposition to the People's Party regime that remained.

I had been asked to attend the trial and write a series of articles about it by an American newspaper publisher whom I had met once or twice when he had been visiting London. The request had surprised me. I had never written anything of that kind before and had thought at first that my name had been mistaken for someone else's. However, there had been no mistake and I had decided to accept.

At some time or other, I suppose, most writers who have never done newspaper work indulge in the belief that, should the occasion arise, they would make brilliant reporters. Some of them, of course, are right. My case is different. With a solemnity that in retrospect seems pathetic, I looked up an old *Times* article on Deltchev, bought some of the likely books and lunched with an economist who had once read a paper before The Royal Institute of International Affairs. I felt that I ought to learn something about the country I was going to visit, its people and its problems.

The odd part is that I did learn one thing. It was over that luncheon that I first heard about the Officer Corps Brotherhood. It was referred to as a kind of joke.

Originally, it seemed, this Brotherhood had been a welfare association formed to protect and to help financially the families of a number of army officers who had been shot after the Macedonian *Putsch* of 1925. The founders were brother officers of the victims and sympathetic to their cause; but they were not wealthy men and it was not long before some of them became convinced that the most honourable way of helping and protecting the bereaved families would be to kill those who had condemned their men to death.

By the early thirties the Brotherhood had become a secret society of reactionary extremists and been responsible for at least twenty-eight political murders. Moreover, it was concerned no longer with simple acts of vengeance but rather with eliminating potential sources of injustice which would later call for vengeance. As, in the Brotherhood's dogma, any politician or highly placed official with even remotely liberal ideas was a potential source of injustice, the problem of the Brotherhood became a matter of interest to all parties.

Attempts made by successive pre-war governments to bring actual murderers to justice and to suppress the organisation had been only partly successful because never quite wholehearted. It was easy enough to disapprove of the Brotherhood but courage was required to become actively concerned with an attack upon it. The Brotherhood had survived and, although its earlier 'officers only' membership qualification had been relaxed and psychotics from many other sections of the community had found it congenial, it had retained much of its traditional military background. The symbolic revolver and dagger of other Balkan terrorist organizations had become, for the Officer Corps Brotherhood, the symbolic rifle and bayonet; and, during the occupation, the Brotherhood had snobbishly preferred to collaborate with the German Army authorities rather than with the Gestapo.

This latter piece of discrimination, however, had not deterred the Provisional Government, set up after the liberation, from making the first serious effort to stamp out the Brotherhood once and for all. Emergency powers had been used to the full. Membership of the organization had been made a capital offence and arrests, summary trials and executions had continued over months. So effective, indeed, had been the Government's campaign that there was little doubt in most minds that the Brotherhood had been betrayed from within. However, interest in this aspect of the affair had soon faded. When, during the elections, there had been none of the usual Brotherhood murders, it had been assumed with general relief that the organization was at last dead and buried. Now, astonishingly, the corpse had been exhumed and was being declared alive. For, part of the case against Deltchev contained the incredible allegation that he, who as head of the Provisional Government had set out to destroy the Brotherhood, was in fact a member of it and the organizer of a plot to assassinate the head of the People's Party Government.

I left London at the end of May and arrived in the capital the day before the trial began.

Chapter 2

Over much of South-Eastern Europe the heaviest summer rains have fallen by early June and the hardening mud of the roads is being grated into dust. The tinted walls of the villages glow in the strong sun and the shadows on them are black and sharply defined. Only the higher Balkan peaks still have snow upon them. The corn is becoming tall and rich and, in the river valleys east of the Yugoslav frontier, the fields of roses and white poppies that you see from the train are alive with blossom. But in the cities, the air is humid, and the insects which swirl in the sunshine over the refuse in the streets or crawl from the dark recesses of hotel beds are in their lush heyday. At that time, the human animal has a strange feeling of lassitude; strange because, although the body is sluggish, the mind is uneasily alert, as if it fears that something is being prepared for its discomfort.

I was met at the Central station by my employer's local representative. His name was Georghi Pashik.

I saw him standing on the platform as my train drew in; a short, dark, flabby man in rimless glasses and a tight seersucker suit with an array of fountain pens in the handkerchief pocket. Under his arm he carried a thin, black dispatch case with a silver medallion hanging from the zipper tag. He stood by a pillar gazing about him with the imperious anxiety of a wealthy traveller who sees no porter and knows that he cannot carry his own baggage. I think it was the fountain pens that identified him for me. He wore them like a badge.

I know a lot about Pashik now. I know, for instance, that the black dispatch case which he carried so importantly rarely contained anything but a stale meat sandwich and a

9

revolver, that the seersucker suit was given to him when he was working in a Displaced Persons camp, that one of the fountain pens came from Passaic, New Jersey, and that those facts can be related directly to his death. I know now some of the ways in which his mind worked and of the strange fantasies that possessed it. Then, he was merely a name in conversation – 'our man there, Pashik, will fix you up with all the permits you need' – a figure waiting on a station platform. I was not expecting a man of destiny to meet me.

He shook my hand and smiled in a friendly way.

'I'm delighted to know you, Mr Foster. Have you had breakfast?'

'Not yet. It's very kind of you to meet me.'

He gestured a denial. 'I have my car outside. We'll have to carry your luggage, Mr Foster. There are no porters at this hour.'

He spoke English well with an accent both foreign and American. He was not a prepossessing person. He had a plump, sallow face with several chins and a two days' growth of beard, and his eyes, as brown and limpid as a spaniel's, squinted slightly through the rimless glasses. He was businesslike and very courteous.

'Good journey, Mr Foster?' he asked as he walked out to his car.

'Not bad.'

'Any trouble at the frontier?'

'No more than usual I imagine.'

'I'm very glad of that.'

In the station yard he put my suitcase in a battered Opel with no cushions on the back seats. He took my typewriter from me to put it with the suitcase and then paused, looking at it thoughtfully.

'You know, Mr Foster,' he said, 'sometimes the authorities make a great deal of trouble for visitors who they think may not be favourable to the regime.'

'Yes?'

'Oh, yes.' He put the typewriter in the car and then with

his hand still on the carrying handle of it turned his head. For a moment he seemed about to say something very important. It was on the tip of his tongue. Then he changed his mind. He shrugged. 'Things are difficult right now, Mr Foster,' he said. 'I'm glad they made no trouble for you.'

He had an office in a building just off the Boulevard Marshal Sokolovsky. He called himself The Pan-Eurasian Press Service and represented a number of American and a few British newspapers whose proprietors had not found it necessary after the war to re-establish their own offices in the capital. He was energetic and gave an impression of efficiency. I had to be registered as a foreigner with the police and as a newspaper correspondent with the Ministries of the Interior and Propaganda; I also had to have a special permit for the trial. It was early evening before we had finished.

Although there was a good deal of waiting about in the various offices we visited as well as the ordinary opportunities for conversation, our relationship did not progress during the day. For the most part he remained courteous but reserved, avoiding all discussion of Deltchev or the trial on the grounds, plainly insufficient at times, that we might be overheard, and introducing me to officials with a measured politeness that took no responsibility at all for my subsequent behaviour. He had very much the air of the man on the spot who, while giving the specialist from head office all reasonable assistance, feels entitled to suspect that the results may not justify the trouble taken. This I could well understand; indeed I would have shared the suspicion. What puzzled me as the day wore on was the growing realization that, understandable and appropriate though his attitude might be, it was only partly a disguise for professional jealousy and that he had some quite different anxiety about me to conceal. It manifested itself in curious ways: sudden bursts of cordiality followed by strained silences, moments when I looked up to find his brown myopic eyes contemplating me furtively, as if to assess my

11

bank balance, and other moments, like that at the station, when he changed his mind about what he was going to say as he opened his mouth to say it. Evidently some bad news had arrived for me while I had been travelling or he had a request to make that I would be likely to receive badly. The thought bothered me. Unfortunately, I already had a bad conscience about Pashik. I disliked him because of his smell.

I had become aware of it when we entered his car at the station. It was sour and musty and at first I was not sure whether it came from the car or its owner. I don't think that I have an unduly fastidious nose or that the stinks of urban humanity specially distress me. I have known other people afflicted with what is daintily called body odour without disliking them. Yet Pashik I did dislike. Perhaps it was that the personality expressed by his appearance and manner – the suit, the American glasses, the dispatch case, the touch of complaisance – did not in some peculiar way allow for a bad smell. I remember that when I found that he was the source and not his car, I took note of those with whom we came in contact in case what I was finding offensive was the body smell of a city rather than that of one particular inhabitant. But no; it was Pashik. And then, unreasonably, I had begun to dislike him and so was at a disadvantage for what followed.

The sun had not yet set but the shadows of a church spire and the dome of a mosque stretched like a finger and thumb across the St Mihail Square when we left the Propaganda Ministry for the last time that day and walked back to Pashik's car; but I had my permit for the trial.

He waved my thanks aside mock-modestly.

'We do what we can, Mr Foster.' He had one of his moments of cordiality. 'If you do not mind coming with me and waiting while I clear up at my office I will then take you to dinner. There is a special restaurant I use.'

I would have liked to refuse; instead, I thanked him again.

12

There was a minute ante-room to his office with a frosted glass door on which were painted the names of all the newspapers he represented. The list was long and imposing and after it the office was an ante-climax. It contained a desk, a table, two chairs and several filing cabinets. The window looked out into a tall fire escape well. It admitted warm stagnant air and a grey twilight which left the corners of the room in darkness. Standing on one of the filing cabinets and framed as importantly as if it were a picture of his wife, was a publicity photograph of Myrna Loy with a reproduction of her signature on it.

He turned on the desk lamp and began to go through a pile of message flimsies. Most of them he crumpled and tossed aside; two or three he scribbled on and handed to a youth with a glazed peak cap who had been awaiting his return; others he clipped together in a folder. When he reached the last of the messages he gave the youth some money and sent him off. Then he picked up the telephone and had a conversation, to me quite unintelligible, with a woman whose voice I could hear vibrating tinnily in the receiver. It ended with a brief crescendo of negatives. He stood up and began to tidy the desk. He was frowning and ill at ease.

I watched him from the darkness outside the ring of light shed by the desk lamp. His small hands no longer moved surely. He was making up his mind to a difficult task. He stopped tidying to look at me. Then he sat down again, leaned back and, taking out a packet of American cigarettes, began to open it.

'Mr Foster,' he said very carefully, 'there is a matter about which I have not yet spoken to you.'

Here it was.

'Yes?'

He kept his eyes on the cigarette packet. 'The matter of censorship. You know there is a strict censorship here of course?'

'I was told so.'

'In the ordinary way the procedure is that I submit the matter to the censorship office and then file it as a cable or airmail it.'

'I see.'

'That is in the ordinary way.' He laid peculiar emphasis on the words.

'You mean that you would like me to give my stuff to you for submission to the censorship and onward transmission. Is that it?'

He did not reply for a moment or two and began to rock slowly on the back legs of his chair. 'Mr Foster, these are not ordinary times here in this country,' he said.

I waited. His glasses, reflecting the light of the desk lamp, winked steadily as he rocked. He went on: 'As I understand it, your articles may contain satirical matter hostile and derogatory to this regime.'

'They might do so, yes.'

He shook his head solemnly. 'I can tell you now, Mr Foster. That's out. Right out.'

'Well, we'll see.'

'Didn't they warn you at head office that things might be difficult here?'

I smiled amiably. 'They said that you might be, Mr Pashik.'

He stopped rocking. 'Oh now, Mr Foster, please. You don't at all understand. The censorship is very powerful here. For writing matter antagonistic to the People's Party regime you would be liable under the February decrees to imprisonment and a heavy fine.'

'Yes, but only liable.'

'I agree. In your case there would naturally be no question of enforcing the decree, but your permit for the trial would certainly be cancelled and you would have a very disagreeable interview with the police.'

'I could make an article out of that, too.'

His lips tightened. 'Obviously your papers would be confiscated, Mr Foster. If it amuses you to write articles so

14

that they may be confiscated that is your affair. I am concerned with practical newspaper work.'

He had me there; I was not. But I felt at the moment he was not either. I thought he was trying to show me how helpless I should be without him. I said as calmly as I could: 'Very well, you're the paper's representative here and you tell me it's all very difficult. I understand. Now, how do we get over the difficulty?'

I had to wait while he lit a cigarette and blew smoke at the end of it like a bad actor pretending to think. 'You could try going down into Greece over Saturday night and Sunday and sending your work from there.' He blew some more smoke. 'Of course, the police would guess what you were attempting. An American on a Chicago paper tried it.'

'Yes?'

Now he looked directly at me. 'He just wasted a lot of time, Mr Foster. Of course he had no written matter when they searched him at the frontier; it was memorized; but they made difficulties about his visa, took his passport away to get it fixed and kept him at the frontier station for a week. He had a very uncomfortable time.'

'I see. Well, now you've told me how it can't be done, what's the answer?'

He was rocking again. 'There is no answer, Mr Foster. Other ways have been tried. The crews of foreign air liners were used as couriers for a while, but no longer. It is too dangerous for them. I have tried to make all this clear to the head office, but what is real here does not seem so in New York and London.'

'In fact, you think it's a great waste of time my being here at all.'

'No, I do not say that.'

'In effect you say it.'

'You misunderstand me. I am in favour of these articles. This trial is *dramatisch* . . . er . . .' He broke off, feeling for the word.

'Theatrical?'

'Yes, theatrical. Thank you. The trial of a political leader on ideological grounds is most theatrical to Western ways of thinking. So, I say that to have a distinguished playwright, such as you, Mr Foster, write matter about the Deltchev trial is a very cute editorial idea. I am myself looking forward to reading the series. But' – he leaned forward impressively – 'you cannot write it here and send or take it out of the country; that is, not unless you paraphrase the Propaganda Ministry's official matter and get every page stamped by the censorship. You must resign yourself to that.'

'But . . .'

'See the trial, Mr Foster, memorize' – he stabbed his forehead with a finger to show me where – 'and then go home and write your articles. That is what you must do.'

For a moment or two I did not answer.

I had been in a train for four days and had had very little sleep on the journey. I had arrived at seven o'clock that morning in a strange city under a hot sun and in a sticky, enervating atmosphere. I had left my luggage in an hotel which might, for all I could remember of the geography of the streets, be a hundred yards away or three miles from where I was now; and even if I found the hotel and remembered the room number I would not know how to ask for the key. I had trailed round cafés and government offices, listening to conversations that concerned me conducted in a language I did not begin to understand, at the heels of an aggrieved, self-important Eastern European with fat hips and a bad smell. I had a blister on the sole of my right foot and a grimy face. I was also hungry and well on the way to wishing I had not come. Now I was being told that the fact that I had come at all was a pity but that if I behaved myself and cared to waste my time I might stay and see the fun. Or so it seemed to me then. I felt myself losing my temper and then managed to wait until the moment had passed before replying. I tried to keep my voice level.

16

'Mr Pashik, you know as well as I do that these articles are meant for publication during the trial as a commentary on it. They'd be useless afterwards.'

'Do you think so?' He looked knowing. 'Deltchev will be condemned to death. Your articles will be part of the campaign against the sentence.'

'That's not what I was told. I was asked to send the stuff in as I did it.'

'And why?' He threw up his hands, smiling with teeth like salted almonds. 'In case you, Mr Foster, the distinguished playwright, should find time to enjoy yourself on the expense account, or get an idea for a new play about life behind that sinister Iron Curtain and forget your commission. Editors treat us all like children.'

'Nevertheless, the articles are expected.'

'No, Mr Foster, they are not. I sent a cable to head office saying that they will not be available until you return.'

'I think you should have consulted me before you did that.'

'I am responsible, Mr Foster.'

There was a thin-lipped silence. Then I said: 'Mr Pashik, are you a member of the People's Party? I didn't think to ask you before.'

He smiled again but the American accent became more pronounced. 'Ah, Mr Foster, you are mad at me. I don't blame you. I will be frank with you.'

'Good.'

'If there is any trouble with the censorship over anything that goes out of this office, it will be closed up. That means that I will be closed up, finished. I am responsible.'

'Then you'll still be responsible if the articles are published after the trial.'

'Ah, no. If the Propaganda Ministry admits you to the country it is their affair if you produce hostile matter when you leave. While you are here the responsibility rests with this office that you should not pre-judge the trial by sending hostile matter.' He shrugged. 'It is no doubt for them an expedient. For myself, I am hostile to the regime; but I have been expelled for my opinions before, and Pan-Eurasian representing twenty-seven foreign newspapers has a responsibility to others besides your editor. So you see I must play ball with the regime, Mr Foster.'

I did not know quite what to say. My impulse was to take the trial permit from my pocket, put it on his desk and say that I would leave in the morning. Certainly, that is what he hoped I would do. It was only my awareness of disliking him for a poor reason that made me hesitate. He pushed the cigarettes towards me.

I shook my head. 'When did you send that cable?'

'Four days ago, Mr Foster.'

'Why not before?'

'It was not certain that you were coming.'

'It was settled three weeks ago that I was coming.'

'I did not know that.'

'Have you had a reply?'

'Yes, Mr Foster.'

'May I see it, please?'

'Certainly.' He opened a drawer in the desk and brought out a cable and put it in front of me. I read:

Your 109 of 6 June understood advise Foster and arrange air passage London soonest close trial.

'You could have shown me this before,' I said.

'I did not realize that you did not trust me, Mr Foster,' he replied gently. 'The cable only says to advise you of something and secure an air passage for you. It does not explain what I have been telling you. You still have to believe that I am telling you the truth.'

His smile said that this was the moment when I should feel silly and apologize. Perhaps it was the smile that prevented my doing so. Instead I said: 'I take it that the other foreign correspondents will be under the same restriction?'

'If they are hostile to the regime they will have to be equally discreet.'

'That story about the American who tried to go to Greece for the week-end – I suppose you made that up in case I thought of the idea myself and didn't tell you.'

'It was a way of warning you that the method was known.'

'You go at things in rather a roundabout way, don't you?'

He looked at me thoughtfully. 'One gets in the habit of it, Mr Foster,' he said and then paused. 'Roundabout ways are sometimes safer. However' – his expression changed and he stood up expansively, his smell billowing around him – 'it is good to meet a person who cares for frankness. We can understand one another.' He smiled cheerfully. 'We shall get on well, Mr Foster. We can help each other and that is as it should be. I will show you.'

He went over to a filing cabinet in the outer darkness, opened one of the drawers and began to search through it.

'You know, Mr Foster,' he murmured as he picked through the files, 'being expelled from a country is not dignified and not at all rewarding. For a few hours you are the brave man who dared to tell the truth. But the next day when the hand clasp of friends is forgotten you are just another reporter without a job.'

He came back to the desk with an untidy bundle of papers and a large envelope.

'When did it happen to you?' I asked.

'Italy, nineteen thirty. I was a married man then, too,' he said. He hesitated for an instant, then stuffed the papers into the envelope and handed it to me with the rueful smile of a rich uncle for the rascally nephew whom he likes.

'The office file on Yordan Deltchev, Mr Foster. It will help you.'

'Thank you.'

'Please!' He put up a protesting hand. 'I want to help you, Mr Foster. And I want you to know that I want to. And that is frank. *Avanti!* Now we go to dinner, eh?'

That night I was too tired to sleep. For a while I tried to

do so; then I gave up, switched on the light and began to read the file Pashik had given to me.

At that point, I still had the illusion that I could report the Deltchev trial.

Chapter 3

This is what I learned from the file.

Until the spring of nineteen-forty, when his country had joined two of its Balkan neighbours in coming to terms with the Axis, Yordan Deltchev, although an important figure in the councils of the Agrarian Socialist Party, had had no popular following. Originally a lawyer by profession he had been deputy for a provincial manufacturing area, and then, having served the monarchy and later the republic in various subordinate capacities, had become Minister of Posts and Telegraphs.

At that time he had been regarded by the knowledgeable as a very able man and as either honest or so far insufficiently tempted. That he was not then even considered as potentially a great popular leader is understandable. His special talent was for organization; and while as a speaker he was not without force, the cool logic, dryly delivered, which made him effective in debate seemed unlikely ever to capture the hearts of audiences of peasants. That it did ultimately do so was a phenomenon produced by a peculiar combination of circumstances. Deltchev himself had very little to do with it.

He had been one of the few deputies, and the only Minister, who had opposed the alliance with the Axis at all vigorously; and during the summer of nineteen-forty, at the request of the German authorities, he had been interned. Towards the end of the year he was released but kept under police surveillance. Two years passed before the surveillance became sufficiently negligent for him to embark on the underground political activity with which his name was to become associated.

Before that time, opposition to the pro-German government and its allies had been expressed chiefly by acts of sabotage against war supply installations and by propaganda against the recruitment of divisions for the Russian front. This work had been done by groups led by militant People's Party men but containing a good proportion of Agrarian Socialists. Yet, although it was sometimes spectacular and always dangerous, the amount of inconvenience it caused the enemy was small and its effect on popular morale disappointing. To Deltchev's way of thinking, the policy of the underground opposition should be to leave the winning of the war to those who could fight effectively and to concentrate on planning for the future of the country during the period immediately following the inevitable German collapse. He saw that her fate at the hands of the victorious powers would depend very much on the speed with which she could herself establish a provisional government sufficiently uncompromised to negotiate without cringing and strong enough to prevent civil war.

The resultant Committee of National Unity was not created by Deltchev alone but it was he who made it effective. Clandestine organizations are mostly recruited from among the dedicated, the romantic and the mentally ill-adjusted men and women of a community; and in them, courage and devotion are more easily found than high level planning ability and political skill. Because he was the clearest thinker the Committee had and the only member of it with any practical experience of government, Deltchev became in effect (though in fact he never held any specific appointment) its President, its Secretary-General and, eventually, its spokesman. Hundreds of thousands of people who had never heard of Deltchev, the Minister of Posts and Telegraphs, now came to know of and exult in Yordan Deltchev the patriot. And when the time came for him to speak to them, the dry steady voice and the cool logic seemed, after the hysterical oratory of the war years, to derive from a special kind of sanity and goodness. They felt that he possessed the truth.

If the Provisional Government of National Unity set up

by the Committee in the spring of nineteen forty-four had done no more than sue for peace so promptly it would have justified its existence; for, by this action, it saved all but one of the Northern frontier provinces from devastation and kept the minute army intact and available for police duties. Yet it did do more. It was able to secure recognition, qualified but sufficient, by the United Nations, and contrived, in those days of hasty negotiations and shifting authority, to confuse and postpone discussions of such matters as territorial claims and the dismantling of industrial installations. It ensured, at a minimum cost both to the national economy and to the national pride, that most of the vital decisions affecting the country's future were made not in the heat of the newly won battle, but in the milder atmosphere of delayed peace conferences. The credit for these benefits was given to Deltchev. He began to be nicknamed, affectionately, 'Papa' Deltchev.

Perhaps, but for that nickname, there would have been no People's Party regime, and no Deltchev trial.

When the Provisional Government came into power it was said by neglected members of his own party that the motives behind Deltchev's actions had all along been those of a shrewd, ambitious politician and that, while he could not be blamed for having had greatness thrust upon him, he should not now behave towards his old friends as if he had achieved it. They were soon to wish that they had been entirely right.

One of the main articles of the Committee's original programme had been that insisting on the need for free elections at the earliest possible moment. Its inclusion and the sanctimonious style of its wording were concessions to Anglo-Saxon susceptibilities which, it had been felt, could hurt nobody. Not that the men of the Committee were cynically indifferent to elections; it was simply that, faced with the task of planning for a great emergency of which nothing was then known and only the worst could be expected, they found such talk unrealistic. A cultivated sense of emergency is not easy to discard, and, later on, the early state of mind about elections tended to persist. When, therefore, the People's Party members of the Provisional Government began to press for redemption of the election promise their action was interpreted, and correctly interpreted, as a demand for more power; that is, a larger share of the important posts. Only to Deltchev, apparently, did it mean anything different.

The People's Party had lately grown enormously in numbers and influence. The participation of the Agrarian Socialists in the formation and work of the Committee had achieved its object of enlisting wide popular support; but it had also had the secondary effect of making the Committee a powerful recruiting agency for the People's Party. This mishap had long been a subject of complaints and bitter exchanges within the Government and on one occasion Petra Vukashin, the leader of the People's Party men, had been too frank. 'If,' he had said, 'you are fool enough to introduce your wife to a handsome young man with a bad reputation, you must not complain when you find them in bed together.'

When, to the manifest discomfort of Vukashin and the rest of the People's Party faction, Deltchev took the election proposal seriously and began to argue in favour of it, it was assumed at first by his pathetically gleeful colleagues that 'Papa' Deltchev was merely calling the enemy's bluff. They knew, had known for some time, that the Provisional Government had the approval and support of the Western Powers who would not press for the promised elections while the country was in Soviet occupation. They had evidence that the Russians, not unimpressed by Deltchev's efficiency, were content to let things stay as they were for the present. Some of its members had even wondered if the word 'provisional' might not be dropped from the title of a government with so rich an expectation of life. They could not know that their leader, Deltchev, had already numbered its days.

24

Many attempts were made later to offer more reasonable explanations of Deltchev's actions at that time than the one accepted by the simpler members of the public, namely: that he was a self-sacrificing patriot who had been directly inspired by God. Since, however, most of their other explanations relied on the assumption that he was monumentally corrupt, none of them was much more convincing.

The material facts were simple.

After the meeting at which the election promise was discussed, Deltchev seemed preoccupied and unwilling to pursue the matter in private conversation. To one persistent man, however, he said: 'If we have clean hands they cannot accuse us.' The man took this to be a comment on the strength of the Government's position and the absurdity of the People's Party manoeuvre.

That was on a Thursday. For the next few days Deltchev was at home in bed with a severe chill. On the following Tuesday he was due to make a radio speech about a national campaign then in progress for conserving winter foodstuffs for livestock.

He came to the radio station straight from his bed, looking, according to the director of the station, 'like a man who has been fighting with devils.' In his speech he talked briefly about the conservation campaign and then, after a momentary hesitation, produced a handwritten manuscript from his pocket and began to read a statement from it.

Five minutes later the people knew that, in the considered opinion of 'Papa' Deltchev, the time had now come for the Government to redeem the Committee's solemn pledge to hold free elections at the earliest possible moment.

At the beginning of the statement he had declared that he was speaking only for himself and not for the Provisional Government of National Unity. This declaration was both seized upon as evidence of his cynical contempt for his audience and pointed to as marking his absolute integrity. For the former view it was said that no one but a fool would suppose that, whether he wanted to do so or not, Deltchev could in fact dissociate his private opinions on such a question from those of the Government he led; for the latter it was argued that if you accepted the fact of his honesty (and who could deny it?) you would see that his disclaimer was a simple statement of the truth which he had been bound to make if he were not to deceive the public. As equally divergent constructions could be placed on every other sentence in the statement, neither side could score points. Deltchev himself had returned from the radio station to his bed and, having issued through his secretary the statement that the broadcast speech was 'self-explanatory,' remained there, silent and inaccessible. But, by the time two days had passed, it was clear that the storm over the speech which raged with mounting fury among the politicians was no longer of interest to the people. In their eyes the Provisional Government was now committed quite irrevocably to holding elections in the near future and anyone who attacked Deltchev was attempting to deny the fact. Yet it was the People's Party which profited most from the situation.

Those of the unfortunate Agrarian Socialists who had the wit to see that, whatever they might now say in private about Deltchev, they could not hope to win without him as a figurehead, were in the majority; but they were terribly hampered by a considerable and vindictive minority whose only concern now seemed to be to oppose and revile him in public. The People's Party, while taking full advantage of this mistake, took care not to make it themselves. By referring to Deltchev patronizingly but respectfully as a kind of elder statesman (he was, in fact, only sixty then) they managed to convey the impression that he was in a state of derelict senility which could excuse his continued association with the Agrarian Socialists. Also, by securing the postponement of the elections until the early summer, they gave themselves time to prepare a *coup d'état* which anticipated publication of the election results by a few hours. In the event, it was almost unnecessary. Thanks to

Deltchev, they very nearly came into power by constitutional means.

His response to these events was at first curiously passive. True, he protested against the *coup d'état*, but rather formally as if expressing an appropriate but not heartfelt sentiment; and in the chamber his attacks upon the new Government had about them the studied moderation of a fencing master with a new pupil. For a long time he seemed unaware or unwilling to be aware of the Government's quick, wary moves to make themselves secure. Soon the anti-Deltchev faction within his own party began to find people ready at last to listen to their tale of a great fortune deposited abroad in Deltchev's name the day after his election statement. Even among the general public he seemed to be losing popularity. It was understandable that the Government's supporters should have come to think of Deltchev almost as one of themselves.

Then came the incident of 'Deltchev's football match.'

The occasion was the official opening of a sports stadium. It had been completed in nineteen-forty and immediately requisitioned for use by the German Army as a transit camp. Later, the Red Army had used it as a garrison headquarters. Its return was a gesture of Soviet goodwill which the new Government had dutifully decided to celebrate with as much publicity as possible. It was probably the presence of Western diplomatic representatives at the ceremony which determined that Deltchev as leader of the 'opposition' should be asked to speak.

He began, deceptively, with a tribute to the Red Army, and expressions of his party's recognition of the generous motives which had prompted the early return of the stadium. He hoped that in the near future it would be the scene of a memorable football match with the local Red Army team.

Then, during the mild applause which greeted this suggestion, he moved nearer to the microphones. But this time he took no manuscript from his pocket. He knew exactly what he had to say.

'But meanwhile, my countrymen, there is another, more deadly battle for us to fight – the battle for freedom within the State.'

He paused. There was a silence in which the long banners could be heard flapping in the wind. He went on.

'Two days ago I was invited by the leader of the People's Party, Petra Vukashin, to take the office of Minister of Justice in the government which now has power. My answer was promised for to-night. I take this opportunity of giving him the answer now. I answer that if he thinks that by so betraying my brothers in the Agrarian Socialist Party I should change in any way their determination to fight until this new tyranny is utterly destroyed – if he thinks that, then he is stupid. If our opposition to his party's criminal plans is such that he must try to buy us off with a share of the loot, then he is also frightened. My countrymen, there is no time to lose. These stupid, frightened men are dangerous not for what they are now, but for what they mean to become – your masters. They are not . . .'

At this point the booming public address system in the stadium was cut off. In the deathly pause that followed, Deltchev's voice, high and thin in the wind, could only be heard by those near to him as he completed the sentence.

Then the cheering began. It came across the packed stadium as a rolling, sighing wave of sound that surged up and broke with a roar that shook the air like an explosion. It lasted nearly a minute and subsided only when another sound came to replace it; the steady, massive chanting of Deltchev's name. Suddenly on the far side of the stadium there was a wide swirling movement in the crowd as a fight developed and from closer at hand there was angry shouting. Deltchev, who during the cheering had stood motionless in front of the dead microphones, now waved his hand and turned away. There was another tremendous cheer and more shouting. At that moment, the officer in command of a Russian military band, which had been waiting to lead into the arena the squads who were giving the gymnastic display, decided not to wait for an order to do so. It was a sensible decision and probably averted serious trouble. As the band began to play and march in, the cheering became ragged and in places gave way to laughter and clapping. In less than a minute the incident of 'Deltchev's football match' was over; over, that is, except for the breathless excitement of discussing it and of reporting it to those who had merely heard it on the radio. But nothing about it was forgotten and much that had not happened was remembered. 'Papa' Deltchev had come back to them. He had spoken his mind and they had shown that they were with him in his fight against the 'masters.'

Four nights later an attempt was made to assassinate him.

His house was of the old kind with a walled courtyard. As he got out of his car to enter the house a grenade was thrown. It hit the wall by the entrance and bounced back into the road before exploding, so that Deltchev, who had gained the doorway, was partly shielded from the blast. There were few people about at the time and the man who had thrown the grenade escaped.

The driver of the car was badly cut about the head and neck but Deltchev, although he had been flung against the half-open door and much shaken, was not seriously hurt. In the ensuing confusion, however, his protests that the pain in his shoulder was caused only by a bruise were ignored and he was taken to a hospital with the driver. Within an hour rumours that he was dead or dying were circulating in the cafés and a large crowd gathered outside the hospital. By this time, Deltchev had returned to his home where the police were collecting fragments of the grenade in the presence of an even larger crowd. There was a great deal of hostility towards the police.

It is said that, when the Chief of Police reported to Vukashin later that night that the atttempt on Deltchev was being described openly as the Government's reply to the stadium speech, the Minister exclaimed: 'Did they think we would reply in the Chamber?' The story may be untrue but, in the light of what followed, it is not incredible. Certainly from that moment on there was an ominous change in the Propaganda Ministry's public attitude towards Deltchev and it is likely that the decision to try him was made at this time. The Ministry's official statement on the affair had a sort of angry jocularity about it which did nothing to change the general belief that the Government had known of the attempt in advance. It asserted that the grenade was of American manufacture and went on to suggest that the obvious place to seek the criminal was in the ranks of Deltchev's own party where there were many criminals with Anglo-American Imperialist connections.

The editor of a newspaper which described this statement as 'unsatisfactory, but significantly so' was immediately imprisoned. A series of savage attacks on the Agrarian Socialist Party now began. Their violent tone and the barely concealed threats which accompanied every allusion to Deltchev conveyed unmistakable warnings. The opposition had become intolerable and was going to be liquidated; but first Deltchev must be disposed of. He had a choice. He could escape abroad and be condemned or stay at home and be condemned. In any event he would be condemned.

Deltchev chose to stay. A month later he was arrested.

That was all. For a while I looked out of my hotel window across the flat roofs and Byzantine spires of the city, as still in the moonlight as the landscape of a dead world; and at last I became sleepy.

As I collected up the mass of news cuttings, notes and manuscript which composed Pashik's file and began to put them back in the envelope, I noticed a paper which I had not seen before. It had been clipped to the back of a wad of sheets with cuttings pasted on them and therefore easily overlooked.

It was a page from a memo pad I had seen on Pashik's

desk. On it was typed: *Case of K. Fischer, Vienna '46 – Aleko's hand?*

For me, then, it was not the most interesting thing about the file. I went to sleep.

Chapter 4

Pashik had promised to drive me to the trial and we met for breakfast. He nodded at the envelope I was carrying with the approving smile of a friendly schoolmaster.

'Ah, Mr Foster, you have been reading.'

'Yes. There's a lot of material there. Did you collect it?'

He fingered his chin self-consciously for a moment; he had shaved. 'Why do you ask, Mr Foster?'

'Because a lot of the unpublished stuff was obviously done by someone who knew Deltchev very well and liked him. You?'

'Ah, the memoir;' he looked embarrassed; 'that was commissioned by one of my papers from Petlarov.'

'Who's he?'

'He was Deltchev's secretary and friend – until the elections. Then they quarrelled. He was paid for the memoir but it was not used. It was not the moment.'

'Where is Petlarov now? Is he here?'

'He may be.'

'I should like to talk to him.'

'He will know nothing about the trial, Mr Foster.'

'I'd still like to talk to him.'

'He may not wish to see you.'

'Then he will say so. You said you wanted to be helpful, Pashik. Here's your opportunity.'

He wriggled unhappily. 'Please, Mr Foster. I see I must explain to you.' He lowered his voice. 'You do not understand. After the arrest of Deltchev, Petlarov was naturally arrested too. He is released now but he is still suspect. It would be most indiscreet to have relations with him. I cannot take the risk.'

'You don't have to. Just get a message to him from me. I suppose he can speak German?'

'I do not know. Perhaps not.'

'Send a message as if from me asking him to telephone me at my hotel this evening.'

He sighed. 'Very well, Mr Foster. But I think it will be useless.'

I held up the envelope with the file in it. 'We don't want to take this with us, do we? We could leave it at your office on the way and write a note to Petlarov at the same time. Your office boy can deliver it.'

He pursed his lips together at this. 'I see you still do not trust me, Mr Foster,' he said.

'What do you mean?'

He saw the danger of explaining just in time. 'It is not important,' he said with dignity.

He took the envelope from me. Then I remembered. 'Oh, by the way,' I said, 'what does this refer to?' I showed him the paper with the *Aleko* note on it.

He looked at it blankly for a moment. 'Oh, that, Mr Foster,' he said, and taking it from me put it in his pocket; 'that is nothing. Something from another file.'

When once you know how a person lies it is difficult for him to deceive you again. In Pashik's case it was a special tone of voice he used for direct lies that gave him away; a cold, too matter-of-fact tone. He had used it before in telling me the untrue story of the American journalist who had tried to go to Greece for the week-end.

I supposed the fact that he had lied about this piece of paper to be equally unimportant.

The large courtroom at the Ministry of Justice had been thought too small for a political trial of such moment. It was being staged, therefore, in the main lecture hall at the Army School of Aeronautics, a modern building on the outskirts of the city.

The walls, ordinarily decorated with engineering charts and war trophies, had been hung with flags; those of the

Republic and of the Soviet Union, and, at greater intervals, those of the other sympathetic nations of Eastern Europe. Just above on either side of the judges' dais, two draped Soviet flags bulged over (but, tactlessly, did not quite conceal) one of the trophies, the tail plane of a Russian aircraft presented by a German flak unit during the war. Pinned to some of the flags were notices printed in four languages saying that smoking was prohibited. In the balcony, a row of sound-proof booths had been erected for the interpreters relaying translations of the proceedings to the earphones of the foreign diplomatic and press representatives below. In the balcony, too, on heavy stands or clamped to the balcony rail, were big floodlights pointing down into the court to illuminate it for the Propaganda Ministry's film cameras. Beside the judges' dais, on both sides of the prisoner's rostrum, at the corners of the hall, in the balcony, by the doors and below every flag on the walls, guards were posted. They were all officers or NCOs and armed with machine-pistols which they did not sling but held ready in their hands. It had been explained by the Propaganda Ministry that when the evidence against the criminal Deltchev was publicly known, attempts might be made by the people he had deceived to kill him before justice could be done.

The courtroom was crowded. My place and Pashik's were in the foreign press section below the edge of the balcony and to one side. In the centre was the diplomatic section. On the ledge in front of each seat in these two sections was a pair of earphones and four plug sockets marked with letters distinguishing the Russian, French, English and German interpretation channels. Also on the ledge was a duplicated copy of the indictment in French. There seemed to be no seats for members of the public without tickets, but several rows behind us were prominently labelled with notice cards bearing initials which Pashik said were those of prominent trade union organizations. The occupants of these seats were obviously in their best clothes and on their best behaviour. They all wore badges, and in one row there was a group of peasants in national costume. They looked as if they were attending a prizegiving. The front rows, however, had a different look about them. These seats were reserved for the important Party members and functionaries. Their occupants wore dark neat clothes and either sat with self-conscious, preoccupied frowns or conversed in *affairé* undertones with their neighbours. Aware of being in the public eye, they were concerned to show that they had business there and were not merely favoured spectators. It was warm and most of the women and many of the men had highly-coloured paper fans.

At about ten o'clock the floodlights in the balcony were turned on and the fluttering sound of film cameras began. A buzz of anticipation went round the courtroom; then, as the three black-robed judges came slowly in, all stood up. The judges went to their places on the dais but did not sit down until the national anthem had been played through a loudspeaker. It was all curiously reminiscent of a royal visit to the opera. Even the low murmur of conversation, which began as we sat down again, was familiar. All that was different was that instead of the lowering of lights and the rise of a curtain somebody stood up and called out the name of Yordan Deltchev, and all eyes turned towards a pair of glazed doors beside the dais. Then there was silence, except for the sound of the cameras and the distant throbbing of the generator set which supplied the power for the floodlights.

After a moment or two the glazed doors were flung open and three men entered the court. Inside the door they paused for a moment blinking in the lights that poured down on them. Two of them were uniformed guards; tall, smart young fellows. Between them was an elderly man with a thin grey face, deep-set eyes and white hair. He was short and had been stocky but now his shoulders were rounded and he was inclined to stoop. He stood with his hands thrust deep into his jacket pockets, looking about him uncertainly. One of the guards touched his arm and he walked over to the rostrum and stepped on to it. A chair had been placed for him but for a moment he stood there looking round at the flags up on the walls. He smiled faintly. He still had his hands in his pockets. Then, with a curt nod to each of the judges, he sat down and closed his eyes. This was Yordan Deltchev.

There were twenty-three counts listed in the published indictment against him. They charged (principally in count number eight, though the same charge was paraphrased in two other counts) that he had 'prepared terrorist plots against the state and conspired with reactionary organizations, including the criminal Officer Corps Brotherhood, to secure for financial and other personal advantages, the occupation of the Motherland by troops of a foreign power.' There were other charges concerned with terrorist activity, the smuggling of arms, and plots to assassinate members of the People's Party Government, 'in particular P. I. Vukashin.' Sprinkled throughout were dark references to 'various confederates,' 'notorious foreign agents,' 'hired saboteurs and murderers,' 'reactionary gangsters' and so on; while the name of the Officer Corps Brotherhood recurred with the persistence of a typewriter bell. It was soon evident that the indictment was a propaganda document intended for foreign consumption. It said, in effect, or hoped to say: 'He is the kind of man against whom such charges may seriously be brought;' and: 'He is accused of so much that of some he must be guilty.'

The Public Prosecutor conducted his case in person. His name was Dr Prochaska and he was one of the few members of the legal profession who had joined the People's Party before it had come into power. He was an authority on questions of land tenure and most of his practice had been concerned with cases involving them. He had had little experience of court advocacy of any kind and none at all in criminal proceedings. A stout, pugnacious-looking man with quick, jerky movements and a habit of licking his lips

36

every few seconds, he seemed more concerned to defend himself against accusations of weakness than to present his case effectively. He made scarcely any reference to the official indictment and dealt with only two of the charges in it. If he could prove, or seem to prove, those, then Deltchev would stand convicted on the whole indictment. That, at least, was the impression I had of it. From the commencement of his long opening address he adopted a tone of ranting denunciation that carried little conviction and confused even the more reasoned passages. In spite of the earphones on my head and the voice of the interpreter quietly translating the speech I was constantly distracted by the sight and half-heard sounds of its originator.

His case, however, was dangerously simple.

It was generally known that, at the time of the German retreat in nineteen forty-four, Deltchev, who had been secretly in touch with both the Russians and the Western Powers, had gone to great lengths to secure Anglo-American rather than Soviet occupation of the country. Against the wishes of a majority of the Committee of National Unity, he had at one point gone as far as to propose to the Western Powers that the national army should continue to resist the Russians in the north so as to give the Americans and British time to prepare an airborne invasion from Middle East bases.

It was now suggested by the Prosecution that this proposal had come in fact from the Western Powers themselves and that Deltchev's support of it had been bought with the promise that he would have control of the re-allocation of the German oil concessions. In other words he had tried to sell his countrymen's lives for money and power.

The other favoured charge was the one that had so amused my economist friend. It was that Deltchev had planned to assassinate Vukashin, the head of the People's Party Government, and that he was, in fact, a member of the Officer Corps Brotherhood. If this could seem to be proved, he could quite legally and with full popular approval be sentenced to death. The case against Deltchev was designed to destroy both him and the Agrarian Socialist Party which had produced him, for ever.

I left the court that day in a peculiar frame of mind. I felt as if I had been to the first night of what had seemed to me a very bad play only to find that everyone else had enjoyed it immensely. A Propaganda Ministry bureau had been set up in a room adjoining the court. On the way out Pashik stopped to get the official bulletin on the day's proceedings. The room was crowded and I waited in the doorway. There were a number of tables, each signposted with the name of one of the official languages. As I stood there I saw a bald young man whom I thought I knew coming away from the English table. I had noticed him earlier in the day and been unable to place him. Now as he pushed his way out we came face to face. He nodded.

'You're Foster, aren't you?'

'Yes. We've met before.'

'Sibley, Incorporated Press.'

'Oh, yes.' I remembered, too, that I had not liked him.

'What are you doing here?' he asked. 'Getting local colour for a new play?'

I explained. He raised his eyebrows. 'Very nice too. Still I expect you'll make a play out of it sometime, won't you.'

'I don't know.'

'I should have thought that there were masses of material for you. It'd make quite a nice little paragraph, your being here. Do you mind if I use it?'

'Yes, I do.' I smiled as I said it, but not very cordially.

He laughed. 'All right, I'll spare you. But it'd be nice to send something even a *little* more interesting than these handouts.' He waved the sheets in his hand. 'I'm at our Paris office really. I've been lent for the trial. Why, I can't think. An office boy could file this junk for all of us.' He turned his head as Pashik came up. 'Hullo, Georghi, we were just talking about you.'

'Good evening, Mr Sibley. We must be going, Mr Foster. I have to get to the office.'

'That's our Georghi! Always on the job.' Sibley grinned. 'Where are you staying, Foster?'

I told him.

'We must have a drink together,' he said.

In the car Pashik gave me the bulletin. I glanced through it. Most of it was composed of extracts from Dr Prochaska's address. They were even more idiotic to read than to listen to. I put the bulletin down. The streets leading back to the centre of the city were narrow and crowded and Pashik was a driver who twitched at the wheel instead of steering with it. He squeezed his way none too skilfully between two carts.

'Mr Foster,' he said then, 'there is a suggestion which I think I must make to you.' He looked round at me soulfully. 'You will not, I hope, be offended.'

'Not at all. Look out.'

He twitched away from a cyclist just in time. The cyclist shouted. Pashik sounded the horn unnecessarily and put on speed.

'It is a small thing,' he said – the car swayed unpleasantly across some protruding tram lines – 'but I would not, if I were in your place, be too friendly here with Mr Sibley.'

'Oh? What's the matter with him?'

'It is nothing personal, you understand.'

'But what?'

'He drinks too much and becomes indiscreet.'

'I don't see that that has anything to do with me.'

'His associates will be suspect.'

I thought for a moment. 'Mr Pashik,' I said then; 'as a newspaper man, don't you think that you're a bit too anxious about the censorship and the Propaganda Ministry and the police and all the rest of it?'

A woman missed death by an inch. He sounded the horn absently and shook his head. 'I do not think so. It is difficult to explain.'

'What's so difficult about it?'

'You are a stranger here, Mr Foster. You look on our life from the outside. You are interested in the trial of a man whose name you scarcely know because his situation seems to you to contain the elements of a spiritual conflict. Naturally so. You are a writer of fiction and you make the world in your own image. But be careful. Do not walk upon the stage yourself. You may find that the actors are not what they have seemed.'

'Is Sibley one of the actors?'

'I was speaking generally, Mr Foster.'

'Then I'm sorry but I don't understand what we're talking about.'

He sighed. 'I was afraid not. But perhaps it does not matter.'

I let that one go. A few moments later he pulled up outside my hotel. I got out of the car.

'Shall we meet for dinner, Mr Foster?'

I hesitated. The air outside the car smelt good. I shook my head. 'I think I'll get to bed early to-night,' I said.

Chapter 5

The Hotel Boris had been built by a German company in nineteen fourteen and was one of those hotels in which footsteps echo and only the sound of a toilet flushing in the distance reminds you that you are not alone there. The foyer was a cavernous place with a tessellated floor and a hydraulic lift in a wrought-iron cage. The reception clerk was a slow-moving, mentally-deficient youth with a charming smile. He spoke little English.

'There is a message for you, sir,' he said. He glanced at a scrap of paper that he had taken out of the key-rack with my key. 'Mr Stanoiev called to see you and will call again.'

'Stanoiev? I don't know anyone of that name. Are you sure it was for me?'

He looked stupid. 'I don't know, sir. He went away.'

'I see.'

The lift was deserted. I walked up the wide shallow stairs to the sixth floor.

My room was at the end of a long corridor with upholstered benches set against the wall at intervals along it. As I started down the corridor I noticed that at the far end there was a man sitting on one of the benches. He was reading a newspaper.

It made an odd picture; one never expects corridor furniture to be used except as shelves for trays and chambermaids' dusters. As I approached he looked up casually, then went back to his newspaper. I glanced at him as I passed by.

He was a thin, dried-up man with pale, haggard eyes and grey hair cropped so that the bone of his skull was visible. He had a peculiarly blotchy complexion like that of someone just cured of a skin disease. The hands holding up the newspaper were long and yellow. There was a black soft hat beside him on the bench.

I went on past him to my room. I put the key in the lock and turned it. Then someone spoke from just behind me.

'Herr Foster?'

It made me jump. I turned round. The man who had been on the bench was standing there with his hat under his arm.

I nodded.

'Petlarov,' he said, and then added in German: 'I can speak French or German, whichever you prefer.'

'German will be all right. I'm glad to see you.' I finished opening the door. 'Will you come in?'

He bowed slightly. 'Thank you.' He walked in and then turned and faced me. 'I must apologize,' he said in a clipped, businesslike way, 'for answering your note in this fashion. A native of this country would not find it strange, but as you are a foreigner I must make an explanation.'

'Please sit down.'

'Thank you.' In the light of the room his clothes were shabby and he looked ill. His precise, formal manner however seemed to ignore both facts. He chose a hard chair as if he did not intend to stay long.

'First,' he said, 'I think you should know that I am under surveillance; that is to say I have to report to the police every day. Second; I am officially listed as an "untrustworthy person." That means that if you were to be seen entering my house or talking to me in a public place you would attract the attention of the police and yourself become suspect. That is why I have used this unconventional means of seeing you. I discovered your room number by leaving a note for you in the name of Stanoiev and noticing which box it was put into. Then I came discreetly up here and waited for you to return. You need therefore have no fear that my name is in any way connected with yours or my presence here known about.' He bowed curtly.

'I am most grateful to you for coming.'

'Thank you. May I ask how you obtained my address?'

'From a man named Pashik.'

'Ah yes. I thought it must be him.' He looked thoughtfully into space.

'Do you know him well, Herr Petlarov?'

'You mean what is my opinion of him?'

'Yes.'

He considered for a moment. 'Let us say that I do not subscribe to the common belief that he is merely a disagreeable person whose political views change with the person he talks to. But now that I am here, what do you want of me?'

I had held out my cigarettes. His hand had gone out to them as he was speaking but now he hesitated. He looked up from the cigarettes and his eyes met mine.

'I have some more,' I said.

He smiled in a deprecatory way. 'If you had perhaps a bar of chocolate or a biscuit, Herr Foster, it would, I think, be better for my stomach than tobacco.'

'Of course.' I went to my suitcase. 'I have no chocolate but here are some biscuits.'

I had a box, bought in Paris for the train journey and then forgotten. I opened it. The biscuits were the kind with pink icing sugar on them.

'Not very good for a bad stomach,' I remarked.

He took one with a polite smile. 'Oh yes. Excellent.' He nibbled at it with very white false teeth.

'Pashik gave me your piece on Deltchev to read,' I said.

'Oh, yes? It was considered unsuitable for publication.'

'By Pashik?'

'Yes, but I was not surprised or upset. I knew that it had been commissioned in the belief that because I had had a difference of opinion with Yordan I would therefore write about him in an unfavourable way. If Pashik had asked me I would have told him what to expect. Fortunately he did not ask.'

'Fortunately?'

43

'If he had known he would not have commissioned the article and I needed the money.'

'Oh, I see. I have a bottle of whisky here. Would it be safe to ask the floor waiter for some glasses?'

'I think not. Perhaps I may have another biscuit.'

'Of course, please help yourself. You know, Herr Petlarov, I came here to write a series of articles about the trial of Deltchev. But Pashik seems afraid that I shall offend the censor if I do them here.'

'He is probably right,' he said calmly. 'He is usually right about these things. Yes, I can see. If you offend he will be blamed.'

I must have looked disbelieving. He took another biscuit. 'I will tell you a little story about the regime. A member of the People's Party wrote a novel about the fight of a group of workmen with the capitalists who wish to close a factory. It was a naïve story in which the capitalists were all monsters of evil and the workmen's leader a People's Party man. The Propaganda Minister, whose name is Brankovitch, would not, however, allow its publication. He said that the hero was not positive.'

'I don't understand.'

'The author had not demonstrated that the hero member of the Party was a *good* man.'

'But surely that was inferred.'

'Brankovitch would say that you were in intellectual error, Herr Foster. Inference is not positive. The public must be *instructed* that the man is good, as they must be instructed in all things.'

'You must be exaggerating.'

'In London or New York I would be exaggerating. Here, no. The sequel to this is that the writer was angry and made a little propaganda of his own. He has now been sent to forced labour. Pashik does not see that fate for himself. You see, Herr Foster, those who must be persuaded to obey are no longer important, for shortly we shall cease to exist. Our liquidation has begun.' He smiled significantly.

44

'What do you mean?'

He took another biscuit and held it up. 'This is the third biscuit I have taken,' he said. 'There are twenty-one left in the box. I can eat nine more.'

'You can have the box.'

He inclined his head. 'Thank you. I had hoped that you would give it to me. I had based my calculations on your doing so. If I eat nine more I shall have eaten twelve. That will leave twelve for my wife. Luckily we have no children to share with us.'

I was silent.

'I will explain. It is quite simple. Persons who are listed as untrustworthy are not allowed to work at anything but manual labour. I tried that but I am not strong enough. So, as I cannot work, my wife and I may not have ration cards. We are, of course, very often hungry, and that can make a good argument for obedience.'

I got up and went to the wardrobe for the whisky. Out of the corner of my eye I saw him reaching for another biscuit. He glanced over his shoulder at me.

'Please do not distress yourself, Herr Foster. A bad conscience can, I know, be as unpleasant in some ways as an empty stomach and the person with the biscuits so often has a bad conscience. The trouble is that most of us with empty stomachs also have bad consciences. That combination will prove deadly.'

'I have a metal cup,' I said, 'and also a toothglass. If you like whisky . . .'

'I tasted it once,' he said courteously, 'I thought it better than schnapps and more interesting than our plum brandy. You need not fear, however, that I shall insist on taking it away with the biscuits.'

I gave him the toothglass. He took a small sip and looked at me. 'I know that you will forgive my telling you that before I came to see you this evening I looked up your name in an English reference book I have.'

'You'd like to know what a playwright is doing writing articles about a political trial?'

'Oh no. I see the connection. I was putting myself in your place for a moment. You have been in this city for two or three days perhaps. You do not know the country or the people. You are present at a trial which is like a game played for counters of which you do not know the value. Yet you have to interpret it for Western eyes.'

'Something of the kind has already been said to me once to-day.'

He nodded calmly. 'As a guide you have Pashik, a man so preoccupied with a problem of his own – self-preservation possibly, but we cannot be sure – that he can lead you only to the counter of the Propaganda Ministry.' He took another biscuit. 'Have you seen the official bulletin of the trial to-day?'

'This?' I took it out of my pocket. 'They gave out copies as we left the courtroom.'

'They will do so every day. Tell me, Herr Foster, what will there be in your articles that a clever malicious journalist sitting in London could not contrive for himself from a set of these reports?'

'I'm sure you have your own answer ready.'

'Ah, I have offended you.' He smiled. 'But not seriously I think, if you reflect. What I am suggesting to you, Herr Foster, is that you might find it useful to employ my services.'

'Yes, that's what I thought you meant. How?'

'As a guide. I make this suggestion without embarrassment. You were kind enough to invite me to tell you some things about Yordan, and, of course, I will do so.' He touched the biscuit box. 'I should have been well paid for that. But I think that I could be of further use to you.' His haggard eyes looked up at me with a cold little smile in them. He licked a crumb off his lower lip.

'I'm sure you could,' I said and waited.

'For instance,' he went on, 'I wonder if you have

considered that some of the evidence against Yordan Deltchev might not be as stupid as the Prosecution makes it.' He looked into the toothglass.

An unpleasant suspicion crossed my mind. 'Your difference of opinion with him,' I said, 'was over his radio speech approving the election, wasn't it?'

He was very quick. He said calmly: 'If I were an enemy of his I would not need to beg a gift of biscuits, Herr Foster. I should be a witness at his trial. And if, as your caution may suggest, I am here as an emissary of the Propaganda Ministry to try to corrupt your judgment, then you cannot yet have identified the man whose task it will be to do so.'

'I'm sorry. I don't know what you're talking about. What man?'

'Our friend Brankovitch has been forced to admit a number of hostile foreign journalists for the purpose of reporting this trial. Do you suppose that while they are here he will make no attempt to neutralize their hostility? Of course, he must try. I can even tell you the procedure he will adopt. To-morrow perhaps, or the next day, after Vukashin's evidence has been heard, Brankovitch will call a foreign press conference and answer questions. Then, perhaps the next day, someone will approach you privately with a great secret. This person will tell you that he has discovered a way of getting uncensored messages out of the country. He will let you persuade him to share the discovery. Of course, your messages will not be sent but they will serve as a guide to your intentions which can then be anticipated in the official propaganda. Brankovitch likes, for some reason, to use *agents provocateurs*.' He looked at me sardonically. 'I know his sense of humour. It was I who recommended him to Yordan for a place on the Committee.'

I offered him a cigarette again. He hesitated. 'If I might take two?' he said.

'One for your wife?'

'Yes.'

47

'Please take the packet.'

'Thank you.'

It was not quite full. He counted the cigarettes in it carefully.

'How did you meet Deltchev?' I asked.

He looked up. 'He was my partner,' he said. He seemed surprised that I did not know.

I gave him a box of matches and he lit a cigarette.

'Thank you.' He blew smoke. 'When Yordan first practised as a lawyer, I was his clerk. Later I became his partner. When he was appointed Minister of Posts and Telegraphs I became his assistant and secretary. I was also his friend.'

'What sort of a man is he? Superficially, I mean.'

'Quiet, deliberate, very patient. A sound lawyer. If you were a journalist interviewing him in his office you would probably be irritated by a habit he has of looking past you when he is talking. He keeps his desk very tidy and empties the ashtray as soon as you put your cigarette out. Yet polite. He would tend to put words into your mouth – criticisms of himself – and then answer them. A bad habit for a lawyer, that. A man with a family – wife, son, daughter – of whom he is very fond, but not a family man. A good man but not at ease with himself.'

'The sort of man who would betray a principle for a bribe?'

'Yordan has never valued money enough to be corrupt in that way. Power might have tempted him once. You speak, of course, of his actions over the election promise.'

'Yes.'

'If he was paid to make that radio speech he gave up what he might value – power – to gain what he did not value – money.' He shrugged. 'I have had plenty of time for thinking and much bitterness has gone. At one time I thought of killing Yordan for what he did then, but even in hate I never supposed that he had been bribed.'

'What is your explanation?'

48

'I have none. Yordan was often accused of being merely a shrewd politician. In retrospect that seems as ridiculous as the accusation now that he is a murderer. By unnecessarily bringing about the November elections he committed political suicide and betrayed all the people who were loyal to him. You ask for an explanation.' He threw up his hands. 'It is as easy to say that he was insane as to deny that he was bribed. When I faced him in his room that night he did not look insane. He looked strangely at peace with himself. That made me more angry, and, you know, in anger many things seem clear. "Why?" I shouted at him; "Why?" "It is better so," was all he replied. Then, when I had finished abusing him, I said: "Papa Deltchev has gone and the Minister of Posts and Telegraphs has returned. Papa Deltchev was not strong enough to bear a people's love!"' Petlarov looked across at me and smiled slightly. 'But now I cannot remember what I meant,' he added.

After a moment I asked: 'Will the election matter be raised at the trial?'

He shook his head. 'Not by the Prosecutor. For the regime, the less said about the election the better. But they might tolerate the defence's making play with it to suggest Yordan's fundamental sympathy with the regime.'

'Who is defending?'

'His name is Stanoiev. It amused me to use it here. He is the Party member appointed to defend. His arguments in mitigation will be given prominence. They will serve as the final condemnation.' He frowned. 'What I do not understand is this affair of the Officer Corps Brotherhood. Yordan's attitude towards Soviet occupation – yes, that is something to argue and misinterpret, to deal with speciously. But the Officer Corps Brotherhood is another matter. They make so much of it that they must have something. Yet, the idea is absurd.'

'Surely it's easy enough to manufacture evidence?'

'Yes, but that is not their way. Consider the case of Cardinal Mindszenty. He was accused of an offence against the currency regulations. We know that it was only technically an offence and not committed for his own gain, but he was guilty of it and that was the reason it was used. If he had been charged as a corrupter of youth it would have made much better propaganda and no doubt the evidence could have been manufactured. But no – the currency offence could be proved. The lie stands most securely on a pin-point of truth.' He took the last of his twelve biscuits and shut the box. 'What do you want of me, Herr Foster?'

'You have already given me a great deal.'

'I have a suggestion. Why do you not talk to Madame Deltchev?'

'Is it possible?'

'Yes, for you. She and her household are under protection – that is, they are not permitted to leave the house, which is guarded – but your permits will allow you to pass. I will give you a letter to her. She will see no other journalist, I assure you. You will make a *coup*.'

'Yes, I see that. What kind of woman is she?'

'She was a schoolteacher in the town where we practised years ago. She came of a Greek family. If she had married me instead of Yordan, perhaps I should have become a Minister. But better that you should form your own opinion. If you wish I will come here every evening at this time to give you what information and comment I can.' He leaned forward and touched my knee with his forefinger. 'Is it agreed?'

'Agreed. But what is my part of the agreement?'

He hesitated. 'Money – a little, what you consider fair – and your ration card. Not the restaurant tickets – those you will need and I could not use – but the ration card for bread, meat, butter, milk, eggs and green vegetables. As a foreigner you have one on the highest scale, I think.'

'Yes.'

'You still have it? You have not already disposed of it?'

'No. It's yours. I'll get it now.'

50

He sighed. 'It is as well that my wife is not here,' he said. 'She would weep.'

Later when he had gone, I sat by the window and had a whisky and water in the toothglass. I was beginning to feel perceptive and understanding.

That was the point at which I should have packed my bag and gone home.

Chapter 6

In the afternoon of the second day of the trial, the Prosecutor completed his opening address to the court and began to call witnesses.

The first was Vukashin, the head of the Government. There was a stir as he went into the witness box.

He was one of those politicians who, in their dealings with the public, are like small-part actors who specialize in playing such things as shrewd lawyers, family doctors and wise fathers; their mannerisms of speech and gesture have been cultivated to fit the stock characters their physical peculiarities suggest. He was square and solid with a short neck and he stood awkwardly in the witness box, his big hands clasping the ledge in front of him, the shoulders of his ill-fitting jacket hunched about his ears. He had blunt features with a muscular jaw and full, determined lips. His forehead was low and permanently knitted in a frown of concentration. In the popular edition of his biography published by the Propaganda Ministry he was referred to as a 'veteran front fighter in the class struggle,' and, from the illustrations, you received the impression that he had spent most of his life marching up steep hills at the head of fist-brandishing processions of angry revolutionaries. The role he affected was that of 'simple workman.'

In fact, he was neither simple nor, strictly speaking, had he ever been a workman. His father had been a small but fairly prosperous tradesman and Vukashin himself had been a book-keeper in a timber warehouse during the early part of his political career. It had been a natural talent for accountancy and office organization rather than revolutionary ardour which had raised him first to the secretaryship of a trade union and later to leadership of the party. He had a reputation for the kind of wit that makes a political statement in terms of some excretory or sexual function. He was a powerful man physically and was said to have once made a brutal assault on a colleague who had opposed him. But it was also said that the victim had been alone in his opposition and unpopular and that the assault had been calculated quite coolly for its disturbing effect on the morale of other intransigent colleagues. He was a brusque, direct speaker and very effective with big audiences. 'What are the *real* facts behind this problem?' he would shout; and although he never answered such questions, the sturdy conviction with which he pretended to do so and his way of enumerating his sentences so emphatically that they sounded like hammer strokes of logic, usually concealed the deception.

The Prosecutor's self-effacing deference to him was so abject that it was not even amusing. From a ranting bully who at least existed, Dr Prochaska became suddenly no more than a disembodied, impersonal voice; a prompter who fed the witness with a short question and then waited until the speech in reply was over and another question was wanted from him.

'Minister Vukashin, in March of nineteen forty-four when the armistice negotiations began, what was the attitude of the prisoner, Deltchev?'

'Our policy was peace, immediate peace to save the country from devastation by reactionary led forces seeking to continue their losing battle with our Soviet ally. Every hour of it meant another cottage, another farm destroyed, every day a fresh horror for our peasant workers in the frontier areas. Who could have said "go on"? Not a man with heart and bowels! Only a blood-maddened beast. But there was such a creature. His name was Deltchev!'

'Minister Vukashin, in what ways did the prisoner Deltchev work against the peace?'

'It would be easier, Public Prosecutor, to tell the court in what ways he did *not* work against the peace, for then I could answer shortly: "in *no* way." From the beginning of the negotiations he used his position on the Committee to hinder their conclusion. You may ask why this was tolerated, why he was not immediately removed from his post. The answer to that is simple. We believed at that time that he was in misguided but honest doubt about the terms of the negotiations that were under discussion. We were a responsible group, acting not for a defeated country – we were never defeated – but for a resurgent nation. The terms offered us by Russia, however, contained, as was natural in the circumstances, military clauses which involved our surrendering certain rights of government. The interpretation put upon them depended upon one thing and one thing only – whether or not Russia could be trusted. We of the People's Party did trust Russia, and in the event we have been justified. All the rights surrendered by us then have now been restored. The prisoner took a contrary view – or said that he did, for we know better now – and it was this view that he urged upon us as a justification for delay and for continuing his negotiations with the Anglo-Americans.'

'Did he contend that better terms would be obtained from them than from our Soviet ally?'

'No. The terms were no different in essence. They had been agreed to by the Foreign Ministers at the Moscow Conference of forty-three. According to the prisoner what would be different was the way in which they would be enforced. Or so he said.'

'Minister Vukashin, did the prisoner take part in the discussions with Soviet representatives?'

'Very little. He was too busy licking the backsides of the Anglo-Americans.'

Laughter.

'Minister Vukashin, in presenting his arguments for negotiation with them, what advantages did the prisoner claim would follow?'

'He claimed so many advantages that you would have

supposed us conquerors about to impose our will upon the defeated. But what were the facts at that time? First . . .'

The earphones softly droned out the translation but above this sound his own voice persisted. It was loud and, in the harsh, penetrating quality of its lower notes, disquietingly aggressive. He claimed hostility as urgently as another might claim love, and to hate him was to submit to a seduction. In a way he was impressive.

The voice went on and the grotesque rubbish it talked was passively received in evidence. I watched the judges' faces as they listened.

The floodlights for the cameras were on all the time now. The day was warm, and soon, as the afternoon sun poured in through the high steel-framed windows, those in the lights began to sweat. Most of them wiped their heads frequently and fanned themselves; but the judges, sweltering in their black gowns and biretta-like caps, seemed unwilling to acknowledge their discomfort before the eyes of the cameras. They had been judges before the People's Party had come into power and it was known that all such appointments were under review by the Government. Later, perhaps, in a cool cinema at the Propaganda Ministry, the film would be examined by subtle, hostile men able to construe the wiping of hands or forehead as gestures of disrespect to the Minister and his evidence. No momentary relief from discomfort was worth that risk to the judges. Two of their older colleagues had already been dismissed for showing reluctance to preside at this trial. Now, behind the sweating impassivity of those who had not shown reluctance, there was the terrible anxiety of men who, having sacrificed their principles, fear that the sacrifice may after all go unrewarded.

Only the prisoner did not sweat. He sat with his hands in his jacket pockets and his eyes closed, the back of his white head resting against the wooden rail which separated the lawyers' tables from the body of the courtroom. His face was livid in the glare of the lights and he looked as if he might faint; but, incredibly, he did not sweat. But for the pricking of your own skin you might have fancied that the heat of the place was an illusion and that all the perspiration you could see was simply a visible manifestation of collective guilt.

The afternoon crept on and the shadows moved slowly across the courtroom until there were only narrow strips of sunlight on the walls. There were no more than ten minutes to go before the day's adjournment when the incident occurred.

Vukashin had almost completed his evidence and the Prosecutor was asking him a series of questions about the meeting of the Committee at which it had been finally decided to accept the armistice terms.

'Minister Vukashin, what was the attitude of the prisoner when it was clear that the majority of the Committee favoured acceptance?'

'As always he attempted to obstruct the wish of the majority. He repeated all his former arguments and when these were rejected again by the rest of the Committee he said that he had further discussion with the Anglo-American representatives and that something might yet be done with them.'

'He gave the impression that he was making these proposals to them?'

'He had always given that impression. But now in the heat of the moment he made a slip which revealed his true intention. He said that the Anglo-Americans were only waiting for the word and at the snap of his fingers they would come.'

At that moment a strange voice in the court said something loudly and sharply and, in the dead silence that followed, the interpreter automatically translated.

'That is a lie.'

Deltchev had risen to his feet and was facing the witness box. His hands were still in his jacket pockets but he was standing very straight.

Vukashin looked startled for a moment, then turned his head to the judges.

'The prisoner objects to the truth.'

The centre judge leaned forward. 'The prisoner will be silent.'

Deltchev took no notice. 'I do not object to the truth,' he said. 'Nor do I object to the fantastic perversions of the truth which the court has been listening to to-day, for no person in his senses will accept them. I do however object to lies which attribute to me statements which I have never made.'

The judge shouted angrily: 'Be silent. You will have an opportunity of speaking later.'

'Will Minister Vukashin be available to me for cross-examination?'

'Your counsel may examine the witness if he wishes to do so.'

'He does not propose to do so. He values his own skin too much.'

There was a commotion at this and the thin, dark man, whom I took to be Stanoiev, began to make some sort of appeal to the judges. As several other people including Dr Prochaska were speaking at the same time, the interpreter became tongue-tied. One of the judges began to shout.

'The presiding judges call for silence,' said the interpreter.

Vukashin had been standing in the witness box looking on with a grim smile. Now he raised a hand and, as the noise subsided, spoke: 'I have given my evidence. Let him say what he wants.'

Deltchev faced him again. There was complete silence now. The prisoner's voice was light, but very clear and precise.

'Minister Vukashin,' he said, 'was it with the Committee's knowledge that I made the proposal to the Anglo-American representatives in nineteen forty-four that we should fight a delaying action in the north?'

Vukashin hesitated a fraction of a second. 'Be careful how you answer,' Deltchev put in quickly. 'The facts can be checked. The minutes of the Committee still exist.'

Vukashin made an impatient gesture. 'I am aware of that.'

'Then you see the need for caution. Will you answer the question, please?'

'The reply is not as simple as you try to suggest. The Committee was aware that a proposal was made but it was not aware that you had instructions from your Anglo-American friends to make it appear that the proposal came from the Committee.'

'Your answer is that I *was* authorized by the Committee to make the proposal.'

'Yes, but . . .'

'Let me continue, Minister. If the Committee authorized the proposal and if, as you say, the Anglo-American representatives wished it to be made, will you explain then why they did not immediately accept it?'

'Do not please ask me to explain the actions of the Anglo-Americans.'

Laughter.

'It is not the actions of the Anglo-Americans I am asking you to explain, but your own account of them.'

Vukashin turned angrily to the judges. 'I am here to give evidence, not to answer political riddles. That is enough.'

'You have been very patient. The court thanks you, Minister. The prisoner will be silent.'

Vukashin left the witness box and sat down. As he did so, Deltchev turned with a pale smile to face the courtroom. 'The Minister is afraid to answer,' he said.

It was at that point that Dr Prochaska made a foolish mistake. He had been standing there impotent and forgotten during this exchange. He was irritated. He was the Prosecutor and yet matters had been taken out of his, the responsible hands, and an important battle of words had taken place without him. More serious still, the Minister, whom he should have protected, had had the worst of the battle. Now, he saw his chance of retrieving not only his own dignity but that of the Minister as well. Never once since the trial opened had Deltchev taken his hands from his pockets and Dr Prochaska had found the fact irritating. He suddenly thought he saw just how he might humiliate the prisoner.

'Afraid?' he exclaimed derisively. 'The Minister is *afraid* to answer?' He gave a short laugh. 'It is not the Minister who is afraid. It is you, Deltchev! No wonder you seek to accuse and discredit the witnesses against you. You are in fear of your life. No wonder you tremble. No wonder you keep your hands in your pockets. Do you think we do not notice? Ah, but the people have eyes, Deltchev. You cannot deceive them for ever. You may disguise your fear in other ways but your trembling hands you dare not let us see. Come, show us your hands, Deltchev. Or else be silent while justice is done.'

In the breathless hush which descended there was one single quickly suppressed giggle and then no sound but the fluttering of the cameras. The Prosecutor had a hard ugly little smile on his lips. At that moment he was not absurd. Vukashin looked down at his own hands, frowning. Deltchev stood quite still, his face expressionless. He was making up his mind.

Then he took his hands out of his pockets and held them out palms downward in front of him. They shook with a coarse tremor that must have been visible at the back of the court.

'The prisoner's hands are more truthful than his tongue,' said the Prosecutor.

Without a glance in his direction Deltchev put his hands back in his pockets and raised his head.

'I speak,' he said loudly, 'to the members of the Diplomatic Corps present here and to the representatives of the foreign press.'

There was another commotion in the front of the court

and the Prosecutor began to protest to the judges. The interpreter began to translate the protest and I took my phones off. Others beside me were doing the same. Deltchev had spoken in German.

'You may have formed your own conclusions,' he went on, 'about the quality of the evidence that will be given by the Prosecution in this court. In case you are in doubt, this demonstration will convince you. The evidence of my own hands has now been offered against me. I will explain what it is worth.'

With an elaborate satirical bow in the direction of the diplomatic and foreign press sections, the Prosecutor abandoned his protest and stood, his arms akimbo and an unsuccessful attempt at a smile on his face, looking up at the ceiling.

'I make no defence of myself in offering this explanation,' Deltchev was saying; 'my defence is in the safe hands of the prosecution.' He smiled faintly. 'But perhaps you will be interested in this fact. I give it to you merely as a point of interest.'

He paused and then went on very deliberately: 'Gentlemen, I am a diabetic and have been so for several years now. That has meant, of course, a careful diet balanced with injections of insulin. The amount of insulin I need is not great – twenty units in the morning and twenty at night. I can, of course, call medical witnesses to prove this. When I was first arrested, the prison doctor was authorized to supply me with insulin. He even increased the injections slightly to compensate for the change in diet. Five weeks ago I was moved to another part of the prison and was not allowed to see the prison doctor. For just over four weeks I have been without insulin. The symptoms of diabetes have therefore returned – thirst, fatigue and other disagreeable manifestations which I shall not trouble you with. The trembling of my hands is part of my general weakness and debility. If the Prosecutor had asked me to show you my knees, you would have seen that they also tremble.' He looked round at the Prosecutor for a moment and then turned back to us. 'I think that if he had known of this illness he would not have drawn your attention to it in this way. It is no part of his task to create sympathy for me. I merely ask you to note that he makes wrong deductions even from facts. The fantasies that he will create from the falsehoods his case rests upon I leave to your imagination.'

Then he sat down.

The Prosecutor said something quickly to the judges. The centre judge said something in reply. I put the earphones on again and caught the translation.

'The presiding judges rule that the remarks of the prisoner shall not be entered in the record as they were made in a foreign language not intelligible to the court. The case is adjourned until to-morrow.'

The court rose.

When the judges had gone, Deltchev stepped down from the rostrum and with his own guards walked slowly towards the glazed doors. Nobody else in court moved. They watched him. At the door he paused and looked back. Then with a small, friendly nod he turned away again and went on through the doors.

I looked at Pashik. He was standing stiffly and awkwardly as if caught in the act of rising. He did not seem to notice his discomfort. He looked at me rather strangely. 'A good man, Mr Foster,' he said softly; 'in his way a great man.'

But I did not pay much attention to him. Even now, I can remember everything I thought during that next half-hour. I was very shocked by what I had seen and heard, and full of hatred for the People's Party regime. I think that if I had met Dr Prochaska in the corridor outside the courtroom I should have hit him. But soon I began to think more reasonably.

Nobody, I thought, could share the experience I had just had, without also sharing my passionate indignation at what was being done in that sunny courtroom. If I could convey the scene even with a tenth of the impact it had in reality, I would arouse a storm of anger that might damage the regime appreciably. And then an idea began to form in my mind of how I might write about the Deltchev trial.

This, I thought suddenly, was more than just the crooked trial of a politician by his more powerful opponents. Here, epitomized, was the eternal conflict between the dignity of mankind and the brutish stupidity of the swamp. Deltchev, sick and alone, knowing that nothing could save him from a verdict and a sentence already decided upon, was yet prepared to go on fighting for the truth he believed in. Dimitrov at the Reichstag Fire trial had fought for his life and won. Deltchev's life was already forfeit but he was fighting none the less and might win a greater victory. And the fight was of his own choosing. Months back he could have escaped abroad and made the Government's task easy. He had not done so. Long forgotten sentences began to run through my mind. *'Will you then flee from well-ordered cities and virtuous men? and is existence worth having on these terms? Or will you go to them without shame, and talk to them, Socrates? And what will you say to them? What you say here about virtue and justice and institutions and laws being the best things among men? Would that be decent of you? Surely not? . . . Will there be no one to remind you that in your old age you were not ashamed to violate the most sacred laws from a miserable desire of a little more life?' . . . This, dear Crito, is the voice I seem to hear murmuring in my ears, like the sound of a flute in the ears of a mystic . . .*

I was deeply moved. I was also beginning to enjoy myself.

And then I got back to my hotel and Petlarov was waiting in the corridor.

We went into my room and I told him what had happened.

He nodded coolly when I had finished. 'Oh, yes. Poor Yordan. He is certainly not strong. But how foolish of them not to tell Prochaska how the victim was being prepared! But we may expect foolishness. You see, they have always been able to rely before upon the folly of others. Now that they have to rely on themselves, their deficiencies are revealed. Of course an incident like that will make no difference to the outcome of the trial.'

'No, but it will make a great difference to the comments on the trial in the Atlantic countries.'

'The comments of the West did not save Petkov or Mindszenty. I think it is interesting, however, in quite a different way.' He smiled thinly. 'Why do you think Yordan made this demonstration? What did he hope to gain by it?'

'He saw an opportunity of hitting back and he took it. Surely, that's obvious. It was splendid.'

'He saw an opportunity and took it, certainly. What exactly did he say finally – the last two sentences?'

I had scribbled down Deltchev's words as he had said them. I read the last two sentences again. '"I merely ask you to note that he makes wrong deductions even from facts. The fantasies that he will create from the falsehoods his case rests upon I leave to your imagination!"'

Petlarov showed his white teeth. 'What a clever lawyer Yordan is,' he said. 'Do you not see what he has done, Herr Foster? Oh, certainly he has won the sympathy of the foreign diplomatists and press representatives, and that is very nice; but what else?'

'He made the Prosecutor look a fool.'

'He did more. Consider. He makes the speech in German. Why?'

'Obviously so that he would be allowed to speak. The interpreters didn't relay what he said of course. As far as the public was concerned he was unintelligible. Obviously it was the American and British representatives who mattered to him and Vukashin and the judges and Prochaska didn't want to antagonize them unnecessarily by shutting him up. If they don't care much anyway about Western opinion they could afford to let him talk.'

'If it was the American and British who mattered, why

did he not speak in English? Yordan speaks very good English.'

'Oh.'

'The educated persons of most small nations need a second language to their own. With us it is mostly German. Many of the Party members in that courtroom speak German and some of them are not unfriendly to Yordan. Those were the persons who interested him. What he wanted to do – and what he has done perhaps – is to discredit the Prosecution's evidence in advance.'

'That's not difficult. It discredits itself.'

'So far yes. But perhaps Yordan was wiser than we yet know.'

'I don't understand you.'

'It is quite simple.' He leaned forward with a chilling smile. 'You see, Herr Foster,' he said, 'some of the evidence against him may not discredit itself. Some of it may be true.'

Chapter 7

Deltchev's house was on the edge of the city in an old residential quarter behind the Presidential Park. Petlarov had drawn a sketch map for me of the way there and after an early dinner I walked to it from the hotel. There was a slight breeze and the air seemed cooler. The main streets and cafés were full of people, the women in their shapeless dungarees and cheap wedge shoes, the men in their cloth caps with their jackets over their arms, and their shirts undone at the neck; but beyond the park where there were few shops and scarcely any cafés, the streets were almost deserted and the only sounds came from the radios in apartment houses.

I found the quarter without difficulty. It was off the Boulevard Dragutin; six quiet streets, paved for a short distance from the Boulevard, and then ending casually in a hillside wasteland of scrub and tamarisks. The streets were lined with plane trees and with square solid old houses, each isolated within its own courtyard by a high wall with a heavy wooden door in it. The spaces between the walls of adjacent houses formed narrow lanes which in some cases connected parallel streets but were mostly shut off by tall iron gates and choked with wild vines.

The numbers on the houses were on blue enamel plates over the wall doors, and when I came to the right street I saw that Deltchev's house must be the last in it. But the setting sun was in my eyes and I did not see the guards outside the house until I was nearly upon them.

They were standing in the shadow of the plane tree just by the door. The trunk of this tree was scarred and the lower branches were leafless; the grenade of American manufacture must have exploded just by it. The guards' faces turned towards me as I approached.

They were in the uniform of what I referred to in my own mind as the 'military police,' though perhaps *gardes mobiles*' would have contained a more accurate comparison. They wore the same grey-green uniform as the courtroom guards; but these had rifles instead of machine-pistols and instead of tunics they had blouses bunched in at the waist by greasy leather belts with ammunition pouches. From a difference in their badges I guessed that they were a Corporal and a Private. They were young, bronzed and rather stupid looking. Our eyes met as I came up and I nodded but they did not reply in any way or make any movement to intercept me. I stopped by the door, looked up at the plate to confirm that I was at the right house and then reached up to pull the bell handle bracketed to the wall.

The next moment I received a violent blow on the shoulder. The shock of it made me gasp. I lurched against the door and twisted round. The Private had the rifle raised to prod me again. The Corporal had his rifle pointed at my stomach and his finger was on the trigger. I raised my hands.

The Corporal shouted something and took a pace backwards. I moved away from the door. I started to say in German that I did not understand what he was saying but he shouted again and this time I caught the word for 'papers.' With the heel of my hand I indicated my breast pocket and said '*Papieren*.' The Private jabbed the muzzle of his rifle into my ribs. Then the Corporal, stepping forward, tore open my jacket, snatched out my wallet and stepped smartly away from me.

It all happened in a few seconds. I was absurdly shaken. I must have looked it, for the Private grinned at me then in quite a friendly way, as if my discomfort were a tribute to his efficiency. The Corporal was frowning over my press permit. He looked at the photograph on it and he looked at me. Then he folded the permit, put it back in the wallet and coming up to me began to speak very slowly and distinctly, waving the wallet under my nose to emphasize what he was saying. It was clearly an admonishment. I nodded. Then he gave me back the wallet, saluted negligently and moved away. Behind me, the Private stretched up and pulled the bell handle. A bell clanged inside the courtyard. Then he, too, went back to his post under the tree.

They watched me as I waited, the Private still grinning, the Corporal frowning coldly. My shoulder hurt abominably and I badly wanted to rub it; but a curious shame and perhaps, too, a fear of pleasing them prevented my doing so. I was disconcerted by these unfamiliar and, I could not help thinking, rather childish emotions. I had behaved stupidly and had been roughly treated and humiliated in consequence; but it was no use; my hatred of them welled up like a sickness.

Then I heard footsteps crossing the courtyard inside; the clacking, slithering footsteps of wooden-soled sandals without heel straps. There was a pause and a rattling of bolts. Then the door opened a few inches and an old woman looked out. She had a face like a walnut shell with woolly grey hair and bright little eyes very deep in their sockets.

She looked past me to the guards.

'I would like to see Madame Deltchev,' I said in German.

She snapped out a reply I did not understand.

From behind me the Corporal shouted something. I looked round in time to see him raise his rifle threateningly. She snapped again, then very slowly she opened the door. I heard the Private laugh as I went inside.

The wall of the courtyard was about fourteen feet high and decorated all the way round with big frescoes of pastoral scenes: peasants dancing, a young man wooing a dairy maid, a village wedding. They were crude and conventional like the decorations on Russian toys. The predominant colours were cobalt blue, terracotta and ochre but in some places the paint had flaked so badly that only a faint discoloration of the stones showed where it had been. The floor of the courtyard was paved with square flags on which stood potted plants of various kinds, some of them in brilliant flower. Out of a square space in the flagstones grew a big cherry tree. Beyond it, in a corner, there was a neat wood pile with vine poles leaning against the wall by it.

The old woman had stopped to bolt the door again but now she straightened up and faced me grimly, her arms folded, her eyes bright and full of malice. She said something that must have been: 'Well, now you're in what do you want?' I replied in German that I did not understand. She did not understand that. I got out Petlarov's letter addressed to Madame Deltchev and gave it to her. She took it in her clawed, arthritic hands and looked without comprehension at the writing. I guessed that she could not read. She looked up at me suspiciously for a moment, then held up a hand for me to wait and clacked away round the side of the house.

I rubbed my shoulder and looked at the front of the house. It was about twenty feet from the wall, a blank symmetrical façade in grey stone with white-painted metal shutters fastened over all the windows. Double steps curved up to the front door which was flanked by potted azaleas and looked as if it were rarely opened. I heard the old woman's footsteps on a bare floor inside, and a distant murmur of voices. Then for a bit there was silence. I was a small boy again, calling for a friend with rich parents. The breeze stirred the leaves of the cherry tree and there were other footsteps inside the house. A moment or two later the front door opened and a girl came out. At the top of the steps she paused.

'Herr Foster?'

'Yes.'

She came down the steps with the preoccupied frown of a busy person whose time is being wasted. She was in the early twenties, dark and very pale with high Slavik cheekbones. It was an intelligent face, but had an expression of bland self-assurance too determined to be real.

'I am Katerina Deltchev,' she said.

'I'm glad to meet you.' She had only a remote facial resemblance to her father.

'What is it you wish, Herr·Foster?'

'To see your mother. Perhaps Petlarov's letter did not explain that.' I knew that it·did.

'At the moment I am afraid that is quite impossible. She is very upset, you understand.'

'Naturally. Is she specially upset to-day?'

'Please?'

'I am sure that these are all terrible days for her. I merely wondered if the proceedings to-day had specially affected her.'

'I don't think so.'

'Then perhaps you would ask her when I may see her, Fräulein.'

'I can tell you anything you wish to know, Herr Foster.' She smiled but not very warmly. 'Would you like a drink?'

'No, thank you. Are you quite sure that your mother wishes to be protected from someone who may be of help to her?'

'I don't understand.'

'If you will take Petlarov's letter to her, I'm sure she will explain to you.'

She stopped smiling. 'My mother does not see journalists.'

'So I believe. That is why Petlarov gave me the letter to her.'

She hesitated, then pressed her lips together. 'Very well. Please wait.'

She turned on her heel and went into the house again. She was wearing neat white shorts, a maillot and sandals. I felt a little sorry for her. It is difficult, even for an attractive young woman, to make a dignified exit in shorts.

I waited a few more minutes. The light was going. Then

the front door opened again and this time the old woman came out. She beckoned to me and I followed her.

Inside, there was a large hallway with curtained doorways on either side and a slippery hardwood floor. There was a radiator against the wall between two of the doors. It was all very clean and smelt of polish. Motioning me to follow her, the old woman climbed up the stairs. On the landing there was a shuttered window and by the half light filtering through the slits in the metal I could see a passage running along the width of the house. The old woman turned to the right along it and going to a door at the end scratched on the panel. There was a voice from within. She opened the door.

Red light from the setting sun streamed into the passage through tall unshuttered windows in the room beyond and as I came to the doorway I could see the bare khaki hills outside the city.

The windows gave on to a wooden terrace with an awning and vines growing over trellises at the sides. There was an iron table there with books on it and some cane chairs.

The room was large and filled with massive red plush drawing-room furniture of the kind made for the wealthy tradesmen of pre-Sarajevo Vienna. On the walls there were heavy gilt mirrors and girandoles, and coloured prints in polished wood and ormolu frames. Overhead there was a large gilt electric chandelier. The upholstery was red cut velvet. In winter the room would be quite cheerless but now, with the windows opened on to the terrace and with the gilt touched by the glow of the sunset, it had a certain richness and warmth.

As I came into the room, a woman sitting just out of the sun by the far window put a book down and rose to her feet.

I had a slight shock.

She was someone who had once been a provincial school teacher. Petlarov had said: 'Perhaps if she had married me instead of Yordan, I should have become a Minister.' There

70

was the diabetic husband under sentence of death. There was my pilgrimage to this house to see her and my interview with the attractive young woman whose mother did not see journalists. There was the quiet shuttered house, the smell of furniture polish. Out of all these things an image of the Madame Deltchev I would find had been composed in my mind's eye. She had been an old woman with white hair, in a wheel chair perhaps or even bed-ridden; a wiry matriarch with the evidence of her youthful beauty still discernible in her face, and the vitality, which had served the young lawyer and then driven the ambitious politician, still there in the brightness of her glance and impatient directness of her speech. How this irascible crone had borne a daughter twenty years ago or what disease now immobilized her my untidy imagination had not troubled to inquire. What I was prepared for in Madame Deltchev was the female counterpart of the grey, shaking man I had seen in court that day and with whose mystery and fate I was preoccupied; and I had visualized no other.

What I saw was a slim, erect woman of about fifty in a striped silk blouse and well cut skirt, and with sleek, black hair only slightly touched with grey. Her forehead was broad and high and she had gentle, very intelligent eyes. The bold regular features which her daughter had inherited were in her more masculine, but her complexion was perfect.

She smiled politely as she greeted me. 'Herr Foster, I'm sorry that you were kept waiting outside.'

'It's very kind of you to see me.'

'Please sit down.' She sat down again herself. She had a small lace fan which she fluttered unobtrusively by the side of her face farthest from me. 'My daughter had the best of intentions, but she did not understand Petlarov's motives.'

The girl stood behind the chair. She did not look at me.

'With Petlarov,' she said angrily, 'there is only one motive. He does only what he is paid for.'

Her mother said quietly: 'Please get us some tea, Katerina.'

Katerina laughed shortly. 'English journalists drink only whisky and soda, Mother. It is traditional.' She went over to the samovar. 'Isn't that right, Herr Foster?'

Madame Deltchev frowned and said something quickly in their own language. The girl made a sharp retort. Madame Deltchev smoothed her hair.

'I think that Herr Foster will excuse you, Katerina, if you wish to leave us to talk,' she said calmly.

The girl stood still looking at her for a moment, her face dark with anger. Then with a bang she put down the tea glass she had been holding and walked out of the room.

Her mother rose and, going over to the samovar, began to pour the tea herself.

'All nerves in this house,' she said, 'are greatly strained, Herr Foster.'

'Yes, I can imagine.'

'For my daughter it is perhaps most difficult,' she went on; 'unfortunately she is in political disagreement with my husband. She sympathizes with that section of the Agrarian Socialists which blames Yordan for the present situation. So, her love for her father is in conflict with her feelings towards the man who betrayed his party. It is difficult for her and I cannot help much.' She handed me some tea. 'You see, Herr Foster, it is not without reason that I avoid speaking to journalists. I do not guard my tongue. The regime would be glad to use the fact that Yordan's own children oppose him politically. But Petlarov says that you are friendly and to be trusted.'

'I was wondering, Madame, what there was about Petlarov's motives to be understood.'

She took her tea back to her chair. 'Petlarov is a good friend,' she said. 'Even after his disagreement with Yordan, he remained a friend. When he was released from prison I was able to see him for a short while and I asked his advice about the press. We were already an object of interest you see. He told me that I should see no one until he sent somebody that could be trusted.'

'That is very flattering but frankly I do not see the reason for his choice.'

'Did you not read his letter?' She held it up.

'I'm afraid I couldn't.'

'Oh yes, the language.' She looked at the letter. 'He says that you are going to write a series of articles about the trial and sentence which will be published in America and England. He says that your articles will be well written and acceptable and that although they will be politically naïve . . .' She broke off and looked at me apologetically. 'He means of course that he does not regard you as primarily a political person.'

'He's right.'

She smiled. 'So many of our circle would be offended.' She returned to the letter. '. . . although they will be politically naïve, their simplification of obvious issues and the evident sincerity of their indignation will be admirably suited to the campaign against the outcome of the trial.' She folded the letter. 'Petlarov is interesting, is he not?'

'Very.'

'So very wise and yet not a whole man.' She picked up her tea reflectively. 'His nerves were never strong enough for power.'

'Unlike your husband's.'

She looked up, a little sharply, as if I had interrupted a train of thought. 'Yes, let us talk about Yordan,' she said; 'and about the trial. That is why you are here.'

'I don't wish to distress you but I would like you to know about something that happened to-day.'

She nodded. 'Yordan made one of his demonstrations. I already know it.'

'It wasn't in the official bulletin.'

'No. Every evening since we have been under house arrest an old friend of our family has come to see us. Every evening he is searched by the sentries and every evening

73

the sentries find some money in his handkerchief. They let him pass.'

'I see. The demonstration was moving.'

'Yes, I was told that. It is a great relief. After this they will not dare to withhold his insulin injections.'

There was a curious lack of emotion in the way she said it. We might have been discussing a mutual acquaintance.

'Do you think that was all he hoped to gain from it?'

'What else is there, Herr Foster? Please do not think that you must spare my feelings. Yordan will be condemned.'

'Petlarov had another explanation. He said that your husband seized the chance of discrediting the evidence of the prosecution.'

'Yordan is a good lawyer.'

'From the way your husband used his opportunity, Petlarov deduced that there might be some evidence against him which can only be dealt with by discrediting it.'

She looked slightly puzzled. 'Evidence which can only be dealt with by discrediting it?' she repeated.

'Yes.'

She shrugged. 'There will no doubt be many things too absurd even for denial.'

'There is no true evidence that can be brought to support any of the charges?'

She looked surprised. 'Of course not.'

'No facts at all that could be twisted into evidence of corrupt negotiations in nineteen forty-four?'

'Most facts can be twisted, Herr Foster.'

'But in this case not credibly?'

'No.'

'That would be true also of the alleged association with the Officer Corps Brotherhood?'

'Doubly so. The idea is absurd. My husband was the man primarily responsible for the destruction of the Brotherhood.'

'You think that false evidence will be brought?'

'They have no alternative,' she said with a touch of impatience.

'Then it will be easy for your husband to disprove the evidence?'

'If he is allowed to do so, yes. But I do not follow the trend of your questions, Herr Foster? The charges are obviously absurd.'

'That is what troubles me, Madame. If there is no vestige of a case to support them they are too absurd. As Petlarov points out, if they had to fake evidence there were less fantastic charges available.'

'Petlarov is sometimes too clever. It is perfectly simple. Association with the Brotherhood is a capital offence and to-day also a disgrace.'

'You do not expect to be surprised by any of the evidence?'

'Nothing that the People's Party can contrive would surprise me.'

For a moment or two I sipped my tea. There was something difficult I wanted to say. She was sitting attentively waiting for me to go on. The sun was dying and in the faint after-light her face was astonishingly youthful. I might have been looking at the young schoolteacher whom the lawyer Deltchev had married, the young woman of Greek family whose lips may have had even then the same gentle, inflexible determination that I saw now.

'Madame Deltchev,' I said, 'when you were speaking of your daughter you referred to your husband as the man who betrayed his party.'

'I was representing him as my daughter sees him.'

'But you do not see him that way?'

'I understand him better than that, Herr Foster.'

'That might not be a reply to the question, Madame.'

'Is the question important for your understanding of the trial?'

'I do not know your husband. It seems to me important that I should.'

She sat back in her chair. She had just put her tea down on the table beside her and her hands rested lightly on the chair arms. There, they could reveal nothing.

'You saw my husband in court to-day. You could see the evidence of most of the qualities you wish to know about – his courage, his cleverness, his sense of timing, his determination. One thing the circumstances would not let you see – his absolute integrity, and I, who know his heart, will vouch for that.'

The light was very dim now, and in the shadow of the chair her face was difficult to see. Then she leaned forward and I saw her smile.

'And in case you wish to ask me about his weaknesses, Herr Foster, I will tell you. He cannot accept people as they are but only as his reason dictates they should be. Feeling he suspects, reason never, and the idea that in him the two may be connected he rejects completely. Therefore he is often mistaken about people and just as often about himself.'

I was silent for a moment. Then I got up to go.

'May I come and see you again, Madame?'

'Of course, Herr Foster, please do.' Then she paused. 'I shall in any case be here,' she added.

'Afterwards, if you are allowed to do so, will you leave the country?'

'When Yordan is dead do you mean?'

'When there is no more to be done here.'

'Then I shall go on living behind our wall,' she said. 'Did you not notice our wall?'

'It's very fine.'

'You will see such walls round most of our old houses. In Bulgaria and in Greece, in Yugoslavia, in all the countries of Europe which have lived under Turkish rule it is the same. To put a wall round your house then was not only to put up a barrier against the casual violence of foreign soldiers, it was in a way to deny their existence. Then, our people lived behind their walls in small worlds of illusion which did not include an Ottoman Empire. Sometimes, as if to make the illusion more complete, they painted the walls with scenes of national life; but only on the inside, for that was where life was lived. Now that we are again inside our walls, the habits of our parents and our childhood return quietly like long lost pets. I surprise them in myself. This room for instance. Since Yordan's arrest it has been the only room on this floor of the house which has had the shutters open in daytime. My feelings tell me it is better so. But why? No reason except that from all the other windows on this floor one can see the street.'

'Isn't it dangerous to deny the street?'

'For my children, yes. For me no, for I shall not try to impose my private world upon the real. My son, Philip, is a student in Geneva. He will be a lawyer like his father. Already he promises to be brilliant, and Switzerland is a better place for study than here. I hope to make it possible for Katerina to join him there.' She paused. 'Yes, by all means come again, Herr Foster. When you wish.' She pressed a bell-push. 'Rana will unbolt the doors and show you out. I will tell her also to admit you if you come again.'

'Thank you.'

We shook hands and said good-night. As I went to the door I heard the old woman's sandals flapping along the passage outside.

'Herr Foster.'

'Yes, Madame?'

'It might be misleading to pay too much attention to Petlarov's views.'

'I will remember what you say. Good-night.'

'Good-night.'

The door opened and a shaft of electric light from the passage struck across the darkened room. I glanced back; I wanted to see her face again in the light; but she had turned away.

I went past the old woman into the passage and waited

while she was given her instructions. Then she shut the door of the room and led the way downstairs.

The girl was standing in the hall. She was waiting for me. She had changed into a blouse and skirt.

'Herr Foster, may I speak to you a moment?'

'Of course.' I stopped.

She said something to the old woman who shrugged and went away.

'I will show you out myself,' the girl said: 'but I wanted to speak to you first. I wanted to apologize to you for my behaviour.'

'That's all right.'

'It was unforgivable.'

She looked so solemn that I smiled.

Her pale cheeks coloured slightly. 'I have something to ask of you, Herr Foster.'

'Yes, Fräulein?'

She dropped her voice. 'Tell me please. Were you searched by the guards when you came in?'

'No. One of them pushed me in the back with his rifle and they looked at my press permit, but that's all.'

'A foreign press permit. Ah, yes.' Her eyes became intent. 'Herr Foster, I have a favour to ask of you.' She paused, watching to see how I took it.

'What is it you want me to do?'

'To deliver a letter for me.'

'What letter?'

She took a letter from her blouse pocket.

'Can't you post it?'

'I am not permitted. Besides . . .' She hesitated.

'You just want me to post it for you?'

'To deliver it, Herr Foster.'

'Why can't I post it?'

'There is internal censorship.'

'Where is it to be delivered?'

'Inside the city, Herr Foster,' she said eagerly. 'Near the station.'

'Who is it to?'

She hesitated again. 'A young man,' she said.

'Supposing I'm caught with it?'

'You will not be, Herr Foster. Rana said that when she opened the door the guards were friendly to you. Please, Herr Foster.'

I thought for a moment of the guards and of their friendliness. The muscles in my shoulder had stiffened slightly.

'All right, Fräulein. A pleasure.'

'Thank you, Herr Foster.'

I took the letter and glanced at the envelope. The address was in block letters and quite clear. I put it in my pocket.

Her smile was replaced suddenly by a look of anxiety. 'When will you deliver it?'

'To-morrow sometime. When I can.'

She would have liked to ask me to deliver it that night but I was not going to do that. I made as if to go.

'Thank you,' she said again. 'I will show you out now if you wish.'

She had a small hand-lamp. We went out and across the dark courtyard to the door in the wall. She undid the bolts.

'Good-night, Herr Foster,' she whispered and then, standing behind the door so that she could not be seen from outside, she opened it.

The beam of a powerful flash shone in my face blinding me. I stepped through the wall and the door closed behind my back. I stood still.

'*Papieren*,' said a remembered voice.

I got out my wallet and opened it with the press permit showing. The Private was holding the flashlight. The Corporal came into the beam of it. He glanced at the permit without touching it and then, smiling at me grimly, he nodded and with his thumb motioned me on my way. He said something and the Private laughed. They were pleased that I had so quickly learned my lesson.

It was only as I walked away up the street and the beating

of my heart began to return to normal that I realized that, for a moment or two, while the light had been shining on my face and while I had wondered if they might be going to search me after all, I had been very frightened. I fingered the pocket with the letter. It crackled faintly. I smiled to myself. I was childishly pleased. I did not know that I had just performed one of the most foolish actions of my life.

Chapter 8

As usual now, I had breakfast with Pashik.

'Last night, Mr Foster,' he said, 'I telephoned your hotel.'

'I was out.'

'Yes. It does not matter.' In his brown eyes was the faint hostility of the lover determined not to be possessive. 'It was to tell you that Monsieur Brankovitch, the Minister of Propaganda, has called a foreign press conference for this evening. We, of course, have been invited.'

'Oh?' What Petlarov had said about the tactics of the Propaganda Ministry came into my mind.

'Monsieur Brankovitch will speak and also answer questions,' said Pashik solemnly. 'It will be very interesting. The food and drink will be excellent.'

'And there will be a collection taken for the poor of the Parish.'

'I beg pardon?'

'Nothing. A bad joke.'

'The conference will be in the state rooms of the Ministry at six o'clock.'

'Good.'

He dabbled his bread in his coffee. 'Have you seen Petlarov again, Mr Foster?'

'Yes. I thought you'd rather not know about it.' For a moment I wondered if I should also tell him that I had been to see Madame Deltchev, and then decided not to.

'As long as there is no indiscretion, Mr Foster.'

'He comes privately to my hotel room. The reception does not know him.'

He sighed unhappily. 'No doubt he will be discreet for his own sake. Is he still of interest to you?'

'Yes. He is an intelligent man, don't you think?'

'If he had used his intelligence, Mr Foster, I should be more sympathetic towards him.'

'You mean if he had played ball with the regime?'

'Of course. That is the realistic attitude.'

We went off to the trial.

That day, the third, six witnesses were heard. All of them had been members of the Committee of National Unity and all, except one, were members of the People's Party. The exception was a man named Lipka and he was a member of the anti-Deltchev section of the Agrarian Socialists.

For the most part, the evidence consisted of repetitions of the assertions made by Vukashin the day before. A mass of documents, including the minutes of the Committee meetings for the critical period, was produced and there was a great deal of pseudo-legal fuss about which documents could and which could not be admitted as exhibits. The minutes were naturally well to the fore. As minutes they were quite often worse than useless but as ammunition for the Prosecutor they were just the thing. I remember one typical item: 'After some discussion the Committee agreed that Y. Deltchev should meet again with the Anglo-American representatives and urge them to delay the final decision on the proposals previously made.' The Prosecutor's witnesses declared that the 'discussion' in question had been an effort by Deltchev and his henchmen to stampede the Committee into accepting a set of Anglo-American proposals it had not even seen and that the Committee's decision had made Deltchev 'grind his teeth with rage.' The judges had a word or two to say and even the defendant's counsel, Stanoiev, felt it safe to join in this sort of argument. At one point, indeed, there was a fair simulation of a legal battle between the two advocates – a battle between two clowns with rubber swords – and, in the approved fashion, high words were exchanged.

The only effective witness was Lipka. He was one of those angry, embittered men who bear the news of their defeat in their faces; prepared always for hostility, they succeed in provoking no more than weary impatience. A talentless but ambitious man, he had been an Agrarian Socialist deputy for many years without achieving office, and his membership of the Committee had seemed to him the long awaited recognition of his worth and the beginning of his period of fulfilment. In fact, his value to the unconstitutional Committee had resided simply in his status as an elected deputy and when posts in the Provisional Government were being allotted he had been passed over without a thought. From that moment he had nursed an almost pathological hatred of Deltchev. At one time that hatred had been something over which people smiled and shrugged. Now, at last, the People's Party had turned it to account. His mode of attack was stupid but damaging.

Most of those whose work is directly related to the moods and behaviour of the public are inclined to refer to it on occasion in disparaging, even insulting, terms. But, while a gibe at popular stupidity from a harassed bus conductor may be amusing, the same gibe from the mouth of a leading politician has, for many, an uglier sound. What Lipka did was to quote Deltchev's private comments on various matters and contrast them with public utterances made by him at the same time.

'Papa' Deltchev had made a speech officially regretting an incident in which some peasants, misunderstanding or ignoring a Red Army order to keep out of a certain area, had been shot down by Russian sentries. In private he had said: 'It might not be a bad thing if a few more of the damn' fools were shot.' After a speech congratulating the farmers on their public-spirited efforts to send more food to the towns 'Papa' Deltchev had said privately: 'Thank God, they've had sense enough at last to find the black market.' On his own proposals for dealing with the fuel shortage 'Papa' Deltchev had remarked: 'And if they're still cold we can always print a few more copies of the regulations for them to burn.'

There were altogether about a dozen examples given of the prisoner's 'contemptuous disregard of the welfare of the people whose interests he pretended to have at heart.' No doubt there were, as Lipka claimed, many others which could have been quoted. The muttered asides of an over-worked Minister of State grappling with administrative chaos are unlikely to be distinguished for their sweetness or reason, and if he is an impatient man with crude notions of humour, they may be better forgotten. Certainly they cannot fairly be used as evidence of his true mind and intentions.

In his only interruption of the day, Deltchev made this point himself. He said: 'The doctor called out in the middle of a cold night may privately curse all mankind, but that curse does not prevent his doing his best for the patient.'

This remark was immediately excluded from the record as irrelevant. It had its effect in court but I was beginning to see that it was not in the court that Deltchev was being tried.

Petlarov's comments were not reassuring.

'After sitting for three days in that courtroom,' he said, 'you may realize that not one single piece of evidence that could be called evidence in a civilized court of law has been offered in support of the charges and that the only piece of sense uttered has been supplied by the prisoner in his own defence. And yet already much damage has been done. The grocer I now visit again – thanks to you, my friend – is an intelligent man and a supporter of Deltchev. He detests the People's Party and suspects what he reads in the controlled press. Yet the trial is important to him and as he cannot attend in person he must read the official reports in the newspapers. He reads with great suspicion, of course, and he discounts much of what he reads. But where is his standard of measurement? How can he discriminate? He reads that Minister Vukashin's evidence proves conclusively certain accusations against Deltchev. Can he ask by what

84

rules of evidence Vukashin's statements are held to constitute a proof of anything except their own dishonesty? Of course not. He is a cautious man and hard to convince, but when I ask him to-day what he thinks, he is uneasy and does not like to meet my eye. "Evidently," he says to me, "there was much evil that we did not know about. Even if these pigs must find it out, it is best that we know. We are in a mess all right." And you know, Herr Foster, for the Vukashins and the Brankovitches, that is success. The disillusioned do not fight.'

'I thought that it was the possible truth of some of the allegations that was worrying you.'

'The foreign press is not so easily disturbed by official bulletins as my grocer. What did Madame have to say about the Brotherhood?'

'She said quite confidently that the charges were absurd.'

'Did you believe her?'

'I believe she sincerely thinks they are absurd.'

'You were impressed, eh?'

'Yes. She said she thought you were being over-clever.'

'It is possible. I hope so. But remember that the only parts of his indictment which make statements which can be proved or disproved are those referring to the Brotherhood. You may create a haze of misrepresentation to prove that a man had evil intentions and cast doubts on his denials; but if you claim that on a certain date, he went to a certain place and saw a certain person and he can prove that he did not, you are lost. Because the court invites your contempt, do not suppose that Prochaska and Brankovitch are fools.'

'What does Katerina Deltchev do?'

'She was an art student.'

'Was?'

'Is, for all I know. But of course she cannot attend classes at present.' He looked at my wristwatch. 'It is time for you to go. You must not miss Brankovitch.'

I went to the Press Conference in a gloomy frame of mind.

The Ministry of Propaganda occupied one of the wings of what had once been the royal palace. It had been built, during a period of national prosperity towards the end of the eighteenth century, to the design of an Italian architect who had seen Versailles. Only a quarter of the building planned had been completed but the resultant structure was imposing and quite large enough to contain three ministries and the National Bank. The Propaganda Minister's press conference took place in a large stateroom with a painted ceiling and two vast chandeliers. Chairs had been ranged in a semi-circle round the marquetry desk at which the Minister was to stand. To one side there was a long table arranged as a buffet with napkins covering the food on it.

Among the American and British correspondents, Brankovitch was known as Creeping Jesus; he had a peculiar way of walking with his head and shoulders slightly in front of the rest of his body while his arms remained at a position of attention at his sides. By the French correspondents it was said that the posture was imposed upon him, as, in his imagination, Brankovitch carried two portfolios under his arms: that of his own Ministry on one side and that of the head of the Government on the other. He was a pale, dark man with a massive head and supercilious eyes. A graduate of Warsaw University, he had once been a mining engineer and his connection with politics had begun with pamphlet-eering. He had made a name for himself before the war as the arch-opponent of the foreign oil companies. He was a clever, ambitious man who never missed a chance of referring most emphatically to his loyalty to and admiration of Vukashin. There were many jokes made about these fulsome references to his leader; but it was said that, while he did not laugh at the jokes when they were reported to him, neither did he frown. It was believed that Vukashin disliked him personally but respected his judgment.

There were about sixty persons in the room; about half

of us were foreigners. Brankovitch came in briskly followed by two male secretaries bearing files and note-books, and those who had been standing about talking took their seats. Brankovitch waited, looking round, until the movements had ceased. Then he began.

'Gentlemen of the press,' he said in German, 'I have invited you to meet me here with three objects in mind. First, I wish to help you as far as possible in your work by giving you certain information necessary to your understanding of the evidence soon to be given in the criminal trial you are reporting. Next, I wish to give you an opportunity of asking me questions on matters of fact, and also' – he smiled slightly – 'on matters of opinion to which you may feel you already know the answers. Thirdly, I wished for the pleasure of renewing acquaintance with those of you I already know and of meeting those I don't know. But business before pleasure as the English say. I will speak briefly and then there will be time for questions.'

He glanced at his watch. He had a sort of brusque amiability which was not displeasing; he did not much care what we thought of him or mind if his amiability were not reciprocated. He was the busy man prepared to waste a little time on fools and so, logically, indifferent to foolishness.

'Let me tell you,' he said, 'about the Officer Corps Brotherhood; not about its origins – I feel sure you know about those – but about its later activities and its methods. Terrorist societies are not recent institutions. Most countries have suffered from them. Many countries, including the United States of America, still do suffer from them occasionally. It is the duty of all civilised governments, when these occasions arise, to seek out and destroy the criminals. It is the duty, I say; yet, of course, the duty is not always performed. Sometimes the government is itself terrorized. In other cases the government may sympathize with the terrorists' aims and secretly wish them well. I need hardly tell you that the Government of the People's Party is neither intimidated by nor in any degree sympathetic to the Officer Corps Brotherhood. We will not tolerate crime of any sort. The workman who kills his mate in a moment of rage and the fanatic who kills his ideological enemy in cold blood shall have the same justice.'

'From a People's Court?' somebody in the row behind me murmured; but if Brankovitch heard, he took no notice. He went on:

'Under the reactionary governments of the pre-war years, the Brotherhood became a great and terrible burden to our people. It is not known for certain how many murders it was responsible for. Without doubt the number must be reckoned in hundreds. I can tell you with more precision that the number of violent attacks on the person committed by the Brotherhood in the ten years between nineteen thirty and nineteen forty was about one thousand four hundred. This figure includes only those cases serious enough to need hospital treatment. The reason for the greater precision is, of course, that those persons lived to explain what had happened. The injuries included bullet wounds – approximately six hundred cases; stabbing – approximately two hundred cases; acid throwing – approximately thirty cases; flogging – approximately two hundred cases, and severe bruising and beating with truncheons, rods and other weapons made up the remainder.'

He had been referring to notes in front of him. Now he pushed them aside.

'But statistics can give little idea of the emotional consequences of this state of affairs, of the hatreds and fears aroused and of the effect on the social life of the community. I will tell you therefore of one typical case among the known cases and leave the rest to your imaginations. It is the case of Kyril Shatev, who was Prefect of this city in nineteen-forty. A man named Brodno, a criminal pervert and a member of the Brotherhood, had been arrested on suspicion of murder. There was plenty of evidence on this occasion and Shatev determined to bring this man to trial. Immediately, he began to receive the usual threats from the Brotherhood. He ignored them. I will be quite honest with you; past experience told him that when the case came for trial the attention of the Brotherhood would turn from him to the judge trying the case. The judge might yield but that was not Shatev's business. However, he miscalculated. The probability is that the evidence against Brodno incriminated senior members of the Brotherhood and was for them too dangerous to be heard. The Sunday before the date of the trial was to be set, Shatev, with his wife, his two young children and two female servants, was at his house about ten kilometres out of the city. They were about to sit down to the midday meal when a car drove up and three men got out. They said they wanted water for the car. A servant unthinkingly opened the outer door and the men pushed past her, knocking her senseless with a pistol butt. They then went into the house. Shatev tried to defend his family and was immediately shot. Unfortunately for him, he did not die at once. The men had a bayonet, and the two children were killed with it. Shatev's wife was then forced to witness her husband's sexual mutilation, also with the bayonet. She was then killed herself. The other servant was not harmed. She was to serve as a witness, they said, that the sentence of the Brotherhood had been carried out. She was threatened, however, that if she attempted to identify the murderers she too would be killed. The murderers were never identified and Brodno was never tried.'

He paused for a moment and looked round. 'One typical case,' he said and sighed. 'No doubt,' he went on, 'much could be said about a government which allowed itself to be intimidated by such means, but it is easy to miss the point. There were, in fact, many members of the Brotherhood in government circles. This we have found out later for, of course, membership was always secret. Who were these men? We know of two who were ministers and twenty-seven in posts of high authority in the civil service, the police and the army. There were certainly others in these high places. The plain truth is that membership of the Brotherhood ran through every class of society except that of the ordinary workman. This Brotherhood is a bourgeois disease. It is difficult to conceive, I grant you, that a man, presumably of more than average intelligence and ability, who has made his way to a position of authority and responsibility, could have any direct relationship with, for example, the murderous perverts who entered the Shatevs' house that Sunday or with others equally vile. But we found it so. When, during the life of the Provisional Government, we began the attack upon this evil, we had many terrible surprises. Yes, I say, *terrible*. To despise a man politically is one thing. To discover that he is a criminal lunatic is another. It is difficult to believe the most incontrovertible evidence in such cases. Yet we must.'

He paused again and there was dead silence. We knew that now he was talking about Deltchev. He clasped his hands in front of him.

'Let me give you an example from history, gentlemen,' he said; 'not the history of our own country but that of Italy and France. In eighteen thirty there was in Italy a young exile named Louis Bonaparte, a nephew of the first Napoleon and once his adopted grandson. In Italy also at that time there was a secret terrorist society called the Carbonari – the Charcoal Burners. Among the members were nobles, officers, landlords, government officials, peasants and priests. The members called each other "cousin" and the only form of resignation ever accepted from a member was his death. This young Bonaparte became a member of the Carbonari and a year after was imprisoned by the Austrian police for his part in a murderous affair. He was not then a very important or responsible person. But twenty-eight years later when that same man was Napoleon the Third, Emperor of France, the Carbonari had need of him and sent a reminder by an assassin named Orsini. The reminder was a gift of three bombs and they exploded one evening in the January of eighteen fifty-eight as the Emperor was arriving at the Opera in Paris. Eight innocent bystanders were killed and a hundred and fifty wounded, but Cousin Bonaparte was quite safe. What the Carbonari wanted from him was help to make a bourgeois revolution in Italy. He did not hesitate. The responsibilities of Napoleon the Third, Emperor of France, towards the people he ruled were as nothing beside those of Cousin Bonaparte towards the Carbonari terrorists. And so the Italian Risorgimento was paid for with the blood of the French soldiers that soaked the fields of Montebello and Turbigo and Solferino. It is not a pretty story, no prettier than that of Shatev and his family.'

There was silence for a moment.

He added quietly: 'Gentlemen, our people will fertilize no more fields for the "cousins" or "brethren" of this century. We intend to seek out all the murderers whether they sit on café chairs or on the thrones they have made for themselves above the heads of the people. The People's Party and its great leader Vukashin are pledged to that.' He looked round at us again and then sat down. 'I will answer questions,' he said.

It was quite well done and for a space nobody moved; then an American in front of me got up.

'In December of last year, Minister,' he said, 'the People's Party Government announced that the Officer Corps Brotherhood had been completely . . . *eliminated*. I think that was the word used. Are we to understand now that that announcement was incorrect?'

Brankovitch nodded. 'Unfortunately, yes. At that time, of course, we believed it to be true. Later developments have shown that we were mistaken.'

'What later developments, Minister?'

'I would prefer not to anticipate the court proceedings.'

A small dark man got up.

'Minister, was not Deltchev himself responsible for the

91

very vigorous proceedings taken to eliminate the Brotherhood?'

'He was certainly responsible for the action against the Brotherhood which we now know to have been ineffective, but the decision that there *should* be action was taken by the Provisional Government as a whole. In other words the People's Party participated in the decision but not in the carrying out of it.'

Others began to rise and now the questions came quickly.

'Minister, can your allusion to Napoleon the Third be taken to mean that the Government links the allegations about Deltchev's peace negotiations with the allegations about his membership of the Brotherhood?'

'You may draw that conclusion if you wish.'

'The charge is that Deltchev was to be paid for his efforts. Aren't the two suggestions inconsistent?'

'Possibly. But remember that Napoleon the Third also had his reward – Nice, The Riviera, Savoy.'

'Minister, do you consider that the evidence heard so far in court has gone any way towards proving any of the charges against Monsieur Deltchev?'

'The evidence must be considered as a whole.'

'By whom was defending counsel appointed, Minister?'

'By the Government. In all cases when a prisoner fails to appoint counsel to defend him that is done.'

'Did this prisoner fail to appoint counsel? Did he not, as an advocate, wish to defend himself?'

'On a criminal charge a prisoner is not by law permitted to conduct his own defence. The law was made for the benefit of poor persons certain of conviction who feared to burden their families with legal costs.'

'Minister, could not the law, clearly not intended for persons in Monsieur Deltchev's position, be waived in this case?'

'Are laws waived in England for the benefit of persons of high position?'

'Then you agree, Minister, that it would be to Monsieur Deltchev's benefit if he could defend himself?'

'It would be to the benefit of you gentlemen, I have no doubt. I apologize for our reluctance to have the court turned into a circus entertainment.'

'Will the Minister say if, as a result of the Prosecutor's unhappy efforts yesterday to provide the court with entertainment, the prisoner will now be allowed proper medical attention in the prison?'

Brankovitch rose to his feet with a smile. 'The prisoner is receiving ample medical attention,' he said, 'and as much insulin as he wishes. It was nothing more sinister than a stupid administrative blunder which prevented his having attention a few days ago. Disciplinary action has been taken against those responsible. Naturally the prisoner took the utmost advantage of his plight to gain sympathy . . .'

'When driven to do so by the Prosecutor.'

'Or when a favourable opportunity presented itself.' Brankovitch smiled again. 'We interpret motives from the standpoint of our own prejudices. But please note that the prisoner was not prevented from addressing you.'

'What he said was not reported in the official press, Minister.'

'Quite properly. The fact that a man is diabetic surely does not affect his responsibility to the community for criminal acts. Gentlemen, perhaps you would care to continue our discussion over the refreshments. I hope you will not think I am attempting to corrupt you if I say that there is champagne and caviare for you to sample. I am merely performing another of my functions as a Minister in introducing to you two products of our agricultural and fishing industries which we are anxious to export. The champagne is not French, of course, but it is a dry, sparkling wine of pleasing character and I think you will like it.'

There were one or two murmurs of amused assent and a scraping of chairs. Waiters entered, obviously in response to a signal, and whisked away the napkins from the buffet.

'He is clever, the Minister,' said Pashik seriously.

'Yes, he is. Shall we go?'

He looked shocked. 'Do you not wish to ask questions, Mr Foster?'

'What about? Napoleon the Third?'

'I think it would be impolite to go,' said Pashik earnestly. 'The Minister will surely wish to meet you. There is protocol to be observed.'

'There are others going.' Though most of those present had moved over to the buffet and stood in groups talking I noticed several making unobtrusive exits.

'Those are local agency men, Mr Foster. They have met the Minister before.'

'All right. Shall we go over?' Brankovitch was talking to a group which included Sibley, the man who drank too much and was indiscreet.

'No, Mr Foster. Let us quietly have some refreshments. Presently matters will arrange themselves.'

We were joined after a moment or two by an American I had chatted with once or twice at the courthouse. A waiter brought us wine and caviare sandwiches. One of the secretaries delivered copies of a long blood-curdling piece on the Officer Corps Brotherhood.

'Did you know that Byron was a member of the Carbonari?' the American was saying. 'I think we ought to rechristen our friend Brankovitch. When Ferdinand of Italy tried to liquidate the Carbonari he had his Minister of Police set up another secret society called "the braziers of the counterpoise," *Calderai del Contrappesso*. The Minister recruited all the worst characters in the country for it and what they did to the Italian liberals makes Little Bo Peep of that Shatev story. The minister was a man called Prince Canosa. What about Creeping Canosa for our friend?'

Pashik had left us. I talked to the American and ate sandwiches. After a few minutes Pashik came back rather breathlessly with one of the secretaries, a stony-eyed young man with over-neat clothes.

'This is Monsieur Kavitch,' he said; 'he is of the Minister's bureau.' The secretary bowed and we shook hands. 'The Minister is most anxious to meet you, Herr Foster,' he said stiffly.

'I shall be honoured.' I caught the American's eye and he put his tongue very obviously in his cheek.

The secretary stared hard at me. 'Have you yet had time, Herr Foster,' he said, 'to visit any of the well-known beauty spots which abound in the vicinity of our city?'

'I'm afraid I haven't.'

'At this time of year,' the secretary continued steadily, 'there are many varieties of the most remarkable rose blooms in the world to be seen and savoured. Our country is very beautiful. However, it is to be hoped that you will wish to be present on Saturday at the official parade and celebration in honour of the twenty-seventh anniversary of the founding of the People's Party.'

'I don't . . .'

'Herr Foster's special pass has already been applied for,' Pashik put in smartly.

'Ah, then he will see some of the beauties of the country brought to the city,' pursued the secretary steadily. 'This year the parade will be a symbolic integration of peaceful husbandry and armed might – the plough and the sword in harmony together.'

'Very interesting.'

'Yes. It is of the utmost importance that all our visitors leave us with a correct impression. I will myself see that you have an advantageous place, Herr Foster. Here, now, is the Minister.'

He stepped aside nimbly, like a compère effacing himself for the entry of the star. Brankovitch, with the other secretary in attendance, had stopped to say a word to a Scandinavian group. Now he turned in my direction. The secretary beside me said something in his own language with my name in it. Brankovitch held out his hand and turned on a watery smile.

'How do you do?' he said in English. His warm hand released mine almost as soon as it touched it. He nodded to Pashik as I answered him. 'You have not been to our country before, Mr Foster?'

'No, Minister. But I'm finding my first visit most interesting.'

He nodded. 'Much fiction has already been written about it but mostly by strangers. Now that cultural activities are being widely encouraged, however, perhaps a native school of writers will emerge. There is the language difficulty of course. A knowledge of our language is rare. Yet Ibsen, also writing in a narrowly spoken language, achieved world fame.'

'Ibsen's heroes and heroines were not obliged to be positive, Minister.'

'Ah, I see you have heard of our special problems. Yes, we are compelled to consider the standard of education of the public here. We must pay still for past injustices. The percentage of illiteracy is high and those who are literate are for the most part still uneducated in the western sense of the word. But in other cultural fields – the visual arts and music for example – greater freedom is already possible.'

'Ideas do not have to be expressed in words to be dangerous, Minister.'

'We do not hinder truth, Mr Foster, only the facile repetition of lies. But we must have a long undisturbed conversation about such things for I would be glad to hear your opinions. Tell me, how did you find Madame Deltchev last night? In good health?'

I sensed rather than heard Pashik's sharply indrawn breath. Brankovitch's gaze rested on me with unwavering affability.

'She seemed very well.'

He smiled again. 'She is not being persecuted?'

'Not that I am aware of.'

'We have tried to spare her as much as possible. Naturally

her position is difficult and we have to protect her against possible demonstrations. But I am glad to hear that she is well. You are the only journalist who has interviewed her, I think.'

'I think so.'

He nodded vaguely. 'I am so glad to have had this opportunity of meeting you, Mr Foster,' he said. 'We must have another talk. Most interesting.'

He nodded again and turned away. The secretary slid past me after him. The interview was at an end.

I looked at Pashik. His face was quite expressionless. He stepped up to me.

'Do you wish to go now, Mr Foster.'

'Yes, I think so.'

'You did not tell me that you had seen Madame Deltchev,' he said as we walked away.

'No. I thought you'd prefer not to know.'

'We must hope no harm is done.'

'What harm can be done?'

He shrugged. 'Such things attract attention.'

'Does that matter?'

'We must hope not. But I would have preferred that you had told me. I could at least have prevented the embarrassment.'

'What embarrassment? The sentries on the house looked at my permit. They reported. What of it?'

'You do not understand.'

'I'm afraid I don't. I think you're over anxious as I've said before.'

'I think my opinion about that may be better informed, Mr Foster.'

'I'm sorry, Pashik. I certainly have no wish to compromise you, but I have a job to do.'

'I have the responsibility, Mr Foster.'

'You must try to shoulder it.'

Before he could answer, there were quick footsteps

97

behind us. Pashik turned round as if he expected to be attacked. It was Sibley.

'Hullo there,' he said breezily; 'how are you, Foster? And you, Georghi my friend? What a dreadful party? When are we going to have that drink? Now? I feel the need.'

'Please excuse me,' said Pashik hastily, 'I must go to my office. Mr Foster, you have messages to send.'

'I'll see you to-morrow.'

He hesitated. We had reached the door. He gave up. 'Very well. Good-night, Mr Foster. Good-night, Mr Sibley.'

'Good-night.'

He went, leaving a slip-stream of malodorous disapproval.

Sibley chuckled. 'Poor little man,' he said.

Chapter 9

We went to a nearby café and ordered drinks. Then Sibley disappeared to make a telephone call. When he came back the drinks had arrived. He picked his up, peered into it as if it were a crystal ball, then downed it at a gulp.

'Well, what do you think?' he said grimly.

'About this evening's performance?'

'Performance! Exactly.' He snapped his fingers at the waiter for another drink. 'Incredible, isn't it?'

'In what way do you mean?'

'Oh, all of it. That old, old routine! Prejudice, friends? Not a bit of it! Anyway judge for yourselves, friends. Here are the simple facts given as simply as we know how – the facts about the Brotherhood. What has that to do with Deltchev? Who said it had anything to do with him? You're drawing the conclusions, friends, not us. We're only giving you the nasty facts. And to show you that the facts are really nasty we'll pull an old atrocity story out of the bag. Castration and rape, friends! Yes, we thought that'd get you where it hurts. What has that to do with Deltchev? Well, we don't say definitely that it *has* anything to do with him but . . . well, you're drawing the conclusions and we can't stop you, can we? In fact, although we're not exactly saying so, the same ugly thought is beginning to cross our minds now. How clever of you to think of it first, friends! But it does seem fantastic, doesn't it? Though, wait! Isn't there a historical precedent that fits the situation like a glove? Of course there is. And doesn't history repeat itself? Of course it does. In fact there is one point of coincidence we didn't mention. When Murat decided to destroy the Carbonari he gave the job to his Police Chief. The Police Chief destroyed a lot of people and Murat thought the job was done until he found out that the Police Chief had always been a Carbonaro himself and that the Cousins were stronger than ever. Strange, isn't it, friends? How clever of you to remember without our telling you! Any more questions? Yes? Well, let's not get into tiresome arguments. Let's have some caviare and a nice glass of aerated cat water. They make me tired.' He swallowed another large plum brandy and sat back.

'Another drink?'

'For God's sake, yes.' He leaned forward, his face slightly flushed, his lips still wet with brandy. 'How does one deal with it, Foster?'

'Brankovitch's press conference?' I signalled to the waiter.

'All of it. The whole phoney business. Perhaps it's all right for you. You've got plenty of time. A series of articles, weeks hence. But I'm supposed to be sending news. All I've got through so far are those damned official bulletins. I suppose Pashik sends those to your people?'

'Yes.'

'Do you know what I'd like to do?' His dull, hot eyes brooded on mine.

'No, what?'

'I'd like to put it across them. I'd like to split the whole damn' business wide open.' He frowned suddenly as if with irritation at himself. 'Take no notice. I had drinks before the party.' He smiled slyly and lowered his voice. 'Can you keep a secret, Foster?'

'Yes.'

'The funny thing is I can do it.'

'Do what?'

'What I said . . . break it open.' He looked round cautiously and leaned farther forward. 'I've found a way round this bloody censorship.'

'Oh, yes?' My heart began to beat rather unpleasantly.

'I can't tell you the details because I swore not to, but there's a little man in the Propaganda Ministry who doesn't like the regime any more than we do and he'll play. Of course, if he was found out he'd be lucky if they hanged him quickly, but he's prepared to take the risk. There's only one snag.' He paused. I waited. 'He can't do it more than once and the deadline's to-morrow.'

'That should give you time.'

'It's a risk.' He frowned at the table as the waiter put fresh drinks down. 'A big risk. If I'm caught, I'm out. Of course that wouldn't matter to you. It's not your living. But, by God, it's a risk I'd like to take.'

'The little man in the Propaganda Ministry must think it worth while.

He laughed shortly. 'You're right. It's funny, isn't it? One minute I'm breathing fire and murder and the next I'm worrying about a little risk.' He laughed again. His performance was deteriorating rapidly. I was not helping him and he would have to come to the point himself. I waited, fascinated.

'Would *you* take the risk?' he asked suddenly.

'I don't know. The question would have to arise.'

'All right, supposing – ' I thought I detected a note of genuine exasperation in his voice ' – just supposing you had a chance to file a short message with mine. Would you take it?'

'Is that an offer?'

'Don't be silly. Why should I give you a beat?'

'I don't know. Why should you?'

'You'd have to make it worth my while.'

'What's that mean?'

He did not answer. He was pretending to debate with himself. 'Look, Foster,' he said then, 'let's be serious for a moment. If I'd thought you were going to fasten on to the thing like this, I tell you frankly I wouldn't have mentioned it.' He paused. 'But since I have, I tell you what I'll do. If you'll undertake to confine your message to pure comment on the trial as a whole, I'll put it through with mine.'

'If you do send one, of course.'

'Oh, I'm going to send one all right. Don't you worry. And now you can buy me another drink.' He sat back with a tremendous air of having sold his birthright. 'I make only one stipulation. I'll have to read your stuff before I pass it on. Honestly, I wouldn't trust my own brother in a thing like this. Right?'

'I understand.' To give myself time to think I looked round for the waiter. I had had it all now: the confidence-promoting diatribe against the regime, the brandy-laden indiscretion, the indignant denial, the burst of generosity, the second thoughts, the grudging commitment. Petlarov would be amused. Pashik would purse his lips. I looked at my watch. I did not want to have to talk to Sibley any more. The waiter had disappeared. I put some money on the table.

'I have to go,' I said.

It took me five minutes and another hastily swallowed drink to do so but at last I stood up and put on my hat.

'About you-know-what,' he said; 'you'd better give me the stuff to-morrow morning. Two hundred words maximum.'

'Oh, that.' I smiled and shook my head. 'I don't think I'll bother.'

'Are you mad?'

'No. It's different for you. For me it's not worth the risk.'

He looked at me coldly for a moment. Then very elaborately he shrugged. 'As you will, *mon brave*,' he said.

'Good-night.'

Still seated at the table he gave me a heavily ironic bow. 'Don't change your mind to-morrow, Foster *mio*,' he answered, 'it'll be too late.'

'I won't change my mind.' I nodded to him and walked out of the café. Outside I hesitated. Now that the disagreeable part of the encounter was over, I was curious. Sibley the *agent provocateur* and employee of Brankovitch interested me as Sibley the breezy newspaper man never could.

I had an impulse to go back into the café, sit down and try to lure him into explaining himself. I did look back. He was sitting looking down at his drink, his elbows on the table, the thin, fair down on his sunburnt scalp glistening faintly in the evening sun. As I looked, he put his hands up to his head and there was something so hopeless about the gesture that it was quite moving. Then one hand dropped to the stem of his glass and twirled it between a finger and thumb. The other came down too. The money I had put on the table was still there and now a finger of this other hand crept out rather stealthily towards it and gently sorted it over to see how much there was there. Then he looked round for the waiter. I turned away. For the moment there was not much more I wanted to know about Sibley.

I went back to my hotel. I did not eat much dinner. I remembered that in one dim corner of the hotel foyer I had seen a framed map of the city on the wall. After dinner I went to it and got out Katerina Deltchev's letter. The address on the envelope was short: *Valmo, Patriarch Dimo*, 9.

With some difficulty I located the street on the map and set out. The girl had said that the street was near the station. It was, but it was also on the other side of the main line and to get there I had to make a wide detour through a crowded street market to a bridge and walk back along the far side of a freight yard. By the time I had found the church which I had noted as a reference point on the map it was almost too dark to read the lettering of the street names.

It was not an inviting locality. On one side of the main road there were tall warehouses and a power station interspersed with ugly apartment blocks; on the other side were small shops and steep lanes of wooden houses, the roofs of which were patched here and there with sheets of rusty corrugated iron; the old slum. There was a tram terminus a short distance down the road and I considered riding straight back into the city without troubling further about the letter. Then I decided to give the search for the street five minutes. If, as I hoped, I had not found it by then, I would go back. I found it almost immediately.

The street of the Patriarch Dimo was one of the steeper and shabbier lanes. There was a dimly lit wine shop at the corner and behind it a decrepit wooden building that seemed to be used as a stable for oxen. I walked up the hill slowly. The girl had said hesitantly that her letter was to 'a young man.' I had, I think, imagined Valmo to be a fellow art student of hers, a handsome lad with other girl friends who would have no scruples about taking advantage of Katerina's enforced absence. Now my ideas had to change.

Number nine was a house much like the rest but with the ground floor shutters crossed with planks and nailed up. There were no lights in any of the upper rooms and the greasy-walled entrance passage at the side was littered with pebbles and marked with chalk lines as if children had been playing a game in it. The house looked empty. I walked along the passage to the door and struck a match.

At some time recently the building had been a lodging house for there was a board with names painted on it. The match went out and I struck another. None of the painted names was Valmo. Then, as the second match was going out, I saw it. The top name had been scratched over with the point of a knife and under it the word 'Valmo' was crudely written in pencil. I dropped the burnt-out match and stood in the darkness for a moment. I was becoming curious about this Valmo. By the light of another match, I looked for a bell and, seeing none, tried the door. It was open.

I went in.

There was a small lobby with a flight of stairs in it. The place was quite still and seemed deserted. I looked round for a light. On the ceiling there was a hook and a smoke shield but no lantern beneath it. I went up the stairs striking matches. There were two doors on the first landing, both open. I looked in. The rooms were empty. In one of them some floorboards were missing. I went on up. I did not stop on the next landing; obviously the house was abandoned. Only one thing delayed my turning back. The rooms I had seen had been deserted for many months. But Katerina had not been confined to her house that long. It was possible, therefore, that Valmo had only recently moved away and had left a notice of his new address.

As I went up the last flight of stairs I noticed a peculiar smell. It was ammoniac and very sickly. It became stronger as I reached the landing under the roof. I struck another match. There was only one door here and it was shut. There was no notice on it. I knocked and waited. The match burned out. I struck another and turned the handle of the door and pushed. The door opened. Then I had a shock; the room inside was furnished.

I raised the match above my head and moved forward into the doorway. As I did so I became aware of a sound; there were flies buzzing in the room.

In the small light of the match I saw an unmade bed, a deal table and a chair with some newspapers piled on it. There was also a packing case.

The match burned down and I dropped it. Then, by the pale arc of light it made as it fell, I saw on the floor a dark mass like a crumpled curtain.

As I struck the next match I took a pace forward into the room. The light from the match flared up.

The next instant my heart jolted violently. It was not a curtain on the floor. It was a man; and his face was black.

I stepped back quickly and with some sort of shout I think. The movement blew the match out or I should have run. I fumbled desperately with the box and managed to get another match alight. I forced myself to look again.

His hair was close cropped and white except where the blackness spread. The blackness was congealed blood and it lay on and about him like spilled wax. His mouth was open and there was a gaping wound by his ear. There was no telling what he had looked like. He was lying on his right side, his knees drawn up to his chest and his elbows nearly touching them. He had on a dark serge suit and leather sandals but no socks. He had been small and thin. The flies buzzed round him. He had been dead for more than a few hours.

I began to retch and went out on to the landing.

A minute passed and I was beginning to get my breath again when I thought I heard a sound from below.

The blood was thudding in my head so loudly and my breathing was so quick and shallow that it was difficult to be certain. Then I managed to hold my breath for just over a second and heard the sound again. Very slowly and quietly, somebody was coming up the stairs.

I don't know who I thought it was; the murderer I suppose; at that moment I would have panicked if a fly had settled on my hand. In the darkness I stumbled back into the room, shut the door, lighted a match and looked feverishly for the bolt. There was a bolt but the socket of it was missing. I looked round desperately for something to jam the door with. I tried to use the chair but the door handle was too low. The match I was holding went out. I fumbled with the box again, opened it upside down, and the matches spilt on the floor. I was shaking with fear now. I went down on my knees and started to pick the matches up. At that moment I heard the footsteps on the landing just outside the door. I remained motionless. Under the door I saw a light flicker. The person outside had a flashlight.

Then the light went out and the door opened.

There was silence for a moment. Suddenly the flashlight went on and swept quickly round the room. It stopped on the body. Then it moved again quickly and stopped on me.

The end of a revolver barrel gleamed just in front of the flashlight. I did not move.

A voice said: 'What are you doing here, Mr Foster?'

It was Pashik.

Chapter 10

I got to my feet.

'Why are you here, Mr Foster?' he repeated.

'I don't know,' I said. 'Do you mind taking that light off my face?'

He turned the light down to my feet. I could see him now and the revolver in his hand was still pointing at me. He had his dispatch case under his arm and the medallion on it winked faintly.

'Well, Mr Foster?'

'I might ask you the same question.'

'I followed you, Mr Foster.'

'With a gun?'

'It was possible that we might not be alone.'

'We're not.' I looked at the dead man on the floor but he did not move the light from my feet.

'I want to know why you are here, Mr Foster, and who told you of this place. And I want to know right now.' There was a very sharp edge to his voice.

'Katerina Deltchev asked me to deliver a letter for her. This was the address on it.'

'Show me the letter.'

'Pashik, do we have to stay in this room? Can't we go outside? Anyway, shouldn't we be calling the police. This man's been murdered.'

'No, Mr Foster, we should not be calling the police. Show me that letter.'

I got it out. He came forward, took it from me and turned the light on it.

'She told me that it was to a young man,' I said.

Without replying he put the letter in his pocket and swept the light round the room.

'Have you touched anything here, Mr Foster?'

'This chair. Why?'

'What did you touch it for?'

'When I heard you coming up the stairs I tried to jam it under the door handle.'

'Wipe the chair where you touched it and also both sides of the door with your handkerchief. Then pick up all the matches you dropped, including the burnt-out ones, please.'

I obeyed him. Just then, the wish to get out of the room was stronger than my disposition to argue. He held the light down while I picked up the matches.

'Did anyone know you were coming here?'

'Only Katerina Deltchev.'

'You told nobody?'

'No.'

'Not Petlarov?'

'No.'

'Mr Sibley?'

'Nobody.'

'Did anyone see you come in here?'

'I shouldn't think so. There weren't many people about.'

'Your clothes are noticeably foreign. Did anyone turn to look at you?'

'You should know if you were following me.'

'I was not close enough to see. Was there anybody in the passage below when you arrived?'

'No.' I had collected all the matches. I straightened up. 'I can't stay in this room any longer,' I said and went out on to the landing.

'Wipe the door, Mr Foster.'

I did so. He ran the light round the room again and came out. 'Shut the door with your handkerchief in your hand, please. Yes, that will do. Now, Mr Foster, my car is at the end of the street by the wine shop. You have your matches. Go down as you came up, walk to my car, get in it and wait for me.'

'What are you going to do?'

'We must not be seen leaving together.'

'Why not?'

'Get going, Mr Foster.'

He still had the revolver in his hand and he handled the thing as if he were used to it. Oddly, there was nothing incongruous about the look of Pashik with a gun.

He held the light for me as I went down the top flight of stairs. After that I struck matches again. It was a relief to get into the street. By the time I reached his car I had done a good deal of thinking.

I smoked the greater part of a cigarette before he joined me. Without a word he climbed into the driver's seat, took his gun and flashlight from the dispatch case and, putting them in the door pocket, stuffed a greasy rag over them. He started the car. 'And now,' he said, 'we'll go see a friend of mine.'

'What friend?'

'He will advise us what we must do. He is of a special kind of police.'

'What special kind?'

'You will see, Mr Foster. Perhaps the ordinary police should be told. I do not know.'

He twitched the wheel suddenly, swerved across the road and swung uncertainly into a turning on the left.

I threw away the cigarette I had been smoking and lit another.

'Why did you follow me, Pashik?'

'I had a hunch that you might be about to do something foolish, Mr Foster.'

'But you did follow me?'

'You will agree that I was justified.'

I looked at him. 'I came through a street market that was difficult to get through on foot. How did you follow me in a car?'

'I cannot answer questions while I am driving, Mr Foster.'

'Then let's stop for a few minutes. I have lots of questions and they won't keep.'

He drove on in silence.

'You've been to that house before, haven't you?' I said after a moment or two.

'Why should you think that, Mr Foster?'

'You knew that that man's body was there before you came in. That is, unless you're quite used to finding corpses with shotgun wounds lying about. You paid no attention to this one.'

He had been driving towards the centre of the city. Now we lurched into a quiet boulevard with trees along it.

'Another thing,' I said: 'if you'd followed me and expected to find me there, you wouldn't have shown your gun. As you came up the stairs you heard me move about. If you'd known it was me you'd have called my name. You didn't follow me. You went there on your own account and for your own reasons. What were they?'

'You are making things very difficult, Mr Foster,' he said gloomily.

'Yes. Who was the dead man? Valmo? Who killed him? You?'

He did not answer. Behind the trees that lined the road there were houses with *portes cochères*. He slowed down, then turned suddenly into a space between the trees and drove through into one of the courtyards. He stopped and immediately turned off the lights. We were in pitch darkness.

'Mr Foster,' he said, 'you are arrogant and very dumb. If I were truly a murderer you would be already dead. I have been very patient with you. Now we will see my friend.'

He switched on the flashlight and I saw that he had his revolver again. He put it in his dispatch case and we both got out. I looked up. The bulk of quite a large house was visible against the sky.

'Where is this?' I asked.

'My friend has an apartment here. This way.'

I could see very little. We went through a side door down some tiled steps to a small hydraulic lift with a rope control. The cage bounced as we got into it. Pashik hauled on the rope and we shot upwards with a faint hissing sound.

At the top floor the lift stopped automatically and we got out on to a bare stone landing with a small doorway in it and a steel ladder up to a skylight. Pashik knocked on the door.

After a moment or two a woman in an apron opened the door. She had grey hair scragged back into a bun and a bitter mouth. She obviously knew Pashik. He made some explanation to her. She nodded and looked at me curiously as we went in; then she led the way along a narrow passage and showed us into a drawing-room. There was nobody there. She switched on the lights and left us, shutting the door behind us. If there had been a faint smell of disinfectant in the air, it would have seemed like an appointment with a dentist. The room we were in, indeed, had very much the look of a waiting-room. The chairs stood round the walls and there was a large table in the middle with one small ash tray on it. All that was wanting was a selection of magazines.

'What's your friend's name?' I asked.

Pashik sat on the edge of one of the chairs. 'I will introduce you to him, Mr Foster.'

'What did you go to that house for?'

'You do not believe me when I answer your questions, Mr Foster.' His brown eyes looked at me mournfully. He took off his glasses and began polishing them.

'You never do answer them. Why didn't you tell me that Sibley was working for the Propaganda Ministry? You must have known.'

'How do you know that, Mr Foster?'

'Petlarov warned me to expect an approach from someone pretending to have a way round the censorship. It came from Sibley. If you knew, why didn't you warn me?'

'Would you have believed me if I had, Mr Foster? No.

111

You would have thought that I was trying to stop you sending news out.'

'Yes, I'm afraid you're right. I'm sorry.'

'It is unimportant, Mr Foster. It is simply that you do not like me.' He put his glasses on and stared at me. 'I am used to being disliked,' he added; 'I no longer mind.'

But I was spared the deathly embarrassment of replying to this. The grey woman appeared at the door, nodded to Pashik and said something. He got up and turned to me.

'My friend wishes to see me privately for a moment, Mr Foster,' he said. 'Perhaps you will wait.'

He picked up his dispatch case and went out of the room. I sat down.

Until that moment I had been feeling all right. Now, suddenly, the smell of the dead man was in my nostrils again. I felt sick and giddy. I put my head between my knees and tried to think of other things. I suppose that if Pashik had not arrived on the scene I should have hurried back to my hotel, had several large brandies and a sleeping pill and gone to bed. Instead, I was sitting in a strange room in a strange house with a desperate feeling of having lost all contact with reality. At that moment I would have given anything to be back in London, quietly doing in my own way the work I understood. I had realized that the delayed reaction to the horror of finding a decomposing corpse in a dark room was only the surface of my discomfort. Beneath, there were fears of another kind. I had thought to write about the trial and condemnation of an innocent man. Now, in spite of the obvious injustice of the trial itself, I was having to accept the disagreeable possibility that really the man might not be innocent, that the rubbish Prochaska was talking might have a basis in fact, that the trembling hands of the diabetic Deltchev might have clasped in brotherhood those of the murderers of the Shatev family; and the foolish trouble was that if those things were true I feared to know about them. Petlarov's grocer, I reflected bitterly, was not alone in his ill-informed

112

uneasiness; Mr Valiant-for-Truth, the great journalist, had also caught a whiff of the odour of corruption and was wishing his delicate nose elsewhere. It was curious how preoccupied I had become with smells; they seemed easier to deal with at that time than other ideas; the smell of the dead man, the smell of Pashik, the smell of furniture polish in Deltchev's house; those three things were related. And if I looked for reassurance to the other senses, I could recall the taste of the plum brandy I had had with Sibley, the feeling of the sentry's rifle on my shoulder, the image of Petlarov's white false teeth and the sound of his voice saying: 'Some of the evidence may not discredit itself. Some of it may be true.'

I got up and began to wander round the room. I knew now that the train of thought I had been avoiding could be avoided no longer.

If you accepted the seemingly incredible proposition that Deltchev was, and for years had been, a member of the Officer Corps Brotherhood, it was possible to explain some things about him that had hitherto defied explanation. To begin with you could explain the inexplicable election affair; Deltchev had done what he did, not because he had thought it right or necessary, or because he was a saint, or because he had been bought; he had done it in obedience to the orders of the Brotherhood. And, having said that, you could also explain why he had been able to give no explanation himself for his action. You could explain, though with difficulty, how a prosaic, undistinguished Minister of Posts and Telegraphs had been able to become the leader of a secret nationalistic revolutionary movement and ultimately seize power. You could even explain the 'football match' incident in that context; the fanatically nationalistic Brotherhood, having through fear of the growing People's Party misjudged the election timing, had commanded their puppet Deltchev to retrieve the position. Napoleon the Third had done more for the Carbonari. Besides, had not Petlarov himself admitted that power was a bribe that might be used with Deltchev? In a fantastic way it all fitted. It might be objected that, as a lawyer, Deltchev would not have qualified for membership in the early days of the Brotherhood; but the class distinction between professional men and army officers was not great. His membership was not impossible. It was certainly not improbable. Idealistic young men very often joined societies supposedly dedicated to the human struggles for freedom and justice; and very often, too, they later regretted having done so. When, I wondered, had Deltchev begun to regret the association? Then another objection occurred to me. Why, if the Brotherhood had supported Deltchev, had it also collaborated with the German occupation forces? But this I disposed of easily. What better cover could there have been for the subversive activities of the Brotherhood than half-hearted collaboration with the German Army? Not with the sharp and sceptical Gestapo, mark you, but with the Army. It would be interesting to know about the men who had made the Brotherhood's policy. Perhaps the trial would reveal them.

But, meanwhile, Deltchev's daughter had sent a letter to a cheap lodging where there was a murdered man. I thought about that. Who was Valmo? Katerina's middle-aged lover? I doubted it. This rather too knowing young woman had offered me a drink because she had thought that the engaging way with an irritable reporter; she had said that the letter was to 'a young man' because she had thought, perhaps less incorrectly, that was the engaging way with a reluctant letter smuggler. If I had had the presence of mind to do so, I might have looked more closely at the room for signs of a relationship with Katerina; her photograph perhaps, or a letter in her handwriting. A letter. And that brought me back to Pashik.

I had made a mistake about Pashik. I had thought of him as one of those hapless, over-anxious persons who cannot help entangling themselves in systems of small, unnecessary lies. It had not occurred to me that he might have anything of more than private importance to conceal. Now, I had to reckon with the news that not only could he be concerned quite calmly with the body of a murdered man but also that his tiresome preoccupation with 'discretion' had its origins in something very unlike the old-maidish timidity to which I had attributed it.

At that moment, with a jolt, I came out of the haze of cow-like rumination in which I had been lost and began to think clearly. If Pashik had known that the body was there before he came to the house why was it now necessary to consult his 'friend in the special police' so urgently? Answer: because I had been there, because I had seen the body, because I had seen Pashik, because I had drawn certain conclusions, because I might be indiscreet.

I had been pacing up and down the room. I stopped, then went to the door. From another part of the apartment there came very faintly a murmur of voices. I glanced at my watch. Pashik had been gone five minutes. I was suddenly convinced that it would be wise to leave without waiting to be introduced to Pashik's friend, to leave now, quietly. I hesitated momentarily, then I made up my mind. I put my hand on the doorknob and turned it gently. Then I began to pull. But the door did not move. I had been locked in.

Chapter 11

For a moment or two I stood there looking stupidly at the door as if I expected it to open itself. To find oneself locked in a room and know that the locking cannot be accidental or a practical joke is an extraordinary sensation. My feelings were confused and are not easily described; I was angry and frightened and depressed all at once. Then I broke out into a sweat. I tried the door again, then turned away from it. The room suddenly looked different, very large and empty, and I could see every detail in it. There was something familiar and yet not quite right about it.

When I had been walking about I had noticed an inch or two of string looped round one corner of the carpet. Now I saw it again; I was standing on the hardwood surround just by it. At that moment I was wondering if I should hammer on the door and demand to be let out, or sit there quietly and pretend not to have noticed that I had been locked in. Absently, I reached down to pick up the string. I wanted something to fidget with. I got the string, but the corner of the carpet came up with it. The string was threaded through the edge of the carpet and tied to a label. The label had some figures written on it and a printed name, obviously that of the dealer who had sold it. It was an expensive carpet, a Sparta, yet the owner had not troubled to remove the price tag. It had simply been tucked away out of sight. I was puzzled. I let the carpet fall back into place and walked round the room again. At one end by the windows there was a Buhl cabinet. I opened one of the drawers. There was a small brass screw in it and some dust. I tried the other drawers. All were empty except one which contained a price tag from the same dealer who had supplied the carpet. I went round quickly looking at the wood of the

116

chairs. They had been used a lot and yet there was a certain unused look about them. And then I knew what was familiar about the room; it was like a stage set when all the furniture had just been brought in and placed in position.

At that moment I heard voices and footsteps in the passage outside. I sat down. They came to the door and there was a slight pause. I knew why. The person who was about to open the door was preparing to turn the knob and the key simultaneously so that the sound of the latch would conceal that of the unlocking. If I did not know that I had been locked in, they did not want to tell me of the fact. My heart beat faster.

The door opened and after a momentary pause Pashik came in. He was followed slowly by a small man in a loose tussore suit and a black tie. I stood up.

Pashik put his hand on my shoulder and enveloped me in a broad smile. 'Herr Foster,' he said in German, 'let me introduce you to Herr Valmo.'

I had no time to digest this surprise. The other man came forward with a polite smile and held his hand out tentatively.

'So pleased, Herr Foster,' he said.

He was about fifty, short and very slight, with wispy and receding grey hair brushed back from a sunburnt forehead. It was a thin, pointed face with large, pale blue eyes and an expression that might have been cruel or amused or both. He looked like a retired ballet dancer who has taken successfully to management. In his hand was Katerina Deltchev's letter. It had been opened.

'Herr *Valmo*?' I said.

He smiled. 'I am afraid a little explanation is due to you, *mein Herr*.' He had a quiet, monotonous voice.

'It was not possible for *me* to explain, Herr Foster,' said Pashik. 'I could not break a confidence.'

'Please sit down, Herr Foster, and you, my dear Pashik. A cigarette? Ah, you are already smoking. As our friend Pashik explained to you, I am, you might say, some sort of a policeman, a very – ' he made a belittling gesture with his hand – 'a very confidential sort of policeman.' The woman appeared at the door with a tray and he glanced round. 'Yes, come in, Mentcha. Put it down.' He turned again, pulled round a chair and sat facing me. 'Coffee and a little brandy, Herr Foster. You have had a very upsetting experience, our friend tells me. Thank you, Mentcha. Shut the door. And now,' he went on as she went out, 'we must set your mind at rest. In your coffee, the brandy?'

'Thank you.'

Pashik was sitting deferentially by as if at a conference between his superiors. The hand holding his cigarette was trembling slightly.

Valmo handed me a cup and went on talking as he filled the other two. 'There is one thing,' he said, 'that I must ask of you, Herr Foster. That is that you respect the confidence of what I am about to tell you.' He held a cup out to Pashik, but he looked at me. 'Pashik tells me that you are not friendly to the regime here. I understand. But I am not a politician. I am a civil servant. Our country is a centre for many conspiracies against the law and it is my task to destroy them. Can I be certain that you will respect my confidence, Herr Foster?'

'Yes.' I tasted the coffee.

'Very well.' He put his cup behind him on the table and then leaned forward towards me with his elbows on his knees and his hands together. 'In my role of policeman, Herr Foster, it was my duty to seek out the perpetrators of the bomb outrage against Herr Deltchev which took place shortly before his arrest. I made certain secret inquiries and investigations. It was believed that the criminals had had the Deltchev family under surveillance and members of the family co-operated with me in identifying them. I have said that my function is not political. Herr Deltchev's trial does not relieve me of the responsibility of tracing these criminals. You understand?'

I nodded.

'For reasons with which I will not trouble you,' he continued, 'it became necessary for me to install an agent in the Patriarch Dimo. For convenience and identification, the agent employed my name. Very well. Three days ago my agent reported to me that he had news of the men we were after. That night he was killed.' He paused impressively.

'Who found him dead?' I asked.

He stared at me for a moment. Then he turned round and picked up his coffee cup again. 'I did, Herr Foster,' he said blandly. 'However, let me continue. The agent had collected certain documentary evidence against the conspirators which he kept hidden in the room. I discovered that this had not been stolen. Therefore, I argued, they did not know of its existence. Therefore, if they were made aware of its existence they would return for it. Therefore, I replaced the true document with some false ones which I prepared, and sat down to wait for results.'

'You mean you put a secret watch on the house to catch the murderer when he returned?'

He smiled gently and shook his head. 'I am afraid you do not know the street of the Patriarch Dimo, Herr Foster,' he said. 'That sort of secret could not be kept there. No. I set a different kind of trap. All I wanted was to get the false documents into the conspirators' hands. I had reason to believe that in fact that had happened. To-night, I asked Herr Pashik, who is a friend of mine and also sometimes a helper, to go to the house and make sure.' He spread his hands out like a conjuror. 'He finds you there.'

'With a letter addressed to you.'

'Exactly. Katerina Deltchev had recalled an important piece of evidence. She wrote to tell me of it.'

'Through your agents.'

'Naturally. This address is most confidential, Herr Foster. So you see how it has happened and the need for your discretion.' He sat back with a smile, clicked his lighter and held the letter in the flame of it. As it caught fire, he smiled at me again. 'I'm sure you do,' he added.

I thought quickly. It was just not quite good enough. The man who called himself Valmo and said that he was of the secret police had had a certain initial advantage; he did not look like the conventional secret policeman of fiction. If he had been vaguer and more mysterious about his story, it might even have been convincing. There would have been nothing unlikely about a secret policeman who was secretive. But this man had seen the holes in his story as he was telling it and instead of leaving them had tried to cover them up. For instance, having indicated an official connection between the Deltchev household and Patriarch Dimo street, he had decided that it did not satisfactorily cover Katerina's letter so he had added another detail; that weak one about her recalling an important piece of evidence. It would have been better to let me see the hole and question it. He could then have replied with a knowing shake of the head that he was afraid he could not permit himself to give me that information. And that, in turn, would have prevented my asking the awkward question I did in fact ask.

'Herr Valmo,' I said, 'what I don't understand is why Fräulein Deltchev, who is under house arrest, has to get me to smuggle out a letter to the head of the secret police. Why didn't she just give it to one of the sentries?'

He crushed the ashes of the letter on to the tray. 'She is a girl. No doubt she was afraid I would not get it.'

'She seemed more concerned about the censorship than anything else. She made me promise to deliver it by hand.'

'Confinement affects some people strangely.'

'Shall you go to see her?'

'It may be necessary. I do not know.' He was getting confused now. He pulled himself together a trifle impatiently. 'Those, however, are not matters of immediate concern, Herr Foster. It is your position that we must make clear.'

'Yes?'

'I have given you a great deal of confidential information. It must, please, remain confidential.' His pale eyes stared at me coldly. 'I may add, Herr Foster, that if you were not a distinguished journalist, it would have been considered advisable to put you in prison for a short while to make sure of your behaviour. That, however, we need not discuss. You have already assured me that you will be discreet. I require now three further undertakings from you. First' – he held up a finger – 'that you will not return to the house in the Patriarch Dimo or tell anyone of it. Secondly, that you will not again visit the Deltchev house. Thirdly, that you will make no attempt to identify this house, and that you forget its existence, and mine.'

I did not reply immediately. I knew now the kind of conversation that must have taken place between Valmo and Pashik while I was safely locked up and waiting. My one desire was to get out of the place as quickly as possible. But I had the sense to realize that if I showed my anxiety and agreed to the terms too hastily they would not feel quite safe. They were both watching me narrowly. I frowned, then looked up and nodded.

'All right,' I said curtly. 'I agree. And now, if you don't mind, I'd like another brandy.'

Valmo stood up. 'Yes, of course,' he said perfunctorily. He poured a small one. He could not wait to get rid of me now. 'Herr Pashik?'

'Thank you, no.'

They stood looking at me impatiently while I sipped the brandy. It was the only moment of enjoyment I had had in the whole evening and it lasted about ten seconds. As I swallowed the first sip, I heard the front door of the apartment open and close and footsteps in the passage outside.

'It is my brother,' said Valmo quickly.

Then the door opened and a young man came into the room. He saw me and stopped.

'Good evening, Jika,' Valmo said. 'We are talking a little business. I shall be with you in a minute.'

He was about twenty-five, dark and very tired looking.

He had a raincoat on and his hair was blown about as if he had been in an open car. He looked at us suspiciously. For a moment he did not move; then he turned away slowly and went to the door.

'Don't be too long, Aleko,' he said. 'I have something for you.'

I raised the brandy to my mouth again. I was not looking directly at Pashik but I could see his face and it had gone the colour of mud. He knew that I had seen the 'Aleko' note in the Deltchev file and for some reason was terrified lest I had remembered it. Aleko himself was waiting for me to finish my drink. The use of his Christian name had not visibly upset him. But the situation was delicate. I had seen something I should not have seen, but Pashik did not know if I realized it. The main thing then was to get out of the apartment before he could make up his mind what to do. I drank the brandy at a gulp and held out my hand to Aleko.

'Thank you, Herr Valmo, and good-bye.'

He smiled agreeably. 'I hope your stay is pleasant here, Herr Foster,' he said.

I turned to Pashik. 'Are you going to drive me back to my hotel, Pashik?'

'Yes, Mr Foster, yes,' he said heavily.

We went along the passage to the front door. Aleko came out to the lift with us. Aleko shook my hand again.

'I have liked you, Herr Foster,' he said; 'and with a journalist that is a new experience for me. I have faith in you. Good-bye.'

He might have been sending a promising young dancer on a first international tour.

Pashik was already in the lift. I got in after him. We went down in silence.

It was not until we were in his car and out on the road again that I broke the silence.

'Aleko Valmo,' I said. 'A curious name.'

'In these parts it is quite common, Mr Foster,' he said calmly.

He had made up his mind that I had forgotten the other name.

I was not feeling very friendly towards Pashik and, for a moment or two, I toyed with the idea of asking him suddenly: 'What was the case of K. Fischer, Vienna forty-six about, Pashik, and what had Aleko to do with it?'

Then I decided not to. We did not speak again until he drew up outside my hotel. As I went to get out, he put his hand on my arm and his brown eyes sought mine.

'Mr Foster,' he said, 'it has been a lousy experience for you this evening and no doubt you will wish to forget all about it. That is, if you are wise.'

I did not answer. His voice took on its cautious round-about tone.

'I wish only to tell you,' he said, 'that I understand your feelings and share them. But you have your own profession and need not trouble about what happens to dead-beats and bums far away from your home. Men are dying all over the world for the causes they believe in. You cannot fight their battles.'

'Are you telling me that I should mind my own business?' I asked.

'Ah, please, Mr Foster!' He spread his hands out. 'You are mad at me.'

I was exasperated. 'I'm not mad at you, Pashik. I'm merely trying to get you to say straight out what you mean without all this double talk. I don't mind being advised to mind my own business. That's all right. I don't have to take the advice if I don't want to. I'm still capable of deciding what is my own business and what isn't. I'm not fighting any battles. I'm trying to find out what goes on here.'

'That is what I mean, Mr Foster. It does no good to try.'

'You mean I won't be able to find out?'

He looked away from me and picked at the steering wheel. 'You force me to be frank, Mr Foster.'

'What's the matter with frankness. Why has it to be forced?'

'You say you fight no battles, Mr Foster,' he said quietly; 'but I tell you, you are wandering like a fool between the opposing forces of those who are. That is a crazy thing to do. Once, years ago in Vienna, I saw street fighting between troops and revolutionaries. The fighting went on for many days. But there was one street that was swept equally by the fire of both sides and neither could advance. Then one afternoon something very silly happened, as so often it happens in war. Into this empty, silent street there came a man. We heard his footsteps first. Then we saw him. He staggered from a side turning right into the middle of the street and stood there swaying. He belonged to neither side. He was drunk and did not know where he was or what he was doing. He began to sing and wave and call out for a woman. At first the soldiers laughed and shouted jokes at him. But after a while their officer noticed that the enemy was taking advantage of the distraction to run across the far end of the street in ones and twos so as to outflank the troops. He shouted a warning and they opened fire. The enemy replied with covering fire and the street was swept from end to end with machinegun bullets. The drunk was killed immediately. You see, Mr Foster?'

'Which side were you on?'

'I was a soldier then. I have been many things, Mr Foster.'

'Yes. Tell me. The reason that your friend Valmo doesn't want me to go to the Deltchev house again is that he doesn't want me to ask Katerina Deltchev to confirm his story, isn't it?'

'I don't know, Mr Foster. As long as you keep faith with Mr Valmo it does not matter. One thing I have to ask of you myself, however. I thought it discreet not to mention your connection with Petlarov; it would have complicated the affair. None of these things must on any account be mentioned to Petlarov. Or Mr Sibley. That is most important.'

'All right.' I was tired of the whole business now. I wanted to get to bed. I opened the car door. Pashnik put out his hand again.

'You will think over what I said, Mr Foster,' he said anxiously. 'It is for your own good I ask.'

I got out of the car. 'I'll be very sober,' I said. 'That I promise you. Good-night.'

I was about to slam the door. He leaned across and held it open. His glasses flickered in the light from the hotel entrance as he looked up at me.

'I hope so,' he said slowly. 'But if you do not intend to take my advice, Mr Foster, it might be less painful to be drunk. Good-night.'

Then he shut the door and drove off.

I did not sleep well that night.

Chapter 12

It was on the fourth day of the trial that the evidence connecting Deltchev with the Brotherhood was given.

When the court opened a man named Kroum was called into the witness box. He was about fifty with a bald head and glasses and an erect, military appearance. He looked shrewd and brutal. He described himself as a Brigadier of Police in the detective department of the Ministry of the Interior. He was carefully washed and brushed and his manner was irritatingly complacent.

Prochaska began his examination in what was for him an unexpected way.

'Brigadier Kroum, how long have you been a member of the police?'

'Thirty years, sir.'

'How long have you held your present appointment?'

'Twelve years, sir.'

'Are you a member of any political party?'

'No, sir.'

'Have you any political affiliations?'

'No, sir.'

'None at all?'

'I do not interest myself in politics, sir. I have my work to do.'

'An excellent citizen! Have you ever arrested a man or ordered his arrest for political reasons?'

'The only reason for any arrest, sir, is that a man breaks or is suspected of breaking the law. I do not make the law. It is my duty simply to enforce the law under the constitution. That is the duty of every police officer,' he added. Someone near me sniggered at this; but my impression was that Brigadier Kroum meant what he said.

Prochaska glanced at a paper. 'In March,' he said, 'were

you concerned with the arrest of eight persons on the charge of trading illicitly in prepared opium?'

'I was responsible for the arrests, sir.'

'Did you also examine the prisoners?'

Kroum hesitated. 'Unofficially, sir, and solely for the purpose of obtaining information about other members of the gang. The examining magistrate was responsible, of course, for the official interrogation.'

'You were not usurping the magistrate's function but merely doing your duty as a police officer. Is that correct?'

'Yes, sir. That is correct.'

'But you gave the prisoners the impression that they were making official depositions?'

'It is sometimes necessary, sir.'

He had a blubbery mouth with bad-tempered creases round it. Interrogation by Brigadier Kroum would not be an agreeable experience.

'Was one of those arrested a man named Rila?'

'Yes, sir.'

'Did you interrogate him?'

'I did, sir.'

'Tell the court about this interrogation.'

'Yes, sir. This Rila is a criminal well known to the police. He is an old man who has served many prison sentences. I knew that his eldest granddaughter was pregnant for the first time. I told him that this time he would surely die in prison and never see his great-grandchild, but that if he assisted the police by telling all he knew, a permit might be obtained for the child to be brought for him to see.' He looked doubtfully at the Prosecutor. 'It is customary to offer such inducements to prisoners. No regulations would be broken, sir.'

'No, no. Continue please.'

'At first he refused to talk. Said he knew nothing. The usual.' Kroum was gaining courage. 'But the following day, when I saw him again, he was in a better mood. He had thought over my offer and he was worried. After a while he asked if I would protect him from any consequences there might be of his talking. That, too, is usual with criminals informing,' he added confidentially.

'Yes. Continue, please.'

'I asked him for the names of the other members of the gang. He said there were no other members and that we had them all and that there was no information he could give about that case. But he wanted to see his great-grandchild and there was other important information he could give in return for the concession. I said that if the information was valuable it might be possible.'

'Continue.'

'He then told me that there was in existence a conspiracy to assassinate Minister Vukashin and that the conspirators were members of the Officer Corps Brotherhood.' He paused.

'And did you believe him – this criminal who wished to purchase a concession with information?'

'No, sir. At first I thought it was merely an impudent lie and sent him back to his cell. But on thinking it over I decided to question him again. Even though I thought that what he had said must be fantastic, the suggestion was so serious that I felt it necessary to make quite sure. I felt it my duty,' he added virtuously.

'Yes, yes. So you questioned him again.'

'Yes, sir, and again he began by asking for protection. Again I reassured him. Then he told me a strange story. He lodged in a house in the Maria Louisa quarter. One of his fellow lodgers was a man named Pazar.' He paused. He was at his ease now, talking more as an experienced policeman and less as an applause-hungry functionary. 'We know that house,' he went on; 'it is a place for crooks; and because we do know it we let it be; but anyone living there is automatically suspect. Pazar, however, was new there. Rila was curious about him. For Rila there was always the possibility that a stranger might be a police spy. So he took note of this man's movements and was watchful. All he discovered to begin with was that on certain evenings Pazar would be visited by three or four men unknown in the Maria Louisa quarter. They did not look poor, and Rila wondered what they were up to. It is probable, I think, that all along he had an idea of joining in what he thought might be a profitable racket, but this, of course, he denied when I suggested it. He gave another explanation. However . . .'

'Just a moment, Brigadier. What was the explanation he gave?'

Kroum looked embarrassed. 'He said, sir, that he was an old man and only interested in human nature.'

There was some laughter. Prochaska frowned. 'Go on,' he said shortly.

'Yes, sir. Rila said that Pazar had been living there for about a month when one day he stopped Rila on the stairs and asked to speak to him privately. Rila agreed and they went to his room. After a lot of talk Pazar came out with what he wanted. Someone had told him that Rila dealt in illicit drugs and Pazar wanted some heroin for a friend. Rila's first thought was that Pazar was a police spy after all and he pretended to be shocked. But after a little more talk Rila became convinced that Pazar himself was a heroin addict and needed the stuff badly. Now Rila is quite frank about what followed. Pazar had little money and asked for credit. Rila refused. With heroin addicts one might as well give the stuff away as give credit. Instead, he referred to Pazar's well-dressed visitors and said that if he, Rila, could afford smart clothes like that he would be very grateful to the person who helped him. In other words, he asked for a share in the profitable business he thought was being done by Pazar's friends. Pazar refused angrily and went away. Rila shrugged and waited. Pazar would have to have his stuff and, if he had been driven to ask Rila for it, that meant that his old source of supply had for some reason been stopped. Two days later Pazar came again to Rila, who repeated his price. Pazar again refused but this time he did not get angry; he pleaded with Rila. His friends he said were nothing to do with any trade. They were political. He went on pleading and Rila went on refusing until Pazar became desperate. He begged on his knees and when Rila told him to go away he broke down and wept. Then it came out. Pazar and the friends who visited him were members of the Brotherhood.'

Kroum paused. He had his audience now. There was dead silence. He went on.

'At first Rila did not believe him. When he did believe, he was worried. Our criminals have never liked the Brotherhood. They have been resentful of the extra vigilance it has caused, but also they have been afraid. It is curious,' Kroum went on thoughtfully; 'a man who kills for money they understand, but the Brotherhood killer troubles them. This old criminal Rila talked about the Brotherhood as a boy might talk about ghosts and demons.'

'Yes, yes. Continue.'

'Pazar worried him very much for he knew the ways of heroin drug addicts, as I have said, and he knew that they were treacherous and spiteful. If he refused Pazar and Pazar told his mysterious friends of the Brotherhood that their secret was known to Rila, then Rila would be in danger. So to keep Pazar quiet he gave him some heroin. After a few days, Pazar came back for more and soon Rila was supplying him regularly. Pazar would come into his room and stay and talk, and gradually he became more indiscreet.'

That word! I glanced at Pashik next to me. His face was quite impassive but his hands were tense.

Kroum had paused again. Now he went on very slowly.

'One day – Rila cannot remember which day – Pazar began to tell him of something he called the secret of power. He was very mysterious about this secret but Rila let him talk and after a while Pazar took a round of machine-pistol ammunition from his pocket. "This is the secret of power, my friend," he said, "for this beautiful little thing can make a revolution." Rila was afraid to ask him what he meant,

130

but Pazar told him eventually. The Brotherhood were planning to assassinate Minister Vukashin.'

The Prosecutor nodded and looked up at the judges. 'The man Rila made a deposition to the effect of what the witness has told the court,' he said. 'The deposition is signed by him and properly witnessed.' He picked up a bundle of papers. 'I submit it to the court in evidence, together with three certified copies.'

The copies were passed to the clerk of the court who handed them up to the dais. The centre judge glanced at the top paper, nodded gravely and said something.

'The Presiding Judges accept the documents in evidence,' said the interpreter's voice, 'and call upon the Prosecutor to continue.'

Prochaska turned to the witness box again. 'Brigadier Kroum, what action did you take as a result of what you had heard?'

Kroum had prepared his answer. 'I considered it my duty, sir, to inform the Minister of the Interior at once so that those responsible for the protection of Minister Vukashin might be warned.'

'And then?'

'Then, sir, I set about investigating the truth of the story.'

'You doubted it?'

Kroum very nearly permitted himself a tolerant grin. 'The police, sir, are obliged to think suspiciously of persons who wish to help them,' he said; 'especially if they may gain an advantage by doing so.'

'Very well. You investigated. What did you discover?'

'That there was a man named Pazar at the house in Maria Louisa, that he did occasionally receive the kind of visitors described and that he had a reputation for drug-taking. He was not known as a criminal. He was believed to have been at one time a schoolmaster. He had made a living as a language tutor.'

'And then what did you do?'

'There were three possible explanations, sir: that Rila had made up the rest of the story or that Pazar had invented it to impress Rila and get drugs from him; second: that Pazar was mentally unstable as a result of drug-taking and not only invented the story but also believed it to be true; thirdly: that it was in fact true. Although we believed this last possibility unlikely we decided that no harm would be done by acting upon it. We therefore set a watch on the house with the idea of identifying Pazar's visitors and possibly confronting them in Pazar's room. On the evening of the third day Pazar did not return to the house at the customary time. That same evening a man arrived at the house and was identified by the woman who kept it as one of the regular visitors. He went straight to Pazar's room which was on the second floor. He received, of course, no reply to his knock, and waited for a time. Then he decided to go. When he was stopped by one of my men he immediately drew a revolver and began to shoot, wounding two policemen. He then attempted to escape but was shot down. He was identified as a man named Eftib, a university student with a reputation for fanatical views of the kind associated with the Officer Corps Brotherhood.'

'He was killed?'

'Unfortunately he died before we could question him, sir.'

'Continue.'

'The fact that Pazar had not returned and that only Eftib had arrived for a meeting suggested to us that Pazar had been warned of our activity and had passed the warning to the other conspirators. This view was confirmed by the fact that Eftib had been visiting his parents in the country and had only that evening returned. He, therefore, had not received the warning. In any case, our interest in the house was now exposed. We therefore entered Pazar's room and made a search of his belongings.'

'And you found?'

'The complete dossier of a conspiracy to assassinate

Minister Vukashin on the occasion of the Anniversary Celebration, including a plan of the operation and detailed orders for the five men participating in it.'

A stir ran round the court. Prochaska looked up at the judges. 'I ask the Court for discretion in this matter,' he said. 'I have the dossier here and will with permission proceed to offer it in evidence. I ask leave, however, to withhold that part of it concerned with the actual plan of the attempt. It is of great ingenuity and, for reasons that will appear in a moment, unsafe for publication at present. It is in any case not essential to the Prosecution's case.'

'The permission asked for is granted by the Presiding Judges.'

A bulky file was handed to the clerk of the court. Prochaska continued: 'The witness is, of course, not quite accurate in describing what he found as a dossier. He found the operation plan concealed under the floorboards of the room and, in other hiding places, a number of documents. These things were later collected into dossier form.'

The centre judge nodded.

Prochaska turned to Kroum again. 'I will ask you now to identify the various items. Item one.' He nodded to the clerk who handed Kroum a clipped wad of papers.

Kroum looked at it.

'Do you recognize those papers?' asked Prochaska.

'I do, sir. I identify them as those I found concealed beneath the tiles of the stove in Pazar's room.'

'Have you ever seen papers like that before?'

'Yes, sir. These are pledge forms used as part of the initiation ceremony of the Officer Corps Brotherhood. I recognized them at once. They were secretly printed by a member of the Brotherhood now dead. His name was Markoff. He was arrested, tried and hanged in January forty-five. But these were his work.'

'Read the pledge to the court.'

Kroum cleared his throat. He said: 'The form is headed: *Brotherhood of the Officer Corps for the Holy Protection of all*

Kindred Families and of the Sacred Motherland which gave them Birth and Honour. Then follows the pledge: *I, Brother X, having, from the dictates of my own heart and conscience and for no other reason, submitted myself to the judgment of my Brethren in honour, and having, through the mingling of my blood with theirs, received absolution before the Mother of God for all acts committed in their name, do hereby dictate my soul and body to the service of the Brotherhood until and unto death. Recognizing that between Brothers thus specially united by ties of blood there may be no contention or preference or inequality, I swear unconditional and immediate obedience to all orders given to me by Brothers to whom authority has been delegated by the Brethren assembled, and should authority be so delegated to me I swear to accept it and use it faithfully in the knowledge that the responsibility is shared by all equally and that my loyalty to the Brotherhood is superior to all other loyalties and avowals, private or public. My reward for faithful service shall be the honour and love of my Brothers and their protection of me and of my family. But should I betray or in any other way fail the Brotherhood my own death with be only part of the price to be paid for the offence, for by this oath now taken I bind my whole being, and in betrayal of it, all that I hold dear is forfeit. All this I understand and accept. All this I believe just. All this I freely swear to on my blood, my honour and my life and by this act become of you my Brothers.'* Kroum looked up. 'That is all, sir.'

'A licence to commit treason and murder,' commented Prochaska, 'as the acknowledged crimes of this fraternity have long since proved.' He nodded to the clerk who handed up another document to Kroum.

Kroum looked at it.

'Do you recognize that document?'

'I do, sir. It was hidden in Pazar's room with the papers I have just read from.'

'What is it?'

'A list of names under the word "Active".'

'Is the name of Pazar there?'

'It is.'

'And Eftib?'

'Yes, sir.'

'Is there any other name there familiar to the police?'

'Yes.' He hesitated. 'The name of Deltchev.'

There was dead silence in the court now. Deltchev was sitting in his usual position with his eyes closed. He did not move.

'Is there any other peculiarity about the list?'

'Yes, sir. Certain names on it are underlined.'

'Which names?'

'Those of Pazar, Eftib, Vlahov, Pechanatz, Radiuje and Deltchev.'

There was a faint murmur in the court. Deltchev opened his eyes and looked at Kroum thoughtfully.

'Did you say that the plan to assassinate Minister Vukashin required five persons to operate it?'

'Yes, sir.'

'Then the sixth person might be the leader?'

'It seemed likely, sir.'

'What action did you take?'

'I informed the Minister of the Interior, and warrants for the arrest of Pazar, Vlahov, Pechanatz and Radiuje were issued.'

'Did you execute the warrants?'

'Pechanatz and Radiuje were found to have already left the country. Vlahov was arrested while attempting to do so. It was at the airport and he was placed in the waiting-room to await an escort. The arresting officer had neglected to search him and while in the waiting-room he shot himself. Pazar has not yet been traced.'

'What action has been taken about the other names on the list?'

'I ask permission not to answer that question, sir.'

'I understand, Brigadier.' He turned to the judges. 'I would point out to the court that at least one man connected with the conspiracy is still in the country and free and that he may attempt to find other confederates even now. It is for that reason that all information cannot yet be made public.'

'The Presiding Judges acknowledge the point.'

Prochaska bowed and nodded to the clerk. More papers were handed to Kroum.

'Do you recognize those documents?'

'Yes, sir. I identify them as from Pazar's room.'

'Describe them.'

'They are messages, mostly typewritten or inked in block letters on plain paper.'

'Read from them.'

'The first reads: *"Meeting for Thursday to take place Friday. Notified V. and P."*'

'No signature?'

'None is signed, sir.'

'Continue.'

'The second reads: *"Await advice as arranged."* The third: *"P. remains incomplete. Progress others."* The next: *"V. unsuccessful. Will expedite."* Next . . .'

Prochaska interrupted him. 'One moment, Brigadier. I do not think we need trouble you to read all the messages. I wished only to show their character. They continue like that?'

'Yes, sir. There are over thirty of them.'

'Do you understand their meaning?'

'I think so.'

'They have a direct bearing on the assassination plan?'

'Yes, sir.'

'Then we will be discreet. I come to another point. Do these messages constitute a correspondence or are they only messages received?'

'Messages received, sir.'

'What initials appear in the messages?'

'V., P., E., R. and D.'

'Referring to?'

'Vlahov, Pechanatz, Eftib, Radiuje and Deltchev, I believe.'

'It seems likely. What is the general character of these messages? Are they, for example, instructions?'

'I would say they are reports.'

'To the leader of the conspirators?'

'I think not, sir. It is difficult to say, but in my opinion Pazar, who received the reports, was responsible for co-ordinating the information. We learned that he received no messages at the house. My belief is that the others used a café or a shop as a post office and that he collected the messages from there, copied them and redistributed them for information to those concerned. The nature of the plan would call for constant communications of that sort during the period of preparation. No doubt each conspirator had an accommodation address.'

'Very well. The messages have been numbered for convenience. Please find message number twenty-seven.'

'I have it here.'

'Read it please.'

'It reads: "*V. in difficulty. Advise D. urgent.*"'

'Is that written or typewritten?'

'Typewritten.'

'Is there anything else on the paper?'

'Yes, sir, some pencil writing.'

'Read it please.'

'It reads: "*Strumitza, twelve.*"'

The courtroom stirred.

'Is that an address?'

'Yes, sir. It is the prisoner's address.'

'What explanation have you for its being there?'

'It is in Pazar's handwriting. I suggest that as the message was urgent he did not deliver it to the usual accommodation address for the prisoner but took it direct to his home. The pencil note was a memorandum of an address which Pazar would not normally use.'

I looked at Deltchev. His eyes were closed again. He had not moved. It was impossible to believe. And yet . . .

Stanoiev did not cross-examine. Kroum left the witness box reluctantly, like an ageing prima donna on a farewell tour, and one of his colleagues took his place. The questioning was resumed. What Kroum had said was now elaborately confirmed. I no longer paid much attention. I was trying to digest what I had already heard.

Chapter 13

It was true; of that I had little doubt. Prochaska had an air of confidence that was not of the kind he could assume. Perhaps clever cross-examination could have made much of Kroum's evidence look weak; Deltchev was not an uncommon name and when you pointed out that the prisoner's identification with the D. of the messages rested solely on a pencilled note of an address alleged to be in the handwriting of a man who could not be produced, you might have shaken a jury's belief in the whole story. But here there was no jury to be shaken and, after the massive certainties of Vukashin and the rest, the very flimsiness of the thing gave it probability. Someone named Deltchev who lived in Deltchev's house had been in close touch with persons desperate enough, as Eftib and Vlahov had been, to shoot when confronted by the police or to commit suicide when arrested. Madame Deltchev? Absurd. Katerina Deltchev? By the time the luncheon break came, I thought I was ready for Pashik.

'Well,' I said, 'what do you think?'

'It is very interesting.'

'Yes. Where do you think Pazar is now?'

He shrugged elaborately. 'It is a mystery.'

'So they say. When do you think they'll find that man in Patriarch Dimo?'

The brown eyes looked at me steadily. He did not reply.

I stared back at him. 'I would guess that it's Pazar's body in that room, wouldn't you?' I said.

'What makes you think that, Mr Foster?'

'Just an association of ideas. Somebody in Deltchev's house sent messages to a man named Pazar. That man is now missing. Someone in Deltchev's house sends a message by me to a man who lived in Patriarch Dimo. That man is now dead.'

'That's bad logic, Mr Foster.'

'It might be good guessing. Do you believe that Deltchev was in a conspiracy to assassinate Vukashin?'

'It could be so.'

'Yes, it could be, but do you think yourself that it was so?'

'Who else could there be, Mr Foster?'

'Katerina Deltchev could be the D. of those messages.'

He showed his brown teeth in a smile. 'A nice young lady of twenty in a Brotherhood conspiracy? That is a very funny idea, but it is no more than funny. The Officer Corps Sisterhood! Ah, please, Mr Foster!'

'Yes, it's silly. I'm trying to find a reasonable explanation, that's all.'

'The reasonable explanation is the one already given. Mr Foster, we are newspaper men, not attorneys for the defence. We need only observe and report. We are lucky.'

He had a bland, non-committal look on his face. At breakfast I had not mentioned the events of the night before. In the morning light they had assumed the proportions of a bad dream and until I could talk to Petlarov I was content to leave them so. Besides, I was tired of Pashik's denials and warnings and had made up my mind to discover something about the case 'K. Fischer, Vienna '46' before I tackled him again. It looked now as if he thought I had taken his advice. I put aside a temptation to correct the impression.

'What was the Brotherhood plan they're being so secretive about?' I asked.

'I know no more than you, Mr Foster.'

'Doesn't Valmo know? Surely a man in his position would know such things?'

'I am not in his confidence to that extent.'

'Did you know Pazar or Eftib?'

To my surprise he nodded. 'Eftib I knew. He was a

young man with a great dislike of dogs. A dog he found tied up one day he beat to death with a piece of chain. The other students feared him. He was not sane I think.'

'How did you know him?'

'The dog he killed belonged to one of the Professors at the University. There was a scandal. I reported it for a newspaper but his family paid to avoid the publicity. By now,' he added thoughtfully, 'they may wish he had been safely put in prison.'

The waiter came up with our food. This particular section of the restaurant was reserved for the pressmen attending the trial, and across the room I could see Sibley talking earnestly and confidentially to one of the Americans. Then out of the corner of my eye, I saw Pashik looking at me. He looked away almost as I saw him but not quite fast enough. He had to cover up.

'Yes,' he said, 'Mr Sibley is busy still. He may succeed with someone who has no reason to suspect him. It is very strange.'

I smiled. 'There's something I find even stranger, Pashik.'

'Yes, Mr Foster?' He was on his guard again.

'I find it strange that although you are quite ready to serve someone you say is of the Government secret police, you put obstacles in the way of Sibley who is trying to serve the Propaganda Ministry.'

He stared at me for a moment and I thought that he was about to reply. Then, he changed his mind, cleared his throat and picked up his knife and fork. 'Mr Foster,' he said heavily, 'I think we should get on with our eating.'

I could get nothing more out of him. After the luncheon break, the conspiracy evidence was resumed. Now that he had something like real evidence to deal with, Prochaska spread himself. Every detail of Kroum's evidence was sworn to by three or four different persons, every document certified and proved. Had you not heard the earlier days of the trial, you might from Prochaska's attitude have supposed the judges to be pettifogging martinets hostile to his case. When you remembered the rubbish that had already been admitted as evidence by that pathetic trio, the present solemnity was funny. But not for long. Presently it became boring. Only one thing kept me there; the possibility of Deltchev's speaking in his own defence. But he seemed as bored as I was. As witness after witness was brought in to swear to the authenticity of the message with his address on it, I expected a protest from him. It would have been easy enough.

'These conscientious policemen swear to the presence of my address on this piece of paper. Nobody disputes that it is there. Why waste the time they might be devoting to more useful duties? Produce a really serious witness: the man who wrote it or who saw it written or, even better, the man who can tell us *why* and in what circumstances it was written down there. Those questions are important, gentlemen, for I, too, have been plotted against by assassins. They threw a bomb and badly wounded my chauffeur. That was outside my house, and to find my house you need the address, and to remember it you have to write it down. I have no wish to deprive Minister Vukashin of his martyr's laurels but if I am to be convicted of plotting against his life, at least make sure that the evidence you use is not part of an old plot against *my* life. For a new plot new evidence should be manufactured. Economy in such matters is discourteous.'

But Deltchev said nothing at all and the afternoon drowsed on. Curiously, it was only the diplomatic and press sections who seemed bored. For most of the spectators it was an exciting afternoon. As each witness appeared there would be a buzz of interest, then dead silence while he gave his evidence, then breathless whispering as he stepped down. It was the factual nature of the evidence that did it. There must have been many in that courtroom who had been unwilling to believe in Deltchev's guilt and privately uneasy about the trial. Now they were enjoying the illusion

142

that the legal forms were being properly observed and that they were free of the responsibility of condoning an injustice. I was glad when the afternoon was over.

Pashik had nothing to say as he drove me back to my hotel. He knew that I was going to see Petlarov and was saving himself for a farewell admonishment on the subject of discretion; so I thought at least; and I was tired of him; I was tired of his dreadful smell, of his admonishments, of his evasions and mystery-making, of his long-suffering brown eyes, of his dirty seersucker suit and of his bad driving.

He stopped jerkily outside the hotel and turned to me. 'Mr Foster . . .' he began.

I interrupted irritably. 'Look, do you have to go on calling me "Mr Foster" all the time? Can't you make it "Foster" or "you"? It would be easier for you, and I shouldn't feel so stiff-necked.'

He began again picking at the vulcanite covering of the steering wheel. He already had most of it off and the metal beneath looked bare and squalid.

'I am sorry, Mr Foster,' he said, 'I wished only to be polite.'

'Yes, of course. It's not important.'

But he was upset. 'I am afraid you are not a good-tempered man, Mr Foster,' he said.

'No, I'm not. I apologize. You wanted to tell me to be discreet again, didn't you?'

He picked for a moment or two in silence. He was working on a big piece and it peeled away like a strip of sunburnt skin.

'I don't know what more I can say to you, Mr Foster,' he said. 'I have tried to warn you not because I like you or even because I have a responsibility to the New York Office, but in the spirit of any man who sees another by accident going into a danger he does not realize. I can do no more. There are things more important than the safety of a stranger. You will not take advice, then you must take your chance. I will not discuss the case with you further. The services I am paid for are yours, however. To-morrow I will be getting your press ticket for the Anniversary Celebration. When the end date of the trial is known, your return passage by air will be available. If there is any other service you wish performed you must tell me. Meanwhile, when we meet we can talk of other things.' He turned and looked at me. 'Good-night, Mr Foster.'

'Good-night.'

I got out and went into the hotel. I was both impressed and depressed. As I walked up the stairs I decided that I would take his advice. I told myself that it was only my personal dislike of the man that had prevented my taking it before. That was really stupid. My task was to write articles about the trial, not to play policeman. I had stumbled on a political murder in a country where political murder was a commonplace. The fact that for me it was a novelty did not give me a licence to inquire into it. I should remember that I was a foreigner, there on sufferance, that I had a very lucrative profession to return to and that in my temporary role of newspaper reporter I had done very well to get an exclusive interview with Madame Deltchev. That was enough. I would now mind my own business. And it might be a good idea to apologize to Pashik. He had been very patient with me and I had behaved with the bumptiousness of an amateur. And, by the way, since when had Mr Foster been entitled to object to being called Mr Foster by someone who wished to be courteous. Mr Foster was making a very tiresome fool of himself. He'd better stop.

Petlarov was sitting stiff and straight on his usual seat in the corridor. Without speaking he followed me into my room and sat down. I went to the wardrobe and got out the whisky. He took the tooth glass with his usual polite bow and then glanced up at me.

'You look tired, Herr Foster.'

'I've had a tiring twenty-four hours.'

He nodded politely. He did not even look a question.

'What about to-day's evidence? What do you think?' I asked. 'It's more or less what you feared, isn't it?'

He considered for a moment, then he shook his head.

'No. I don't think it is. You see, I expected something possible. I thought that Yordan might have committed some indiscretion capable of being shown badly. But not this. It is really very funny. I know Yordan and I know that he is incapable of this kind of association. And with men of the type of Eftib and Pazar, it is grotesque.'

'He associated with Vukashin and Brankovitch?'

'He did not like them but he recognized their importance. Both are considerable men, leaders. But conspiracy with this delinquent riffraff? It is impossible! Yordan is too much of a snob.'

'What sort of indiscretion did you expect?'

He shrugged. 'Many things are possible. For example, it would not have greatly surprised me to learn that some of the exiles were planning a *coup d'état* and had nominated Yordan their leader. If they appealed to him he would be flattered. He might temporise but he would treat with them. In transactions of that kind many foolish things are written. Now with this, all is different. We have circumstantial evidence of the kind that is used to convict ordinary criminals – the piece of paper with the note on it, the scribbled address, the conspirators who escape and those who do not, the mysterious Pazar who is missing but really dead – it is all a different pattern.' He shrugged again. 'But that is only what I feel.'

'What did you mean by saying that Pazar is really dead?'

'If he were alive they would certainly have found him before the trial. They could not risk his being found unexpectedly. He might be an inconvenient witness and it would look bad if he, too, were killed resisting arrest.'

So then, of course, I told him. Whatever else was not my business, the problem of the evidence against Deltchev certainly was, and I had come to rely upon Petlarov's opinions. I told him about the letter I had carried, of the

145

dead man in Patriarch Dimo nine, of Pashik's arrival, of the visit to Aleko and of the Aleko note. He listened in silence and was silent for a time when I had finished. I noticed that he had gone very pale. Then he put down his drink and stood up.

'Herr Foster,' he said slowly; 'I, too, have something to tell you. Every two days I have to report to the police to get my papers stamped. It is part of the control to which, as an untrustworthy person, I am subject. To-day, when I reported I was warned. I was told that I had recently made an undesirable association and that if I did not wish to be removed with my wife to a labour camp, the association must cease. That was all. Your name was not mentioned.' He hesitated. 'When I came here this evening, Herr Foster, I had almost made up my mind to ignore the warning. I thought that if it had been a serious matter I should not have been warned but arrested. I see now that I was wrong.'

'What do you mean?'

But he did not reply. He was fumbling agitatedly in his pocket. He got out the ration card I had given him and held it out to me.

'I am sorry, Herr Foster,' he said; 'I cannot keep our bargain.'

'That's all right. I understand.' I didn't, but he was so obviously upset that I wanted to soothe him. 'Keep the ration card anyway. I don't want it.'

He shook his head. His face looked pinched and there was sweat on his forehead. I had a curious sense of shock. I had come to think of Petlarov as some kind of genie who inhabited the corridor outside my hotel room, ready to explain, to enlighten, to serve when I needed him. Because his own account of himself had been quite calm and impersonal, because he had not exuded the self-pity I should have been so quick to condemn, I had not found it necessary to think of him as a human being. Now suddenly he was a human being; he was frightened. The realization gave me a curious feeling of discomfort.

'Herr Foster,' he said, 'please take the card. I cannot use it any more and if I am arrested I do not wish to have it found in my pocket.'

I took it. He picked up his hat and went to the door.

'Just a moment,' I said.

He stopped. The effort he made to control his agitation was almost painful to watch. He just wanted to be gone.

'Can't you give me any ideas what this is all about?' I asked.

For a moment I thought he was going without answering. Then he swallowed and licked his lips. He looked at his hat as he spoke. 'I will tell you one thing, Herr Foster. K. Fischer, Karl Fischer, you mentioned him.' He hesitated before he went on with a rush. 'He was a Left Wing politician, very popular in the working-class quarters of Vienna. A good man and a fearless speaker. He was in principle for the Soviets, but in forty-six he protested against the Soviet kidnappings of Austrians from the American sector. An honest man. He did what he thought right. He was murdered.' He hesitated and swallowed again.

'Yes?'

'In September it was,' he said. 'He went out one evening to see his married daughter in Favoriten. Next day the railway police found his body behind a shed in the marshalling yard outside the Ostbahnhof.' He paused and looked up at me. 'You said that the man you saw at Patriarch Dimo had been killed by a bullet wound in the back of the head, by the ear.'

'Yes.'

He nodded. 'That was how Karl Fischer died,' he said. 'That was the hand of Aleko.'

Then he went.

Chapter 14

That was on Friday, the fourteenth of June. The assassination took place on the Saturday.

I have since been described in the People's Party press as 'a well-known agent of the English Secret Service,' 'the leader of a foreign gang.' 'Anglo-American spy and pervert,' and in other less reproducible ways. In one article the fact that I am a writer was acknowledged by a reference to 'the notorious pornographer and English murder-propaganda lackey, Foster.'

That part of it has been less amusing than I would have thought. Some of the stuff was reproduced in London papers and among my friends the 'notices of Foster's Balkan tour' were quoted hilariously for a day or two. But when the news of the Deltchev verdict came and the mass executions of Agrarian Socialists began, the attacks on me became related to events that were anything but funny. I began to be asked questions which the Foreign Office had suggested I should not answer.

With the newspapers it was not difficult; I did as I had been asked and referred them to the Foreign Office. With friends and acquaintances it was less simple. It is, I find, extraordinarily embarrassing to be described in print as a member of the British Secret Service. The trouble is that you cannot afterwards convince people that you are not. They reason that if you are a member you will still presumably have to say that you are not. You are suspect. If you say nothing, of course, you admit all. Your denials become peevish. It is very tiresome. Probably, the only really effective denial would be a solemn, knowing acknowledgement that there *might* be some truth in the rumour.

But I can never bring myself to it. Foreign Office or no Foreign Office, I have to explain what really happened.

To begin with, I think I should make it clear that I am not one of those persons who enjoy danger. I take pains to avoid it. Moreover, my timidity is speculative and elaborate. For instance: in Paris at the time of the Stavisky riots, I was living in an hotel room overlooking a street in which the police fought a revolver battle with the rioters. My first impulse was to lean out of the window and watch. The firing was several hundred yards away and I knew perfectly well that at that distance a revolver is about as dangerous as a water pistol. What I remembered, however, was that James Elroy Flecker had had a similar impulse of curiosity in Mexico City and died of it, absurdly, with a stray bullet through his head. Instead of leaning out of the window, therefore, I had knelt on the floor by it and tried to use my shaving mirror as a periscope; but by the time I had arranged all this, the battle was over and I saw nothing but an indignant woman with an upset shopping bag.

The war did nothing to make my attitude to danger bolder or more philosophic. I do not have heroic impulses. The news that a bomb had killed my wife in our London flat had many other effects on me but it did not send me out in a murderous rage to exact retribution on the enemy, nor did it make me volunteer for some suicidal duty. For a long time my life felt less worth living than before but I did not for that reason become careless of it. Accounts of great bravery sometimes move me deeply but they arouse in me no desire to emulate them. The spirit of romantic derring-do runs somewhat thinly in my veins.

The truth about my part in the Deltchev affair is untidy. I did not even blunder into the danger; I strayed into it as if it were an interesting-looking tangle of streets in an old town. Certainly I had been warned that they were dangerous; but only to those who warned, I thought, not to me. When I found out that I was mistaken and tried to get out, I found also that I was lost. That was how it felt. The last

149

moment at which I could have turned back was when Petlarov went out of my room that evening. If, at that point I had shrugged my shoulders, had another drink, gone out to dinner and spent the evening at the cinema, I should have been fairly safe. And I very nearly did do that. I had the drink – it was the last of the whisky – and I looked at a cinema I could see from my window. It was called *LUX* and was playing a dubbed version of a German film called *La Paloma* that I did not want to see. I considered opening a bottle of plum brandy I had bought, decided against it and then caught sight of the typewriter I had brought with me but not yet used. I thought of the solemnity of my departure with it from London ten days or so before, and felt absurd. Images came into my mind of those groups of toys you see mounted on highly coloured boards in the shops at Christmas time; the Boys' Conductor Set (complete with ticket punch), the Boys' Detective Set (complete with disguises), the Boys' Tank Commander Set (complete with binoculars). I spent a self-abasing minute or two thinking of a new one: the Boys' Foreign Correspondent Set, complete with typewriter, whisky bottle, invisible ink, and a copy of John Gunther's *Inside Europe*. Then I did a foolish thing: I decided to pull myself together and be sensible.

What, I asked myself over dinner, were the facts? Quite simple. I was supposed to be reporting the trial of a man named Deltchev who was accused of planning an assassination. Probably, he was innocent. Yet some of the evidence against him had a ring of truth about it. Moreover, his daughter had been in touch with someone concerned in the assassination plan. I had found that person dead, killed in the same way as an Austrian politician and most likely by the same man, Aleko. Aleko had pretended to be of the secret police but was probably an agent of another kind. Who had employed him? Deltchev? Or the People's Party, to implicate Deltchev? But why should either employ Aleko when they had dangerous psychotics like Eftib and Pazar ready to hand? It didn't make sense. And where did

Deltchev come in? That was the important thing. I was preparing to defend him before a very large public. It might be just as well (might it not?) to make sure that I had the facts right. *Might* be! A fine fool I should look if the noble Deltchev I had postulated turned out to be in reality as murderous as his persecutors but rather cleverer at concealing the fact. 'Mr Foster, what steps did you take to check the validity of your impressions?' 'Well, none really. I thought it better not to be inquisitive. Too risky.' Oh dear, oh dear! By the time the wine arrived I no longer had any doubts. Nothing I already knew about the case seemed either logical or in any other way satisfactory. Far too much was hidden. Well, it must be revealed; and if the intimidated Petlarov did not want to help me, I would find it out for myself. The first thing for me to do anyway was to see Madame Deltchev at once – that evening – and hear what she had to say about the day's evidence. Then I would give myself the pleasure of an interview with little Miss Katerina, tell her the news about her friend, Valmo, and ask her the questions that Aleko did not want me to ask. After that I would decide what to do next.

I finished my dinner and walked out to the Deltchev house. As I turned into the street where it was, the mood of hearty resolution in which I had started out suddenly weakened. The guards I had passed before might not be on duty. A different set might have taken over. Then, as I approached, I saw that the same guards were there. It made no difference; my anxiety deepened. I realized that the real source of it had nothing to do with the guards but with the undertaking I had given to Aleko and my too ready disposal of it. If, I had reasoned, Aleko had really had any police powers he would not have asked for an undertaking not to visit the Deltchev home again; he would simply have issued an order to the guards not to admit me. Therefore, I had concluded, he had no police powers and I might call his bluff. But it was one thing to have arrived at a theoretical conclusion and quite another to act upon it in this way. All sorts of unconsidered possibilities occurred to me as I walked toward the house. Supposing, for instance, he really did have police powers and had planned to test my good faith by including this prohibition in the undertaking. For a moment I hesitated and was about to turn back; then I realised that the Corporal had seen and recognized me. Retreat was impossible now. I walked on up to him and took out my press permit. He nodded curtly but examined the permit carefully again while the doltish Private stood grinning at me. At last the Corporal handed back the permit with a faint shrug (ominous?) and nodded to the Private. The latter hitched his rifle sling more snugly on his shoulder and, crossing to the door in the wall, pulled the bell.

It was as before. I waited. They watched me. There was the clacking of old Rana's sandals on the paving of the courtyard. The door opened cautiously. But then she recognized me and held the door for me to go in. Inside she said something and signed to me to wait. She was not long. Soon I heard her sandals flapping down the stairs inside the house. She opened the front door and beckoned me in.

I went upstairs. The same slippery floor, the same smell of furniture polish, but this time no Katerina. She, I thought, would be standing with her man-of-the-world air behind her mother's chair. I hoped, uncharitably, that my arrival would alarm her.

But Madame Deltchev was alone. She was standing facing me by the window as I came in. The light was behind her but there was tension in the way she stood. On the table by her were two empty tea glasses. The old friend had delivered his report for the day.

She turned quickly. 'Good evening, Herr Foster. It is good of you to call again.'

'You are very kind, Madame. I am afraid I have more questions.'

'Naturally. Please sit down.'

'Thank you.'

There was a *grande dame* artificiality about her manner

which accentuated the feeling of strain she meant it to conceal. 'Although,' she went on, 'I think it unlikely that I shall be able to give you the information you need. Tea?'

'No, thank you.'

'Of course. You have dined, and the English do not drink tea after dinner.' She smiled mechanically and, picking up one of the glasses, went over to the samovar. 'With us it is a habit,' she said; 'Russian, of course. Most of our habits are Russian or Turkish or German or Greek. We have few of our own.' Boiling water spluttered from the tap into the glass. 'You see now why our patriots mean so much to us here. Their unquestioning belief that we are indeed a nation with our own cultural and political identities, and not merely a marginal tribe with some curious ethnological affinities, is a great comfort. The truth about many of our great traditional patriots is ugly or ludicrous; but it makes no difference. They are defended angrily. National feeling in small states is always angry; it must be so, for its roots are in fear and self-doubt and for those things reason is no protection.'

She spoke as glibly as a journalist quoting without acknowledgement from an article he has just written. I was not sure whether she was talking for concealment or whether I was being offered an elaborately wrapped hint. Was there perhaps an ugly truth to be known about patriot Deltchev?

'Your husband has meant a great deal to his people,' I said carefully.

'Yes, yes, he has.' She had carried her tea over to her chair. Now she sat down facing me. 'They will not give him up easily, no matter what lies are told about him. A cigarette, Herr Foster?'

'Thank you; I'm sure you are right. Have you heard about to-day's court proceedings, Madame?'

'Yes, I have heard about them.'

I lit the cigarette she had given me. 'Do you consider

153

that the evidence was false in itself or that it was false only in relation to your husband?'

'Some of his witnesses may be truthful but their testimonies compose a lie.'

'May I put a hypothetical question? Supposing that the evidence were all true, that your husband had in fact been involved in this plot, would you have known about it, Madame? Would he have confided in you?'

She did not answer immediately. Then: 'He always confided in me. I should have known.'

'It would be a dangerous secret to confide to anyone.'

'If it had existed; yes, very dangerous.'

'For comparison's sake, Madame, can you tell me if your husband confided in you his intention to make that radio speech about the elections before he made it?'

She sat quite still for several moments staring out through the window at the bare hills. I almost wondered if she had heard what I had said. She had heard, I knew, and understood, too, but her air of preoccupation was very nearly convincing. Then, with a slight puzzled shake of her head as if to banish other thoughts and face the immediate reality, she turned her gentle, intelligent eyes towards me.

'I am very sorry, Herr Foster,' she said with a faint, confused smile. 'I am afraid I was not paying attention. I had other thoughts.' She put her hand to her forehead as if she had a headache. 'It was inexcusable.'

It was not badly done; I have known actresses make a worse job of it; but if I wanted to parody a particular style of drawing-room comedy, I would have that speech, and the performance that goes with it, well in mind. She must have seen it in dozens of bad plays. Probably she was expecting from me one of the two conventional reactions to it; the guilty ('Forgive me, you're tired') or the aggrieved ('I'm a busy man and my time is valuable'). However, I felt neither guilty nor aggrieved. I did feel intensely curious.

I repeated the question.

Her lips twitched with annoyance. 'Herr Foster, what is the point of this question? Please be honest with me.'

'Certainly. You deny that there is a word of real truth in the evidence put before the court to-day. I wish to know what value I may put upon that denial. Is it based on knowledge or an emotional conviction? You must see that that is important.'

'What I see, Herr Foster,' she said coldly, 'is that this trial is beginning to have the effect intended by the Propaganda Ministry.'

I felt myself flush with anger. By the light of the setting sun she did not see that, but I did not reply and after a moment she began to apologize. I must forgive her; she was tired and overwrought; she had not slept for many nights; she was distracted with worry. I listened carefully. What she was saying was all quite reasonable and genuine but it was also a protective screen. Something had happened to her since our first meeting; some inner certainty had gone. Before, she had been facing with calm courage the prospect of her husband's conviction and death. Perhaps that courage had rested upon a belief in his innocence which no longer went unquestioned. Perhaps the unworthy doubts of which she now accused me were merely the projections of her own misgivings.

I tried a different way.

'In the theatre,' I said, 'a little fact will sustain a lot of illusion. As Petlarov says: "the lie rests most securely on a pinpoint of truth." Brankovitch is not a fool. He knows that although he can impose any nonsense he likes upon the people of his own country, abroad it will not be so easy. With that trumped-up case he cannot hope to deceive the outside world. But what he can do is to confuse it by mixing with his lies a little truth. This plot against Vukashin. Why is it there? To prove that your husband is a member of the Brotherhood? Nonsense! Better evidence could be invented. Besides, even a stable government will regard an assassination plot as bad propaganda and try to conceal it if they can. No, this evidence is there because it is specially valuable. It is valuable because it is true. And those in court to-day recognized that it is true. It was not much – a few statements confirming a small set of facts – but it was true, and already in their minds this truth had grown and obscured the great mass of falsehood that surrounds it. You say, Madame, that there may be truthful witnesses but that they compose a lie. But how much of a lie? Where does the truth end and the lie begin? You cannot defeat the Prosecution's case with blank denials. It is not as simple as that. You have to give the whole truth and that is what I want.'

There was a long silence. She looked stonily out of the window and when she spoke she did not turn her head.

'Herr Foster, there is not a court of law in the civilized world that would accept the case against my husband. I have been well advised of that.'

'No civilized court of law is going to be asked to accept it,' I retorted. 'If the truth is not told, the final judgment will be delivered here. A few persons may doubt and speculate but they must all come to the same conclusion.'

'What conclusion?'

'That there must have been something in the accusations against Deltchev, that the conspiracy evidence was never seriously disputed, that if he wasn't the criminal they tried to make him out, he was something very nearly as bad – a fool. Forgive me, Madame, but what you do not seem to realize is that any protest against your husband's trial is a political act. No foreign office and no responsible newspaper is going to make that protest unless it is absolutely certain that he is innocent. They must know the truth.'

'It isn't true. The case against him is a lie. What else can I say?'

'To what extent did your husband confide in you?'

'What does it matter? If I tell you he always confided in me you will say that this particular matter might have been too dangerous to confide. If I say that he did not confide it is no different.'

'If he were in any way involved in this conspiracy would you have known?'

'Yes. He was not involved.'

'Did you know that he was going to make that election broadcast before he made it?'

'Yes, I did.'

'Did you know why he was going to make it?'

'Yes.'

'Why was it?'

She shook her head hopelessly. I knew she was lying.

'Was it because at one time, long ago, your husband had been a member of the Officer Corps Brotherhood?'

For a moment she was quite still. Then, slowly, she raised her head and stared at me. 'Is that a serious question, Herr Foster?' she asked coolly.

I knew suddenly that it was not a serious question but part of a fantasy in a locked room. I began to mumble. 'It was a faint possibility, Madame.' She still stared at me. 'It could have been a youthful indiscretion, a mistake . . .' I petered out.

She smiled in a twisted sort of way. 'Yordan does not make that kind of indiscretion. He is always an intelligent man. Are there any other questions, Herr Foster?' she added.

If I had had any advantage it was suddenly quite gone. 'Have you ever heard the name of Pazar before?'

'It is a Turkish name. I know no one who has it.'

'Or Eftib?'

'No. Nor any of the other persons mentioned to-day.'

'Aleko?'

'Was that name mentioned?'

'No. Do you know it?'

'It is a short name for Alexander. That is all I know.'

'Valmo?'

'It is a fairly common surname but it means nothing in particular to me. Should it do so?'

'I don't know.' I stood up. 'Thank you for receiving me, Madame.'

'It is nothing.' She stood up too and switched on a reading lamp.

'Before I go, I should like, if I may, to speak to your daughter,' I said.

She stiffened. 'Why?'

'I should like to ask her some questions.'

'Perhaps I can answer them for you.'

'Perhaps.' I hesitated. 'When I left here two nights ago, Madame, your daughter asked me to take out a letter for her and deliver it to a man named Valmo.' I paused.

She tried unsuccessfully to smile. 'My daughter is an attractive young woman. She has her affairs of the heart.'

'Yes, that was the impression of the letter she succeeded in giving to me. I agreed to take it.'

'That was chivalrous of you.'

'The address on the letter was Patriarch Dimo, nine. I found the place. It is a disused house in a slum.'

'And did you find the young man?'

I shook my head. She relaxed perceptibly.

'If you will give me the letter, Herr Foster, I will see that it is returned to my daughter. It was good of you to take so much trouble.' She held out her hand.

I said: 'I did not find a young man, Madame. I found a dead one. He had been shot.'

Very slowly she sat down. 'Had he shot himself?' she asked softly.

'No. The wound was in the back of the head.'

She did not move. 'A young man?'

'No. Grey-haired, about fifty I should think. Why do you ask?'

She straightened up a little. 'I thought perhaps some poor young student . . .' She broke off and drew a deep breath. 'There are so many tragedies. You must have gone to the wrong house, Herr Foster.'

'No. It was the right house. But if the dead man was the person who had called himself Valmo, then your daughter knew Pazar. For that was the dead man's real name.'

There was a silence. She did not look at me.

'Did the police tell you that?' she said at last.

'I did not go to the police. It would have been difficult to explain how I came to be visiting the Brotherhood assassin they are supposed to be searching for. Difficult and embarrassing for us all.'

'We are in your debt, Herr Foster.'

'Perhaps you would prefer your daughter to explain,' I said.

She looked at her handkerchief. 'My daughter is not here.'

I was silent.

She looked at me. 'I am speaking the truth, Herr Foster.'

'I understood that everyone here was under house arrest.'

'My daughter is not here. She has gone.'

'Do you mean that the police took her away?'

'No. She escaped.'

'How? What about the guards?'

'Katerina has lived in this house all her life, Herr Foster. There are other ways of leaving it than by the gates.'

I hesitated. 'A few minutes ago, Madame, I asked you if you had heard of Pazar before. You said that you had not. Do you still say that?'

'Yes. It is the truth.'

'But others in this house do know him?'

'I do not.'

'Do you know where your daughter has gone?'

'No.'

'When did she go?'

'This evening.'

'Can you think of any reason why she should go?'

'Herr Foster, I am very tired.'

I waited a moment or two but she did not look up again. 'I'm sorry,' I said; 'I think I might have been of help to you.'

'I have told you all I can.'

'You have told me all you think it advisable for me to know, Madame.'

'Good-night, Herr Foster.' She pressed the bell-push.

I said good-night and picked up my hat but as I got to the door she spoke again.

'Herr Foster.'

I stopped.

'My daughter's letter. Will you give it to me, please?'

'It is burnt.'

'Are you sure?'

'Quite sure.'

She hesitated. 'Forgive me, but do you know what was in it?'

'I did not open it. In any case I cannot read your language.'

She came a little way across the room towards me. 'Herr Foster,' she said, 'I have not been helpful to you but I would not like you to think that I am ungrateful for your kindness and patience. I do most sincerely thank you.'

I bowed. I could not think of anything coherent to say which would not have deepened my embarrassment. The sound of Rana's sandals flapping along the passage outside came like the answer to a prayer.

'Good-night, Madame,' I said and got out of the room as quickly as I could. It did not occur to me until I was walking down the stairs that my twinges of guilt were unnecessary. Beside the monumental evasions to which I had been listening for the past half hour my own reticences were trivial.

Chapter 15

It was very dark outside the house. The old woman had no lamp to guide us and I blundered rather than walked after her across the courtyard. The fact contributed somehow to the feelings of inadequacy, futility and blank exasperation which were beginning to grow in me.

I stubbed my foot against the edge of a flag stone and said, 'Damn!' violently. The old woman opened the door in the wall and the flashlight from outside shone in my face. I scowled at it and hauled out my wallet as the door closed behind me. The light left my face and I saw the Corporal.

'*Passieren, vorwaerts!*' he snapped and waved me on peremptorily.

'Don't you want to see my permit, you fool?' I inquired in English.

'*Passieren, passieren!*' he repeated and waved me on again.

'Grinning lout,' I said with a smile to the Private.

He nodded, grinning, and saluted.

I walked away. The Corporal was not troubling to examine my permit any more. The Corporal had decided that I was harmless. The Corporal was absolutely right. Tomorrow, I decided, I would send a cable to the man who was paying me, tell him that he was wasting his money and my time, then take the first plane I could get out of the place. It was high time I stopped this foolishness and got back to work again. Not, I thought savagely, that the trip had been a complete loss. I had increased my knowledge of Napoleon the Third. I had also had two interesting experiences; that of finding a dead body in a strange house and that of being locked in a room in another strange house. In the unlikely event of my ever wanting to write the kind of play in which incidents like that occurred, the knowledge would be useful. Meanwhile, to hell with it!

I turned into the Boulevard Dragutin.

It ran in a gentle curve round the high boundary wall of the Presidential Park. It was a wide road, lined with big plane trees and cobbled. Most of the buildings in it were apartment houses; there were no shops or cafés. The lights were on tall standards set among the trees on the building side of the road. I walked on the other side. Beneath the dense foliage of the trees it was very dark.

I walked slowly. The air was pleasant and after a while something happened to make me forget my immediate troubles. Before I had left London I had been trying to write the third act of a new play and had got into difficulties with it. Indeed, I had practically made up my mind to scrap the whole thing. The commission to report the Deltchev trial had come at an opportune moment; it had given me a reason for suspending work on the play that left the real reasons for doing so in abeyance. But now, quite suddenly, I found myself thinking about the play again and seeing quite clearly the point of the problem which I had missed before. The shape of a third act began to emerge. Of course! The wife's lover wasn't her own choice but her husband's and it was her realization of this fact that made it possible for her to leave him. Of course! It was the key to her whole attitude towards her lover. He was not *her* choice. Of course. How curious it was. I had practically sign-posted the thing all the way through without realizing the fact. Why? My mind nosed round the discovery suspiciously, like a terrier at a strange lamp post. There must be a mistake. But no, it was all right. I had been too close to it before and too anxious. Now, all was well. I drew a deep breath. Forgotten were the Deltchevs and the enigma they represented. I had just finished a play. I felt light-hearted and alive, I quickened my pace.

Then I heard it. It was only a slight sound and it went almost immediately; a sort of ringing of my footsteps on the paving stones. But I was very much aware of everything at that moment; of the soft, warm breeze that was beginning to stir the air, of the smell of the trees and of the slow movement of a distant point of light. At this moment of heightened sensibility, the ringing of my footsteps was a matter for appreciation and curiosity. The pavement was solid enough. Where did the rest of the sound come from? I slowed down a little and heard it again; a kind of echo. From the wall? I stepped out again but in a more emphatic way this time. Then I understood. It was not an echo I was hearing. Someone was walking behind me.

It is easy to separate sounds once you know they are there. As I walked on, I could hear the other set of footsteps quite plainly. I slowed down again. The sounds separated and then again they coincided. Even then it took me a moment or two to grasp what was happening. The person behind me was varying his pace with mine. He did not want to change the distance between us. I was being followed.

My heart suddenly beat faster. I looked round. I could just see him, a faint thickening of the shadows under the trees about thirty yards behind me. I walked on fighting down a desire to run. Perhaps, I was imagining it all, like a neurotic spinster with fantasies of being raped. But no; the footsteps kept pace with mine. Wild ideas of turning quickly and challenging the follower went through my mind but I kept on walking for a bit. The calves of my legs began to ache. Then, suddenly, I turned and crossed the road to the lighted side. Out of the corner of my left eye I tried to see if he was crossing too. I could hear his footsteps. They had slowed down. He wasn't going to cross. He was going to stay among the shadows. For a moment or two a feeling of relief flooded over me. It was not until I was nearly to the pavement that I realized why he had not crossed. A hundred yards or so ahead there was a stretch of road with no buildings and no lights. I remembered walking along it earlier. He was going to cross there.

163

I reached the pavement and hesitated. Then I bent down and pretended to tie my shoelace. I wanted time to think. If I went back the way I had come I could stay in the lights. I remembered also that I had seen two policemen yawning and spitting on a corner. But what was I to do then? Explain to them? But there was nothing to explain. The only thing was to wait about like a frightened child until someone else came along with whom I could walk in company through the dark. Ridiculous! What was there to be afraid of? Someone was following me. Very well. Let him follow. What did it matter? There was nothing to be afraid of in that. Nothing at all.

I stood up again and walked on stiffly towards the darkness.

It lay at the end of the lighted strip of pavement like the black mouth of a tunnel. The building I had to pass before I reached it was a huge baroque mansion which, judging from the lighted windows, had been converted into flats. I looked across the road. I could see him moving along under the trees now, a little behind me but at the same speed. The darkness came nearer and I began to see a short way into it. The footpaths ran on between a stone wall and the trees but the surface of it changed from stone pavement to dust. At the end of the pavement I paused. The leaves above stirred faintly, there was a radio playing somewhere and the breathing sounds of distant traffic; but that was in the background; the darkness before me was quiet and still. The gritty dust crunched beneath my feet and the branches seemed to close in as I walked on again. I had gone about thirty paces when I heard the sound of an approaching car. It passed, going in the opposite direction. Then, as the sound died away I heard the footsteps on the road; the man from the shadows was crossing it behind me. I went on faster, stumbling slightly over the swellings in the path made by tree roots. My heart was beating sickeningly now and I could feel the cold sweat stealing down my body. I fought against the desire to run. It was absurd, I told myself. I had been in situations fifty times more dangerous. Here there were no mines or alarm wires to tread on, no machine-guns or mortars waiting to open fire. All I had to do was to walk along a path beneath some trees in a badly lighted city street, followed by someone who might or might not be ill-intentioned. He might be a detective, one of Brankovitch's men instructed to report on my movements. Petlarov had been warned off me by the police. They might now be checking to see if I had any other contacts. Indeed, the man could have been following me about for days without my having noticed the fact. Yes, that must be it. I almost chuckled with relief and slowed down, listening for the footsteps behind me. But there were none. Perhaps they were muffled by the dust. Perhaps . . .

I stopped dead. Something had moved in front of me.

I stood quite still for a moment trying to control the thudding of the blood in my head, so that I could hear. Something had moved, a shadow, something. I took a step forward and my foot grated on a pebble. The next instant there was a blinding flash of light.

It came from a powerful hand lamp a few yards in front of me and lasted for less than a second. And that, too, was the time I took to react. As the light went out I fell sideways, sprawling at the foot of a tree.

I only heard the first shot, a thudding crack that made my ears sing; but the next two I saw; yellow blots of flame that seemed to be exploding in my face as I rolled over and clawed for cover behind the tree. Then there was silence.

I was gasping for breath as if I had been held under water but my brain was working all right. He had missed me three times and then lost track of me. He would have to risk another flash from the lamp to locate me again; and it would be a risk; he could not be sure that I was unarmed. In any case, I was prepared now and unless he were a first-rate shot or very lucky he had not much of a chance. For the moment, I had forgotten the man behind me.

Five seconds went by. I was slowly straightening up and

easing round away from the tree when the light flashed on again. It was not directly on me and in the fraction of a second it took him to realize that, I had begun to move. I was half way towards the next tree when he fired. The bullet whipped past my head. I reached the tree and swung round it as if to take cover again, but immediately scrambled on to the next one. The shot he fired at that moment was yards wide. But he had learned one thing; I was not going to fire back. The lamp shone out again and this time it stayed on. He did not fire. He moved forward. He was going to make sure of it this time. Bent double, I scuttled on again. I saw my shadow twist among the long casts of the trees as the light swung round. Then, as I pulled up against the next tree, a different pistol fired.

The bullet tore through the bark an inch or two from my right eye and a splinter of wood stung my cheek. I dived for the ground again. The other gun, I thought, had been a .38 but this had a heavier sound. I could see how it was. If I had not crossed the road, the man behind me would have shot me in the back. The second man had been there to make sure I did not get away. Probably he had crossed ahead of me while I was still in the lighted section.

I was out of the light for a moment now; but both pistols fired again and the bullet from one of them ricocheted off the road. They were getting worried. Nearly half a minute had gone by since the first shot and I could hear shouting in the distance. The lighted stretch was only a hundred yards away now, but if I broke cover and made a dash for it I would have to pass the heavy pistol with the other man's light behind me. It would not do.

At that moment the man with the light began to run forward yelling hoarsely. The heavy pistol fired again as I rolled sideways and found myself on the edge of the road. I hesitated for only a split second. Then I scrambled to my feet and ran, swerving like a rabbit, for the trees on the other side of the road. They both fired but by then I was a hopeless target for a pistol. I dived through the trees, came up against the boundary wall and ran along it towards the lighted section.

I was safe now. I stopped to get my breath. There were people from the houses standing on the pavement opposite, talking and pointing towards the trees where the sound of the firing had come from. The two policemen I had passed farther back were approaching at a run. I was out of sight. My breath was beginning to come back and with it my wits. I had not seen either of the attackers. I had no information about them to give. But even that would take a lot of explaining to the police and they would certainly detain me while an interpreter was found and my story checked. If I could avoid the police altogether, I should do so. If, while they searched among the trees for the dead and wounded that were not there, I could make myself scarce, I would be saving them trouble. If, in fact, I now did what I should have done five minutes earlier – kept my head, walked back to a café and there telephoned to the hotel for a car to fetch me – everyone would be much better off. I had begun to tremble violently. My ears were singing and felt deaf. I leaned against the Presidential wall fighting down a desire to vomit. Through the singing in my ears I could hear shouts from farther up the road. Then my head began to clear. Reaction or no reaction, if I were going to get away unobtrusively I would have to be quick about it. Keeping close to the wall, I started to walk.

It was an hour before the car arrived at the café and by that time I had had several plum brandies. I was not drunk but I felt sleepy. It was silly of Aleko, I thought, to want to kill me. Very silly. I was perfectly harmless. However, I had now acquired another useless piece of information; I knew what it felt like to be shot at in civilian clothes; it was exactly the same as it felt when you wore a uniform. That was interesting. In the car I went to sleep and had to be wakened by the driver when we got to the hotel.

The reception clerk was asleep. I took my room key from the rack myself. The lift was not working. I walked upstairs slowly, yawning. I was really very tired. I was also beginning to feel stiff and bruised. If the water was hot (and late at night, when nobody wanted it, it usually was hot) I would have a bath and attend to the knee I had cut on a stone. My suit was a mess too, but that could wait until the morning. A bath, then sleep; that was it. I felt curiously relaxed and happy. The odd thing was that this feeling had almost nothing to do with the plum brandy. It was because I had survived an ordeal.

I opened the door of my room. There was a small foyer with a cupboard and a hat rack between the door and the bedroom itself. I switched on the foyer light, remembered with a twinge of irritation that I had lost my hat and would have to buy one of the local Homburgs next day, and went into the bedroom.

My hand was on the bedroom light switch when I saw what was there. I stood quite still.

A woman was lying face downwards across the bed. By the foyer light I could see that she had a loose raincoat of some kind spread about her as if it had been thrown there to cover her up.

I pressed the light switch and the room was flooded with the bright hard light from the naked lamps in the gilt chandelier.

Her hair was dark and one of her tightly-clenched hands concealed her face. I walked over to the bed and a loose board cracked loudly. I looked down.

She stirred. Her hands moved and she rolled on to her side. The light poured down on her face and she raised a hand to shield her eyes.

It was Katerina Deltchev.

Chapter 16

I shook the bed, not gently, and she sighed. Then, with a start and a gasp, she was awake. She sat up quickly and the thin raincoat she had thrown over her slipped to the floor.

'Good evening,' I said.

For a moment she stared at me, then she scrambled off the bed and looked round defiantly.

'There's no one else here,' I added.

She drew herself up as if she were about to deliver an oath of allegiance. 'Herr Foster,' she said formally, 'I must apologize for this intrusion but it was unavoidable. I will explain. I . . .' She broke off and looked down as she realized that she was in her stockinged feet.

'They're down there,' I said. Her shoes had slipped off while she had been asleep and were lying beside the bed.

She opened her mouth to say something, then shut it again, went over to the bed and put her shoes on thoughtfully. She was a young woman who was used to being in charge of a situation; now she was casting about for a way of taking charge of this one.

'I am sorry . . .' she began.

'Quite all right,' I said. 'You wanted to see me so you came here. I was out. You waited. You fell asleep. I am afraid I can't offer you anything but a cigarette. Will you smoke?'

For a fraction of a second she weighed the possible moral advantage of a refusal, then she shrugged her shoulders. 'Yes. Thank you.'

She took a cigarette and I lit it for her. She sat down again on the bed and looked at me calmly.

'Herr Foster,' she said, 'it is not really quite as simple as that for you, is it?'

'No, not quite.'

I went into the bathroom, dipped a towel in water and wrung it out. Then I went back into the bedroom, sat down in the armchair, rolled the trouser leg up and went to work with the towel on my cut knee. She watched uncertainly.

'Who told you I was staying here?' I asked.

'There were three hotels where you might have been staying. This was the second one I telephoned.'

'How did you know the room number?'

'By asking for another room number when I telephoned. Of course I got the wrong number. The operator corrected me.'

'Who let you in here?'

'The floor waiter. I said I was your lover and gave him some money. Does it matter?'

'Not a bit. It's just that at the moment I am in a suspicious mood. Now then. How do you get out of the house without being seen? What do you do?'

'Our neighbours are friendly. Between our wall and theirs, there is a tree. With two vine poles one can crawl from the top of our wall to the tree. From the tree one uses the branches to reach their wall. For a child it is easy. For a heavier person there is some danger, but it can be done.'

'Then why did you ask me to deliver that letter for you, Fräulein? If it was so important you could have delivered it yourself.'

'I did not wish to risk my life if there was another way.'

'Are you risking your life now?'

'Yes, Herr Foster. I am also risking yours.'

'That I guessed.'

'But only if I am found here.'

'Splendid.'

'If I get back to-night without being seen, I shall be safe, too. The guards inspect us only in the morning.'

'Good.'

'I would not have come, Herr Foster,' she said severely, 'if it had not been absolutely necessary to see you.'

'You didn't have to leave the house to do that. I was there myself an hour ago.'

She shrugged. 'I did not know. I wished to see you because . . .'

I interrupted her. 'Do you know a man named Aleko?'

'Aleko? It is common.'

'Who was the Valmo you sent that letter to?'

'I don't know.'

'I see.'

'It is true. Valmo was only a name I was given to send letters to. The letter was for someone else.'

'Who?'

'My brother, Philip.'

I sighed. 'The one who's studying law in Geneva?'

'He is not in Geneva.'

'Your mother said he was.'

'My mother was lying.'

'I didn't think so.'

'She did not intend you to think so. Will you please listen to me without interruption for a moment?'

'All right, I'm listening.'

'My brother has been in hiding here since before Papa was arrested. My brother, Herr Foster, had five friends. Their names were Pazar, Eftib, Vlahov, Pechanatz and Radiuje.'

I dropped the towel. 'Do you know what you're saying?'

'Perfectly. That is what I came to tell you. This evidence that they have brought against my father is quite true. Only it is not he who is guilty. It is my brother Philip.'

I sat back and stared at her. She was telling the truth. A lot of things were suddenly and appallingly clear.

'When did your mother find out?'

'She did not tell me.'

'Does your father know?'

'He must have known from the beginning of the trial, or guessed. But what can he do? He cannot accuse his own son, and Brankovitch would certainly not let Philip give evidence.'

'Nobody would believe it anyway. They'd laugh. Dutiful son takes blame for father's crimes! I'd laugh myself.' I thought about it for a moment. It explained quite a lot of things but not everything by any means. I looked up at her again. 'What's the idea of telling this to me, Fräulein?'

'I want you to publish my brother's evidence.'

'Does he want to give it?'

She set her lips firmly. 'He must.'

'Does your mother know of this idea?'

'I would not tell her. She would say that it would not help Papa, only condemn Philip.'

'She'd be right.'

'But abroad they must know the truth.'

'Would your mother agree with that?'

'I do not know. She is too clever to be simple. She would discuss the idea and think of possibilities nobody else had dreamed of. Then she would say she was tired. You would not know her real thoughts.'

'What was your brother up to? Is he crazy?'

She shook her head slowly. 'When Papa betrayed the party,' she said, 'he and Philip quarrelled. They were always in conflict but this time my mother could do nothing.' Tears came to her eyes. 'We were all against him, even I was, and when the People's Party came to power, Philip joined a student political club which had for secretary this man Pazar. Pazar always needed money but the students liked him. He talked very amusingly and they used to pay him for coaching. When they formed a club they would sometimes make him secretary and give him a commission on the subscriptions. Philip soon felt that the club was not serious, but he became very friendly with Pazar. Then, one day, Pazar told him that he was a member of the Brotherhood.'

'There must have been pleasure in telling that to the son of the man who had done so much to destroy it,' I

172

remarked. It was all too easy to catch the flavour of those dangerous exchanges of confidence between the middle-aged drug addict and the fanatical youth.

She shrugged. 'Perhaps. I know that when Philip joined the Brotherhood it was only to revenge himself on Papa. He did not mean then to do more than join.'

'But once he had joined, he found that they expected more than a gesture. Was that it?'

She nodded. 'There were six of them elected and Philip was named the leader. Their task was to kill Vukashin at the Anniversary Celebration Parade. But . . .'

'Just a moment. Who was the man who gave them the job?'

'It was not one man but a group of men. They called themselves The Survivors.'

'When did Philip tell you all this?'

'Before he went to Switzerland. Mamma had become worried about him. He looked so ill and tired. She persuaded Papa to send him there to study. Naturally, he refused to go at first, but after a day or two he said no more. That was at Christmas. He had arranged to return in secret when Pazar sent for him.' She paused before she added: 'I knew then that he was not the real leader but had been given the role of leader because of his name.'

'Did you say that to him?'

'He already knew it, I think. But if I had said it he would have made some other foolishness to prove to me that I was wrong. Besides, I thought that in Geneva he might change his mind and forget about it.'

'But he didn't.'

'No. We had arranged a code for our letters and when the attempt on Papa was made, I heard from him that he was returning. I only saw him once. We met secretly at a place near the station.'

'Patriarch Dimo nine?'

'No, another. But he gave me two addresses which I might send letters to. Valmo, Patriarch Dimo nine, was one

173

of them. The other he told me I must use only in case of an extreme emergency if I had to find him.'

'What was in the letter you gave me?'

'I begged him to escape to Greece and publish the truth about the conspiracy against Vukashin from there.'

'What made you decide to come to me?'

She frowned impatiently. 'To-day's evidence, Herr Foster. Surely you see. The police know everything. Philip and Pazar are the only two left. They must be in hiding somewhere, helpless. Philip can do nothing now even if he wished. It must be done for him.'

I thought hard for a moment or two, then I shook my head. 'I don't think that it's as simple as you believe, Fräulein.'

'What do you mean?'

'Well, to begin with, Valmo was the name Pazar was hiding under. When I tried to deliver your letter, I found him dead. He'd been shot through the back of the head and had been there some days.'

'What happened to my letter?'

'That was burnt by a man named Aleko who said that he was of the secret police and that *his* name was Valmo. He also said that your letter was addressed to him and was something to do with the attempt on your father.' I described Aleko. 'Does that mean anything to you?' I added.

She looked utterly bewildered. 'No, Herr Foster.'

'What does your brother look like?'

She gave me a description.

I nodded. 'A young man who looks like that came into Aleko's apartment while I was there. I only saw him for a moment. Aleko called him Jika.'

She stood up quickly. 'That is Philip. He likes his friends to call him that. Herr Foster, where is this place?'

'I don't know for certain but I should think that it may be the other address your brother gave you. Have you got it?'

'Philip made me remember it. He said it was too dangerous to write down.'

'What is it?'

'Pashik, Pan-Eurasian Press Service, Serdika Prospek fifteen,' she said.

I went to the wardrobe, got out the bottle of plum brandy and poured myself a big drink.

'Do you like this stuff?' I asked.

She shook her head.

'All right, Fräulein. You'd better go back now. I think I know how to reach your brother.'

Chapter 17

Pashik lived in a modern apartment house near his office. He had pointed out the place to me on the day I had arrived. I thought now that I could find it without much difficulty. There were no taxis. I walked.

The way there lay through the business quarter and by that time the streets were mostly empty and still. Earlier that day they had been decorated in preparation for the anniversary parade and the bright moonlight, striking obliquely through the flags overhead, cast a multiplicity of shadows that stirred and twisted in the warm breeze. It was like walking through the dark forest of a dream. But I had gone some distance before I became frightened.

It was a very unpleasant sensation. The brandy-engendered resolution with which I had set out seemed to drain suddenly away. I began to shiver uncontrollably and an icy, numbing kind of logic invaded the small corner of my conscious mind not whimpering with the effort required to keep on walking. What I was doing was incredibly foolish. Not three hours ago two men had tried to kill me in the street. I had been very lucky to escape. Now, here I was in the streets again, giving them another chance. For obviously they must be waiting for me. Ruthless determination of the kind they possessed would be intensified by failure. They would not fail a second time.

Soon, every shadow had become a man with a gun, every doorway the place of an ambush. I kept on simply because I was afraid to go back. I walked now simply because I was afraid to break into a run that might precipitate action. My legs ached with the strain. My shirt clung to my back. I had so completely lost my head that I went on fifty yards past my destination without seeing it. There was a frantic ten seconds on the corner of the Boulevard Sokolovsky while I got my bearings. Then I saw the apartment house from a familiar angle. I ran the fifty yards back.

It was a tall, narrow building with massive ferro-concrete balconies from the sides of which rusty weather stains drooled down the walls. In the daylight these stains gave the place a tired, unhappy air – you wanted someone to wipe its face for it – but in the moonlight they were hard shadows that made the balconies seem to project like freakish upper lips. The main entrance doors, ornate affairs of wrought iron and rolled glass were still open, and the lobby beyond was dimly illuminated by a light from the concierge's room.

As I stood for a moment or two recovering my breath, I looked back along the street. There were two or three empty cars parked in it, but they had been there already. Nobody had followed me. I went in and pressed the concierge's bell. Nothing happened. After a minute or so I went over to the lift. Beside it was a list of the tenants. Pashik was on the fourth floor. The lift did not work, of course. I found the stairs and walked up.

At the moment of deciding to see Pashik that night I had had a clear image of the sort of interview it would be. I had seen him already in bed and asleep when I arrived. In response to my insistent ringing he had at last appeared, a bleary, night-shirted figure (I had been sure he wore night-shirts) fetid and protesting. I had cut through his protests decisively. I had given him no time to build up his defences. I had pelted him with the facts I had discovered and watched his features grow pinched as he realized how much I knew. Then, at last, wearily he had shrugged. 'Very well. Since you already know so much, Mr Foster, you had better hear the rest.' And I had sat down to listen.

The reality was somewhat different.

The door to his apartment was at the end of a short passage near the main staircase landing. As I turned into the passage I saw that the door was ajar and that there were lights in the apartment. I went along the passage and up to the door. Then, with my hand on the bell, I paused. Inside someone was speaking on the telephone. Or listening rather; there was a series of grunts, then two or three words I did not understand. The voice, however, was not Pashik's. I hesitated, then rang the bell.

The voice ceased abruptly. There was a movement from within. Then silence. Suddenly, the door swung open and clattered gently against a picture on the wall behind it. For a moment the small lobby beyond looked empty. Then I saw. Between the doors of the two rooms facing me was a narrow strip of wall. On that wall was a mirror and, reflected in it, the face of the man who had pushed the door open with his foot. It was Sibley.

He moved slowly out from the wall just inside the entrance and looked at me. There was a heavy bottle-glass ashtray in his hand. He put it down on the hall table and grinned.

'Well, Foster dear,' he said archly, 'this *is* a nice surprise! A small world, I always say. Do *you* always say that? Of course you don't! Come to see our smelly friend?'

'Naturally. What are you doing here?'

He looked at me oddly. 'I've come to see him too, and also naturally. Doesn't seem to be about though, does he? I've looked high and low.'

'Who were you expecting to have to beat over the head with that ashtray?'

'Somebody else who shouldn't be here. Like me. You're quite a logical visitor, of course. Been here before I shouldn't wonder.'

'No.'

He grinned again. 'I thought not. Come on in and make yourself at home. I was telephoning.'

'Yes, I heard.'

'Don't speak the language though, do you?'

'No.'

'I thought not. This way.'

178

He went through the left hand door. I hesitated and then followed.

It was a sitting-room which had obviously been furnished by the owners of the building. There were built-in cupboards and bookcases and a built-in sofa. There were cube-like easy-chairs, glass-topped circular tables and an oatmeal-coloured rug. You could have seen the same sort of things in any other furnished apartment building in any other European city. The extraordinary thing about this room was the decoration of the walls.

They were covered, every square foot of them, with pages cut from American magazine and stuck on with Scotch tape. There were pictures of film stars (all women), there were near-nude 'studies' of women who were not film stars and there were artlessly erotic colour drawings of reclining seductresses in lace step-ins. All would have looked quite at home in the room of an adolescent youth. Yet, that was the comprehensible part of the display; it was not remarkable that Pashik should have the emotional development of a sixteen-year-old boy. The startling thing was that for every Ann Sheridan, for every sandal-tying beach beauty, for every long-legged houri, there was a precisely arranged frame of advertisement pages. The nearest Betty Grable was surrounded by Buick, Frigidaire, Lux and American Airlines, all in colour. A sun-tanned blonde glistening with sea water had Coca-Cola, United Steel, Dictaphone and Lord Calvert whisky. A gauze-veiled brunette with a man's bedroom slipper in her hand and a speculative eye was framed by Bell Telephones, Metropolitan Life Insurance, General Electric and Jello. The baffling thing was that the selection and grouping of advertisements seemed quite unrelated to the pictures. There was no wit, no hint of social criticism in the arrangements. Many of the advertisements were not particularly distinguished as such. It was fantastic.

Sibley had gone back to the telephone. He had said something into it, listened again and then, with a last word, hung up. He flicked his fingers at the wall as if he were launching a paper pellet.

'Lots of fun, isn't it?'

'Lots. How did you get in?'

'The concierge has a pass key and is corrupt. Would you like a drink? There must be some about.' He opened one of the cupboards and peered inside.

'Do you know Pashik well?' I said.

'Would you believe me if I said yes?'

'No.'

'Then let's say that I think I know a bit more about him than you do. Cigars but no drinks,' he added, producing a box. 'Cigar?'

'No, thanks.'

'No, it's a drink you need. You're not looking your usual cheerful self, Foster dear. A bit pinched round the gills and upset. Let's try this one.' He went to another cupboard.

'I take it you're not afraid of Pashik's suddenly turning up and finding you here searching his room. That wouldn't embarrass you?'

'Not a bit.'

'Was that why you came? Because you knew he wouldn't be here?'

He looked up from the cupboard he was searching and shook his head. 'No, Foster *mio*,' he said softly, 'that wasn't why. I just wanted a little chat with him. When there was no answer I had another thought and fetched the concierge. Silly of me, wasn't it, but I actually thought our Georghi might be dead.'

'Why should you think that?'

'It was just a thought I had.' He straightened up suddenly with a bottle in his hand. 'There now! Our old friend plum brandy!' And then he looked directly at me. 'You know about Pazar, of course?'

'What about him?'

'To-night's police statement that they've found him shot in a derelict house.'

180

'Oh yes, that,' I tried to make it casual.

He reached down and brought out two glasses. 'A house in some street with a funny name,' he said slowly. 'What was it?'

'Patriarch Dimo.' My voice sounded unnatural to me.

'That's it. Who told you? Georghi?'

'Yes. He had the statement.'

He brought the bottle and glasses over and put them on the table. 'When did you see him?'

'Oh, earlier on.'

He shook his head. 'It won't do, Foster dear,' he said. 'No, don't get cross. I set a little trap and you fell into it, that's all. That statement was only issued half an hour ago. I was on the phone to the office when you came in. That's how I know.' He thrust his head forward. 'How did *you* know?'

I was feeling sick again. I sat down.

'*Did* Georghi tell you?'

I shook my head. 'I found him by accident.'

He whistled softly. 'My, my! You *do* get around! What sort of an accident was it that took you to Patriarch Dimo? The same sort that got you into the Deltchev house?'

'Not quite.'

'Doing a little private investigating perhaps?'

'That's the idea.'

He shook his head regretfully. 'Someone must be very cross with you.'

Another wave of sickness came. I drew a deep breath. 'Then that's probably why someone's just tried to kill me,' I said.

He stared at me expressionlessly for a moment. 'A joke, Foster dear?' he said gently; 'a joke in bad taste?'

'No joke.'

'Where was it?'

'In that road that runs round the Park.'

'When?'

'An hour or two ago.'

181

'One man or two?'

'Two.'

'One of them couldn't have been Georghi by any chance?'

'No.'

He seemed to relax again. 'Well, well! Poor Foster! No wonder you look peaky. And here I am chattering away instead of pouring the much needed drink. There.'

I swallowed the drink and sat back for a moment with my eyes closed. I hoped he would believe that I was feeling faint. I had to think and it was difficult. Sibley was Brankovitch's paid man and already I had given myself away appallingly. Pashik was involved with Aleko and Philip Deltchev in a Brotherhood plot to assassinate Vukashin. The wreckage of that plot was being used to convict the elder Deltchev. Now, the dead Pazar, probably murdered by Aleko, had been officially discovered on the eve of the anniversary parade at which Vukashin was to have been assassinated. There was a contrived, bad third act feeling about the whole thing; as if . . .

'Feeling better?' said Sibley.

'Yes, thanks.' I opened my eyes. He was looking down at me coldly. I had not deceived him. He smiled.

'What a busy week you've had! Have you any idea, I wonder, what you know that makes you worth killing?'

'None at all.'

He sat down opposite me. 'Maybe if you were to tell me what you do know, I could make a suggestion about that.'

'Or perhaps find a way through the censorship with it? By the way, how is your little man at the Propaganda Ministry?'

He drank his drink down and looked at the empty glass as if waiting for someone to fill it. 'Do I detect a note of bitchiness and distrust, Foster dear?'

'Yes, you probably do.'

He looked at the bottle and poured himself another. 'Drink will be the death of me,' he said. 'I was tiddly, of course, but it seemed such a good joke at the time.

Although, Foster *amigo*, I won't deny that I should also have been interested to see what your angle on the affair was going to be.'

'My angle was and is that your little man in the Propaganda Ministry was Brankovitch.'

He giggled. 'Who told you they played that trick? Georghi?'

'Not Georghi.'

He giggled again. 'Oh, dear! Not Georghi, you mean, but someone else whose name you don't want to mention in case I'm a Ministry spy who might get him into trouble. Oh dear, oh dear! I do see. I played right into your hands, didn't I? No wonder you were so maddening. The thing was that they'd tried it on me days before. I could send anything I wanted if I knew how. That was the line. It would cost a bit, of course, but that was to make it sound right.' He sighed. 'I don't like being taken for a fool, do you? I was a bit vexed so I decided to amuse myself. I thought at first of pretending I'd fallen for it and sending a really dreadful story I'd heard about Vukashin's sex life. Then I sobered up and thought again. In the end, all I did was to lift their dialogue and try it on someone else. Georghi was my first customer and I frightened him out of his wits – or he pretended I did. And that was the crazy part of it; because it wasn't until I saw him looking at me with those big brown eyes of his and got a breath of that subtle perfume that I remembered where I'd seen him before. Do I convince you?'

'By no means.'

He gazed upwards soulfully. 'It's so sad. I can never make the truth sound convincing. Of course, I *look* so shifty. I should stick to lying, shouldn't I?'

'Where was it you saw Pashik before?'

'Ah, I have your interest. If only I can keep it until the knockout drops which I slipped into your drink begin to work, all will be well.'

Involuntarily I looked down at my glass.

He grinned. 'You're really very tiresome, aren't you, Foster dear? If I didn't want badly to know what makes you worth killing I wouldn't say another word.'

'It's late. I'm very tired. And . . .'

'And it's always so upsetting to be shot at,' he said quickly. 'How inconsiderate of me not to remember that.'

'I wasn't apologizing.'

'Of course you weren't. You were just hoping that I'd cut the cackle. I do understand. These affectations of mine are such a bore. All right. Let's talk about Georghi Pashik, why he exists and in whose image he is made. What has he told you about himself?'

'He was expelled from Italy for writing something Mussolini didn't agree with. He did his military service in Austria. He admires Myrna Loy. The last item I deduced for myself from a picture in his office.'

'She must be his spiritual Mum, don't you think. All right, here it is. Technically, a stateless person. Born in the Trentino, of Macedonian Greek parents who were themselves of doubtful national status. He takes Hungarian nationality. Treaty of Trianon muddle. He does his military service in Austria. He goes eventually to Paris and works for Havas as a messenger. Intelligent, ambitious, a worker. He writes odd pieces. He gets on. Eventually they give him a job in the Rome office. He gets important. Then he's expelled, which is all very difficult because he's married an Italian girl and the squadristi make it hot for her family. He has a lot of trouble squaring things. After a bit his wife dies and he returns here to the home of his forefathers with very peculiar ideas about the way the world ought to be run.'

'What sort of ideas?'

'I'm coming to that. Well, the war breaks out and in nineteen forty Georghi skips to Cairo. For a time he's on a newspaper there, then he decides that it's time to do a little war work and gets taken on as an interpreter by the British. Later on, when the United States Middle East contingent arrives he is transferred to them. In nineteen forty-five he turns up in an American Civil Affairs unit in Germany.

'Still as an interpreter. Only by now he has a bastard sort of uniform and is working in a D.P. camp near Munich. He worked under an American Major named Macready. I had business there and that's where I first saw Georghi and got to know about him.'

'What was your business?'

'Intelligence – the British lot.' He caught a glance I gave him. 'Oh, dear me, no! Not any more. I was just the wartime variety, uniform and everything. I was liaising with an American who was on the same job as me – checking up on the bad boys who'd gone to earth in the D.P. camps and then digging them out – and it was this man who told me about Georghi. Another drink?'

'I think I will.'

'That's good. There's another bottle in there if we run short or if Georghi comes home. All right then. We go back to the time Georghi went over to the Americans in Cairo. Almost the first thing that happened was that he was sent up to a small hill town in the Lebanon with a Lieutenant, a Tech-Sergeant and an enlisted man. The job was to operate a radio station monitoring an intelligence network operating in the Balkans. I believe there was some shortwave oddity that determined their position, but that's not important. The thing was that our Georghi was stuck out in the wilderness for nearly a year with three Americans who didn't like it either and talked about home. I don't know anything about the Sergeant and the enlisted man but the Lieutenant was a radio engineer named Kromak and he came from Passaic, New Jersey. Do you know the Lebanon?'

I shook my head.

'In the evenings the sky is like wine and the shadows falling across the terraces have purple edges to them. Overhead, vines – grape and other things with big flowers and a wonderful smell. Everything is very still and warm

185

and soft. It's the kind of atmosphere in which myths are born and the pictures in your mind's eye seem more real than the chair you're sitting on. I wax lyrical, you see. However, the point is that Lieutenant Kromak talked about Passaic, New Jersey, and read aloud his wife's letters while Georghi listened. He heard about Molly's graduation and Michael's camp counsellor, about Sue's new baby and the seeding of the front lawn. He heard about the new refrigerator and the shortage of gasoline, about his friend, Pete Staal, the dentist, and the Rotary Anns. He heard about the mouse in the cedar closet and the new screens that had been bought for the porch. And when the weekly letter was exhausted, the reminiscences would begin. "Pete Staal, Pete Staal," Kromak would say dreamily, "a good dentist and a lovable son-of-a-bitch but what a crazy guy! I remember the night Kitty and me, the Deckers and the Staals went to Rossi's – that's an Italian restaurant at the far end of Franklin Street – and had ravioli. Ever had ravioli? At Rossi's they make the best ravioli in the world. Well, we didn't want to take two cars so we rode down in mine. A Dodge I had then. Well, right after we'd eaten, Helen said she wanted to go over to the Nutley Field Club. That made Pete mad and he said that if she was going to Nutley he was going to fly down to Wilmington to see his mother. Of course, he knew what Helen really wanted – to see Marie and Dane Schaeffer – I told you about them, remember? Well . . ." And on he went while Georghi listened and drank it in. Do you know Passaic, New Jersey?'

'No.'

'Chemical plants and some light industry and the homes of the people who have to work there. But to Georghi Pashik, looking through the eyes of Lieutenant Kromak who wanted so much to be back with the wife and kids, it must have represented a paradise of domestic security and gracious living. You know how it is? Lots of quite intelligent Europeans have fantastic notions about the way most

Americans live. Sitting on that terrace in a Lebanon hill town, poor, unhappy, exiled Georghi must have been a pushover for the American way of life. Just to put it in terms of food – reason might tell him that the ravioli he'd get in Rossi's on Franklin Street, Passaic, would not be as good as those he'd eaten already in Rome and Florence, but Rossi's ravioli had become the desirable ones. They had the approval of those legendary figures, the Staals, the Deckers and the Schaeffers, and that was what mattered. He began to understand why the Americans didn't like the Lebanese they came in contact with. Lebanese standards of sanitation and behaviour are not those of Passaic, New Jersey. Georghi heard local ways that he had accepted or failed even to notice condemned quite angrily. He was troubled and began to question himself. You see what was happening, of course? Along with his dream of Passaic, New Jersey, he was beginning to acquire an American conscience.'

He paused for a moment to swallow another drink and fill my glass.

'How much are you embroidering this story?' I asked.

He shrugged. 'Not much. But the man who told me was an American and he could reproduce that Kromak stuff so you'd think you were really listening to him. I just give you the bits I remember and fill in the rest. The effect's the same though. Anyway, after nearly a year of the American Way and Purpose according to Lieutenant Kromak, Georghi was shifted back to Cairo. Americans again, only this time the high priest was a dairy chemist from Minnesota and the dream was in a slightly higher income bracket. Georghi read the Declaration of Independence, the Constitution of the United States and the Gettysburg address. After that there was a filling station proprietor from Oakland, California. He was followed by an insurance man from Hagerstown, Maryland. Then came nineteen forty-four and the surrender negotiations between Deltchev and the Anglo-American representatives. There was a British Military Mission operating with the partisans in Macedonia at that time. They controlled quite a large area and had a landing strip, so it wasn't too difficult to arrange the meetings. The Anglo-Americans flew in from Foggia. Deltchev travelled overland somehow. They met in a village schoolroom. Georghi was one of the interpreters. It was after the second meeting that Georghi's little cap went over the windmill.'

'Wait a minute. Had he known Deltchev before?'

'Known of him, that's all. Well now, we get to the second meeting. They had their meeting all right, but storms delayed their return and they had to wait for twenty-four hours in the village. The atmosphere of the negotiations had been quite friendly and the wait produced a lot of general conversation about conditions inside the country, the problems, what was to be done about them, and so on. The man who told me this was on that trip. Anyway, one of the subjects discussed was the Officer Corps Brotherhood. Deltchev was very frank about the problem and the difficulties of dealing with it. Some of his revelations, in fact, were deeply shocking to the Anglo-American brass and they didn't hesitate to tell him so. Deltchev must have wished he hadn't mentioned the thing. But that night Georghi went to see him privately. It must have been a curious meeting. After extracting from Deltchev a lot of secrecy and immunity pledges, Georghi revealed that he was a member of the Officer Corps Brotherhood, had been one since he had returned to the land of his fathers from Italy in thirty-seven. I told you he'd had peculiar ideas then about the way things ought to be. He'd expressed them by joining the Brotherhood. But now, he told Deltchev, all that was changed. He'd seen the light of Western democracy – all the way from Passaic, New Jersey, to Hagerstown, Maryland, he might have added – and wanted to make reparation. The long and short of it was that the Provisional Government's big clean up of the Brotherhood was made possible because Georghi turned stool pigeon.'

'How do you know?'

'Because the man who told me was the officer Deltchev went to for a check up on Georghi. The old man's first idea, of course, had been that Georghi was either an *agent provocateur* or crazy. So he was very careful. But after the next meeting he had another talk with Georghi and a plan was made.' Sibley grinned. 'You know, Georghi did a very brave thing really when you come to think of it. He could have stayed safely with the Americans. Instead, he asked them to lend him to Deltchev and came back here. The risk was really appalling when you think. For all he knew, the Brotherhood might have already condemned him as a traitor. He'd not stayed to collaborate. He'd been in the service of a foreign army. And now he'd turned up again, safe and sound at a time when, for a civilian, the journey from Athens was all but impossible. However, he took the risk and got away with it. I suppose that outside this place the Brotherhood's intelligence system didn't operate and in all the confusion nobody bothered to ask many questions. Georghi rejoined his cell and the game began. There were ten Brothers to a cell. Georghi would turn in the names of seven of them to Deltchev. Then the three survivors, Georghi among them, would attach themselves to another cell, and in the next cell purge the survivors of the first one would go with the rest. All except Georghi. He was the permanent survivor. But because of the secret way the Brotherhood was organized nobody could know how many purges our man had survived. He always arrived with the credentials and code words of the cell just betrayed and he'd always see that those who came with him were at the top of his next list. So there was never anyone to say that where he went disaster followed. It was always the first time with him. But still risky. After a time the word got round that there was treachery and the remainder of the Brotherhood disintegrated. As a safety measure, Georghi had himself arrested on suspicion and then released. He'd done all he could. Deltchev had him quietly shipped back to the Americans. That's when I met him.'

'But why didn't you recognise him at once?'

'He had a moustache then and, as I told you, a uniform. As a matter of fact he was so American it was difficult to believe that he'd never been out of Europe. His boss in Germany, Colonel Macready, was the last of the prophets as far as Georghi was concerned. He came from Texas. You know that seersucker suit Georghi wears? Macready gave it to Georghi as a going away present. It came from a department store in Houston. It was also a kind of consolation prize. Georghi had tried every way he could to get a quota number for America but it was no good. So he came back here and claimed his reward.' He paused.

'What do you mean?'

'Well, just think. Four or five years ago he came back here without a penny to his name. Now he's got this place, which I can tell you is quite expensive by local standards, and an established press agency with a dollar income. How did he do it?'

'He's quite efficient.'

'But no genius. Besides, the Pan-Eurasian was a going concern long before the war.'

'You know the answer?'

'Yes. I did a bit of checking up. The Pan-Eurasian was originally a French company incorporated in Monaco. It took a bit of doing but I managed to find out all about it through our Paris office. I got word to-day from them. Like a little surprise?'

'Yes.'

'All right, then. All the shares in the Pan-Eurasian Press Service were purchased in nineteen forty-six from the French syndicate that owned them. Forty-nine per cent of them are in the name of Georghi Pashik. All of them were bought with a draft signed by the person who owns the other fifty-one per cent.' He stopped and grinned again.

'Well, who is it?'

'Madame Deltchev.'

My mind turned a somersault. 'Are you sure?'

'Sure? Of course, I'm sure.'

'She'd be a nominee, of course.'

He laughed. 'Nominee? That woman? Don't be silly. She ran Papa Deltchev as if he were a family business. And if you've fallen for that holier-than-thou line of hers you'd better think again. I'm a newspaper reporter, Foster dear, and I've met some very tough ladies and gentlemen, but that one is up near the top of the list. When I was here two years ago she was running the country. If there were any nominees around they were her husband and that secretary of his, Petlarov. She did the thinking. She wrote the speeches. She made the policy. Do you think that dried up little lawyer could have got to power on his own? Not on your life! The only thing he ever did without consulting her was to make a damn' fool radio speech which virtually handed over the whole country to the People's Party. Papa Deltchev? Don't make me laugh! They're not trying a man in that courtroom. It's a legend they're after and I bet she's still fighting like a steer to preserve it. Why shouldn't she? It's her work. She's the only Deltchev they're sitting in judgment on.'

I shook my head. 'Oh no, she isn't.'

He stared. 'No?'

'No. You may be right about her husband, but she didn't control all the Deltchevs.'

'What are you talking about?'

'Her son Philip. He's a member of the Brotherhood. He was recruited by Pazar. And he's the Deltchev who was the leader of the conspiracy against Vukashin. You see, they're using the evidence against the son to convict the father, and they know it.'

Sibley stared at me, his face sagging.

'What's more,' I went on dully, 'the conspiracy is still in existence. And Philip Deltchev is still alive. I carried a letter from his sister Katerina to him. The address was

Patriarch Dimo nine, and instead of Philip I found Pazar shot through the back of the head. Then Pashik turned up. Where he is in this I don't know. But he turned up and took me to see a man named Aleko, who says he is of the secret police but isn't. In fact he's a professional assassin who makes a habit of shooting people through the back of the head. He seemed to be in charge of the whole affair. Philip Deltchev was there under the name of Jika. The Patriarch Dimo thing was explained to me as part of a cunning police trap to catch the man who tried to kill Deltchev before he was arrested. I pretended to accept that and agreed not to make any further visits to the Deltchev house. Of course, they didn't want me to ask Katerina any questions. Pashik warned me privately too.'

'But all the same, you went?' Sibley's face was the colour of dirty chalk.

'Yes.'

'And you wonder why they tried to kill you?'

'Not any more. Of course, if the fact that Philip Deltchev was the Deltchev of the evidence were known it would make the trial look rather silly.'

He jumped up.

'Rather silly!' His voice rose. 'You poor bloody fool! Don't you know anything about this country? Don't you see what's happened? The People's Party has taken over the whole conspiracy. Aleko's *their* man, not the Brotherhood's, and he's going to do the shooting. Young Deltchev's only the scapegoat.'

'Scapegoat for what?'

'For to-morrow's assassination, you nitwit! Don't you see? It's Judgment Day! The People's Party are going to liquidate their boss, Vukashin!'

Chapter 18

Sibley had his office car and he drove me back to my hotel or nearly to it. He was so frightened that I thought at first that he was going to refuse to do even this. But in my own panic I had made up my mind to kill him if he tried to leave me to walk, and he must have known it. From the moment we left Pashik's apartment until we arrived we did not exchange a word. He stopped at the corner of the street by the hotel. I looked at him.

'I'm not driving up to the entrance,' he said curtly; 'you can get out here.'

'All right.'

The moment I was out of the car he slammed the door and drove off. I could see his point. If Aleko's men were waiting at the hotel for me it would not be a good place to stop at. I turned the corner and paused. There was a police van outside the hotel entrance. I walked slowly towards it. The revolving doors were set back slightly and as I approached I saw the sleeve of a uniform in the recess. I walked on more boldly. If the police were there, there would at least be no gunmen in ambush.

I reached the entrance and went in, stared at by the policeman. Inside the foyer there was a group of military police and the night clerk in his shirtsleeves. They seemed to be questioning him. Then, as I came through the revolving doors, they all looked at me. The night clerk pointed.

'Herr Foster,' he said.

An officer stepped forward and two of his men moved round behind me.'

'Your papers, please?' He spoke in German.

I fumbled them out somehow. My hands were trembling.

He glanced at them, pulled my jacket open to see if I had a gun, then nodded to the men behind me. 'You are under arrest,' he said to me as the escort closed in. 'You will come with us.'

I turned round and walked towards the revolving door again. I just managed to get through it before, very violently and painfully, I vomited.

I sat with the escort on benches in the van. The officer locked us in and got up beside the driver. I did not see where we went. It was not far. I managed to recover sufficiently to ask what I was charged with, and found that the escort spoke no German. The van turned on to cobbles and stopped. I heard the officer get out. Then there was silence. We stayed there for about ten minutes. When the van was stationary, the roof ventilators did not revolve and soon the air inside became warm and stagnant. I could smell the uniforms and greased leather equipment of the escort and their sour, wine-laden breaths. At last, there were footsteps on the cobbles and the door of the van opened. The officer shone a flashlight.

'Get out.'

The escort clambered down and I followed. We were in a quadrangle with a high entrance arch. On the three other sides the space was enclosed by a building with barred windows. A prison, I thought. The only light came from a narrow doorway near the van.

'Forward!'

Going towards the doorway I stumbled on the cobbles and one of the escorts held me by the arm. I shook his hand away and went inside. There was a long stone passage with the smell of a barracks about it. Led by the officer we marched along the passage and up some stone stairs. Then there was another passage and more stairs. The place was certainly not a prison. At the end of the second passage there was a wooden door with a guard on it. As we approached he unbolted the door. The officer went through ahead of us and the ring of his footsteps was suddenly muted. The corridor we now entered was carpeted. We walked on between heavily ornamented walls reaching up to a vaulted ceiling. At intervals there were marble pedestals with busts standing on them and gilt wall brackets with electric candle lamps. There were no doors. Before we reached the end of the corridor, however, we turned off into a narrow passage like the alleyway of a liner. Then there were several doors. The officer peered at each in turn, then opened one of them and motioned me in.

It was evidently a committee room. There was a long table with a dozen or so chairs placed round it, a table with a telephone, and a bookcase. Over the rich marble fireplace there was a portrait of Vukashin in a gilt frame draped with the national flag. There were green linen blinds over the windows and beside the fireplace a curtained door. The room smelt of stale cigarette smoke.

The door by which I had entered shut behind me and I heard the key turn in the lock. I turned round and found that I was alone. I looked at the time. It was two o'clock. I sat down at the table. My head was aching and there was a horrible taste in my mouth. There was a water carafe and glass on the table in front of me. I drank some of the water. It was strongly chlorinated and made me want to be sick again. I lit a cigarette. Minutes went by. Every now and then I would hear a movement or a cough from the passage outside. The escort was still there. When I had finished one cigarette, I lit another. If I were going to be put in jail, my cigarettes would certainly be taken away. I might as well smoke while I could. However, this feeble effort at a philosophical approach to the situation was not successful. Whether or not I had cigarettes to smoke would probably not seem of much importance in the near future. If Sibley were right – and I knew that he was – my arrest could only mean one thing: that Aleko, having failed to kill me himself, had left me to be dealt with by his employers. It was not a pleasant thought. On the other hand, the Party might have decided that to murder a foreign journalist would not be a wise move at a time when they would be busy denying their guilt of a more serious crime. But supposing their wisdom was of a different kind. Supposing they decided that the inconvenience of killing somebody who knew too much was as nothing compared with the inconvenience of being revealed as the accomplices of their leader's murderer. Death seemed very near at that moment. I hoped that it would come mercifully. Perhaps if the hand were that of Aleko . . .

I turned sharply, my heart pounding, my skin crawling. The curtain over the door on the far side of the room had moved.

I stood up. The fantastic thought went through my mind that if I were going to be shot from behind the curtain, I must stand up so as to present an easy target.

The curtain moved again. A draught from somewhere had caught it. There was the sound of a door closing in the adjoining room, footsteps, then the door behind the curtain opened and a hand brushed the folds aside.

Brankovitch came into the room.

He glanced at me casually before turning to shut the door behind him; then he came round the table towards me.

'Sit down, Mr Foster.' He nodded to a chair and sat down himself facing me. His face was haggard and he needed a shave but he did not look as if he had been roused from his bed. Probably he had been attending a meeting. The hours before a *coup d'état* which was to begin with an assassination would be busy ones for a Propaganda Minister. I must be one of the inevitable hitches.

He sighed. 'A cigarette?' He brought out a case.

'I have one, thank you.' This was idiotic. 'I'm glad to find that you allow prisoners under arrest to smoke,' I added.

He pursed his lips. 'I think it will be better, Mr Foster, if you avoid facetious comment. You are being treated with great consideration, as I think my presence here indicates.

196

It would be polite of you to recognize the fact. You realize, I hope, that you are in a very serious position.'

'It's difficult for me to realize anything, Minister. All I know is that I have been arrested and brought here. I should like to know what the charge against me is and I should like the British Legation informed.'

His dark, supercilious eyes stared at me coldly. 'It would be convenient if you would abandon your pretence of innocence, Mr Foster. It wastes time. If you prefer to be treated as a common criminal, that can be arranged. If you will recognize the fact of my sitting here talking to you as evidence of consideration towards a distinguished foreign writer, we may make progress.'

I was silent.

He lit a cigarette. 'Very well then. Early to-night on the avenue that runs round the Presidential Park, shots were fired by two men at a third. Police pursued the men who had fired the shots. They escaped. So did the other man. But something was found by the police. A hat. It had your name in it, Mr Foster. Was it your hat?'

I hesitated. 'Yes, it was my hat.'

'Why do you hesitate? Were you thinking of lying, Mr Foster?'

His eyes were on mine and at that moment I understood the nature of the interview. Brankovitch knew what Aleko knew. He knew about the letter to Philip Deltchev and my finding of Pazar. He knew that Aleko had forbidden me the Deltchev house and that I had that night ignored the prohibition. He knew that Aleko had tried to kill me and failed. He might know that Katerina had talked to me. What he was trying to find out now was how much I knew, how dangerous I was. If I did not know the truth about the conspiracy against Vukashin I was unimportant. If I did know, or if I had an inkling of the truth, I must be eliminated.

I leaned forward and put my cigarette out in the ashtray by him. Then I smiled ruefully. 'Surely you understand my position, Minister. The last thing I want to do is to get involved in police proceedings. Two armed men attempted to hold me up. Luckily, I managed to get away from them. It happened on a very dark stretch of road. I didn't see either of their faces. What use would I have been to the police?'

'It was your duty to report the occurrence to them. By running away in that fashion you have raised a grave question in the minds of the police.'

'What question?'

'It might be that you were one of the men who fired shots.'

'Do you believe that, Minister?'

'What I believe is not important. This is a police affair. It is referred to me initially as a matter of policy because of your status here as a newspaper representative. But I cannot prevent their dealing with you as a criminal. I can merely advise them of my opinion.'

'If I were a criminal, Minister, would I have been so careless as to leave behind a hat with my name in it?'

'The police argue from the stupidity of the criminal, not from his cleverness. But assuming, Mr Foster, that your version of the affair is true, what do you think was the motive for this attack on you?'

Here it was. I looked puzzled. 'Motive? Robbery, I imagine. What else could it be?'

He pretended to think this over. Then: 'You have not, for instance, made any enemies here?'

I felt relieved. If this was the best he could do I had nothing to worry about.

'Enemies? I don't think so.'

'You have been involved, for instance, in no unusual circumstances that might give a clue to the police?'

I hesitated again.

'I should advise you to be frank, Mr Foster. You see, armed robbery of that kind is a most unusual crime here. I do not imply that we have no violent criminals but that it is unusual for them to be armed with revolvers. The reason is that to carry a revolver here is in itself an offence punishable by death. The law was made to deal with the Brotherhood criminals but, of course, it applies to all. Robbers would try to kill you with knives. These men did not. If they were not robbers then, who were they? That is what the police ask.'

I still hesitated. I was in a terrifying quandary. Obviously, the 'unusual circumstances' he was inviting me to tell him about were my finding of Pazar and my meeting with Aleko. But to which would it be better to pretend – frankness or cunning? Which would conceal from him more effectively my actual knowledge? Frankness had its dangers. He would be able to cross-examine and perhaps catch me out. Or he might decide from my manner that I was less artless than I seemed and unlikely to have been genuinely taken in by Aleko's explanation of the affair. Perhaps an obstinate silence would be better. The silence itself would have a useful meaning. It would say to him: 'This man does not know that I know what he is concealing. His pretence of ignorance shows, therefore, that he is truly ignorant of the important facts.' But it might also add: 'And that is just what he hoped I would think. Clearly he is bluffing.'

'Yes, Mr Foster?' He was watching every movement of my face.

Suddenly, hopelessly, I decided. I drew a deep breath. 'Very well, Minister, I will be frank. I have a confession to make.'

'A confession, Mr Foster?'

'Yes.' And then I had a desperate inspiration. I looked at him angrily. 'That was what you were expecting, wasn't it?'

'Expecting?'

'Minister, with all due respect, I've had enough of this cat and mouse game. I've been silly. I stuck my nose into something that was none of my business and found out some things that I wasn't supposed to know. All right, I admit it. I didn't think Herr Valmo would bother you with it. I was hoping he wouldn't. But since he has, I'm sorry. One thing I can promise you is that no reference to it will be made in any of my articles. I can't say more than that.'

He stared at me. The skin of his face was stretched tightly. It was for a moment a most extraordinary and horrible mask. The lips moved.

'Can't you, Mr Foster?'

'What is there to say? I found a dead body that your secret police had baited a trap with. Naturally, Herr Valmo was annoyed. But he didn't blame me. I acted in all innocence. I didn't see what all the fuss is about.'

'Did you make certain very solemn promises to Herr Valmo?'

I looked embarrassed. 'Yes, I did.'

'And yet you again went to the Deltchev house.'

'Unfortunately, I did.'

'Why did you go?'

'I felt I had to have Madame Deltchev's comments on the trial evidence. To be quite frank, I thought it more important for me to have those comments than to obey an instruction I couldn't really see the point of.'

'Did you speak to Katerina Deltchev?'

I looked puzzled. 'No, it was the old servant who let me in.'

'Who do you think were the two men who tried to kill you to-night?'

'I've no idea. I told you. I didn't see their faces.'

'I think you are pretending to be more stupid than you really are, Mr Foster. How on reflection do you explain those men? If they weren't robbers, what were they?'

For an instant, I thought that I had failed after all. It was the phrase 'on reflection' that did it. If he was thinking ahead to a moment when, with Vukashin assassinated, I was beginning to put two and two together, I was really done for. If he thought that there was the remotest chance

200

of my getting at the truth he would decide against me. I made a last attempt.

I stared at him with sudden horrified comprehension. 'You mean that they were Brotherhood men?'

For about ten long seconds he did not answer. Then, slowly, he nodded. 'You see, Mr Foster, this prohibition of Valmo's which you so irresponsibly ignored was not without reason. Naturally, Valmo did not tell you all the facts but there was reason to believe that the Brotherhood was interested in reaching Madame Deltchev. You were mistaken to-night for one of Valmo's men. You are lucky to be still alive.'

He had swallowed the suggestion whole. And he had given himself away. I sat back with a sigh which could have meant anything but which came actually from a feeling of relief that was almost painful. Fortunately, I still had my wits about me. There was one thing he had not mentioned. If he did not bring it up I would have to and I did not know how. I took another risk.

I frowned suddenly. 'There's only one thing I don't understand,' I said. 'Your office issued a statement this evening saying that Pazar had been found shot. The details sounded as if he was the man *I* found. Why didn't Valmo tell me who he was? Why the secrecy?'

'Would you have respected the confidence, Mr Foster?'

'Of course.'

'As you did your undertaking to Herr Valmo?' He was quite sure of me now.

I tried to look embarrassed.

He smiled unpleasantly. 'I will speak plainly, Mr Foster. I think your behaviour here has been, to say the least of it, unethical. If you were a professional newspaper man I should make a very strong complaint both to your employers and to the British Legation here. As it is, I shall recommend to the police that you are released in the morning. However, I shall withdraw from you all facilities for attending the Deltchev trial. I also advise you unofficially to leave the country immediately – let us say by to-night's train at the latest. In case you decide to ignore that advice, I propose to have your visa and *permis de séjour* cancelled forthwith. Do I make myself clear?'

I protested as convincingly as I could, demanded that an official expulsion order be issued, became angry and finally pleaded. He was obviously and satisfactorily bored with me. It has occurred to me since that he must have been nearly as relieved as I was that the problem I represented had been disposed of. He may even have disliked the idea of having to have me killed. It is possible. The last thing he said to me could be taken that way. To stop me talking he rapped on the door to summon the escort. When they came in he gave them an instruction and turned to go. Then he paused and looked back.

'Mr Foster,' he said, 'I once saw a performance of a play of yours and I enjoyed it. Why not stay in the theatre? I think, for you, it would be much safer.'

I was taken out of the building by the way I had come in. It must have been a wing of the Propaganda Ministry. There was another ride in the van, another oppressive wait, then a cell in a police station. The cell had a bug-infested plank bed but I was too exhausted and shaken to care much about bugs. As the patch of sky I could see got lighter, I fell into a headache-ridden doze. I even slept a little. At nine o'clock the cell door opened and I was taken to a sort of waiting-room near the entrance.

There, dirty and unshaven, in his seersucker suit with the three fountain pens in the pocket and his brief case resting on his knees, sat Pashik.

He rose to his feet as he saw me and nodded.

'Good morning, Mr Foster.'

'How did you get here?' I said.

His eyes flickered warningly in the direction of my escort. He spoke in German. 'I have just been informed that you were arrested by mistake and were here. I understand that an apology has already been given and accepted.'

202

'Yes. Am I free to go?'

'I am told so.'

I shook hands with the escort and followed Pashik down the steps into his car. He drove off and turned a corner before he spoke. His tone was bleak and non-committal.

'What happened, Mr Foster?'

'I was interrogated by Brankovitch.'

'Yes?'

'He wanted to find out how much I knew and how much I suspected.'

He turned to look at me. The car wandered in the direction of an obelisk.

'If we're going to talk, hadn't you better stop?' I added quickly.

He straightened up but did not stop. 'And what did you know and suspect, Mr Foster?'

'That the Brotherhood plot to assassinate Vukashin has been taken over by the anti-Vukashin movement in the People's Party. That Aleko has been brought in to organize the job efficiently. That Philip Deltchev was involved in the original plot and is still involved. That when Vukashin is assassinated at the Anniversary Parade to-day, Philip Deltchev will be executed for the crime. That the story will be that when his father was arrested Philip took over the conspiracy and with the knowledge and approval of the Agrarian Socialist Executive carried it through. That the Agrarian Socialist Party will be made illegal and liquidated. That Brankovitch will take over the Government.'

He kept his eyes on the road. 'And what did you tell him you knew?'

'Only what he must have been already told by Aleko – that I found the body of Pazar and believed Herr Valmo's explanations.'

'And you convinced him?'

'Do you think I'd still be alive if I hadn't?'

'No, Mr Foster, I don't. May I say that I have always had the greatest respect for your intelligence?'

'Thank you.'

'You must have talked with Mr Sibley, of course.'

'Yes.'

'I was sure he had recognized me and that someone had been indiscreet. How much does he know, do you think?'

'He's got the general idea. And he's very frightened.'

'I see. We have much to tell each other, Mr Foster.'

'Yes. By the way, my permit for the trial has been withdrawn and I've got to be out of the country to-night.'

He nodded. 'That was to be expected. There is a train for Athens at five which I strongly recommend.'

'Athens? Why Athens?'

'Because that is where Philip Deltchev is.'

I stared at him. He had a curious smirk on his face. He even began a wheezy kind of chuckle.

'What on earth are you talking about?' I demanded.

He swung exuberantly into the street which had the Hotel Boris in it. Already, crowds were beginning to line the roads in preparation for the parade. He looked at his watch and nearly mowed down a family group in national costume.

'It is now twenty of nine,' he said. 'In an hour, Philip Deltchev will be at the Hotel Splendid Palace in Athens. Apart from Madame Deltchev and myself, you are the only person who knows this. You can be the first newspaper man to interview him, the first to expose the People's Party political murder conspiracy.'

'But how did you know?'

'I think you could have guessed, Mr Foster. I saw him across the frontier myself last night.'

Chapter 19

When Pashik was secretly rewarded for his services to the Provisional Government with shares in and management of the Pan-Eurasian Press Service he was not unduly grateful. He had risked his life to serve a political ideal; but it was an ideal which in his mind belonged exclusively to the United States of America; elsewhere it was not valid. He had performed his service somewhat in the spirit of the prosperous immigrant to that country who endows a public library or a child-birth clinic in his native land. The act is charitable but it is also a reparation, a propitiatory rite that makes the separation final and complete. For Pashik there was little satisfaction in the knowledge that his contribution had been so frankly and practically recognized. His pleasure in the gift resided in the fact that the agency's clients were nearly all American and that he could feel, not preposterously, that as their representative he was in a sense an outpost of the American way of life. One day, perhaps, he would go on a visitor's visa to America; and, perhaps, one day, before he was old, he would get an immigration quota number. Meanwhile, he was in touch. For Pashik, who had learned not to expect too much of life, that was a singular blessing and he enjoyed it. After a while, he could almost forget that the Brotherhood had existed.

The reminder that it had indeed existed and the news that in an attenuated way it still did exist, came as a blow. The messenger was Pazar. He told of cautious overtures being made, of small, tentative meetings, of wary soundings and of half-formed plans. It was as if the Brotherhood had been decimated by a plague and as if the survivors had now begun to raise their heads and look about them, uncertain whether or not the infection still persisted. Gradually, in an atmosphere of intense suspicion and extravagant fears, contacts were being re-established. The security precautions were formidable. All surviving members were invited to re-apply for membership and submit to the most searching investigation. Refusal to re-apply when asked was to be deemed evidence of guilt. There had been no refusals so far, Pazar told Pashik grimly. The Brothers awaited him.

Pashik nodded and went to see his principal shareholder, Madame Deltchev. This was just about the election time and Madame Deltchev advised Pashik to re-apply. Apart from the fact that it would be dangerous for him not to do so – Pashik did not think that this alone would have weighed heavily with Madame Deltchev – she felt that it would be advisable to be informed of the new Brotherhood's activities. She had always had in mind the possibility of the People's Party manipulating the Brotherhood for its own ends. This resurgence might not be merely what it appeared.

So began again a double life for Pashik. He was re-initiated into the Brotherhood and sat in judgment on the applications of others. The purges had proved fatal for nearly all the senior members and soon he found himself being admitted into the higher councils of the organization. Some two months before the arrest of Yordan Deltchev he heard of the membership of Philip and of the plot against Vukashin.

For once Madame Deltchev was at a loss. She had already planned the football match incident and was manoeuvring as best she could to bring about an Agrarian-Socialist *coup* before the People's Party was quite secure. Her son's activities imperilled everything. Whether he succeeded or failed it made no difference. As far as the people were concerned, Philip Deltchev was an extension of Papa Deltchev. The murder of Vukashin by Brother Philip would serve to unite the People's Party as never before and shatter the Agrarian Socialists irretrievably. She could not betray the boy, for to do so would bring the same evil consequences. It was useless, she knew, to attempt to persuade him, for he was too deeply committed. She could not even discuss it with him lest he should identify Pashik as her informant. Not that she would have minded sacrificing Pashik; it was simply that she saw no point in sacrificing him uselessly. All she could do was to instruct Pashik to work within the Brotherhood, to keep in touch with Philip and perhaps undermine his belief in the project. It was a feeble plan, but for the moment she could think of nothing better. Then, events began in the most curious way to play into her hands.

In the days before the purges Pazar had been a comparatively unimportant member of the Brotherhood whose weaknesses had been clearly perceived and carefully reckoned with. He would certainly not have been allowed so much as to know about a plan as important as that he now administered. That he should tell someone of it was inevitable. That it should be the petty crook, Rila, whom he told was very nearly lucky. If Rila had not happened at that time to get into the hands of the police, things might have turned out very differently.

The casualties in the assassination group put the Brotherhood in a panic. The Survivors had raised their heads only to find that the plague was still with them. It was another betrayal, another purge. Within a few hours the great majority of the re-admitted Brothers were dispersed and in hiding. The rest – those who had no means of hiding – sat in their rooms rehearsing denials. Only Pashik was in a position to know that the plague had not returned and that there must be a more banal explanation of this disaster. He made his report to Madame Deltchev and waited.

A week later things began to move. One night Philip Deltchev came to see him. He brought news. He and Pazar had escaped and were for the moment safe. Meanwhile, the Brotherhood had reorganized. Pazar had been superseded as administrator – his nerves were bad – and a new man had taken over. His name was Aleko and he was a dynamo

207

of a man with great determination and drive. But others were needed. Several Brothers had refused, cravenly. Would he, Pashik, come in with them? The plan would now go on to success in which all would share.

Pashik accepted and reported to Madame Deltchev. She agreed with him that the whole affair felt peculiar. Their suspicions were aroused in the first place because of the failure of the police to arrest Pazar and Philip. Pashik knew that there was documentary evidence against them and that in such a dangerous case – a Brotherhood plot against Vukashin – the price of concealment was beyond the fugitives' capacity to pay. And there was Philip's name. Why was the People's Party not publicizing the affair? By way of reply to this question, Madame Deltchev produced her theory that the People's Party would ultimately take over the Brotherhood. Pashik listened respectfully. But he had an unworthy thought; that Madame Deltchev's preoccupation with the idea was dictated by her annoyance at having failed to take over the Brotherhood herself. She was, to Pashik's way of thinking, a remarkable woman but inclined to underrate the cleverness of others.

A day or two later he was summoned to meet Aleko. The meeting took place in the apartment that I had been in, and it was soon evident to Pashik that Aleko was not what he pretended to be. For one thing, he noticed – as I had noticed – that the furnishings had been assembled from second-hand stores and arranged hurriedly in an unlikely way. But there might have been reasonable explanations for that. What decided him was Aleko's way of talking. Pashik had met many members of the Brotherhood and he had learned to recognize the habits of thought and speech which were the private currency of their relationships. For instance, the Brethren scarcely ever talked of killing anybody without at some point using the phrase 'removing an obstacle.' Aleko used the word 'eliminate.' It was a small difference but it was one of many. And there was a mannerism he had which was peculiar. When he spoke of firing a gun he would point with his forefinger at the back of his head and make a clicking noise with his tongue. For the Brethren, a gun was a serious matter; you did not click facetiously with your tongue to convey its moment of power. The whole gesture reminded Pashik of something he knew he would remember later. By the end of that meeting he was sure that Aleko was not a *bona fide* member of the Brotherhood. Yet he was dispensing money and making sound plans to assassinate Vukashin. In the early hours of the morning Pashik came to the conclusion that Madame Deltchev had been very nearly right. Someone had employed Aleko; someone who could hamstring police action and also pay well; someone in the People's Party. But not necessarily the People's Party as a whole. A faction within the Party then? It was probable. Someone was going to get killed and somebody else was paying for the event. Pashik decided to learn more before deciding upon the identity of the principal.

Then came the bomb-throwing attempt on Deltchev's life.

The attempt was organised, Pashik thought, by Vukashin himself and without Brankovitch's knowledge or approval. The press releases which came from the Propaganda Ministry bore marks of haste, improvisation and uncertainty of line which suggested that Brankovitch had been caught unprepared. Moreover, Aleko was disconcerted and talked vaguely about 'bungling.' The term could have referred to the failure of the attempt but Pashik's impression was that it was more in the nature of a comment on a situation that permitted the attempt to take place at all. That was interesting because if the impression was correct it meant that Brankovitch and Aleko had one thing at least in common – ignorance of Vukashin's intentions. And that in turn might mean that they had other things in common too.

The arrest of Deltchev created a new problem for Pashik. Hitherto he had no difficulty in arranging for private meetings with Madame Deltchev. Now that she was under house arrest it was impossible for him to see her personally. He knew that all visitors would be reported and could not afford to have his name on the list. His whole position was, indeed, highly equivocal. He was certainly known to Aleko's employers as a member of the Brotherhood. The faintest breath of suspicion as to his motives would result in his being informed upon and promptly hanged. He had Philip Deltchev on his hands and an obligation to extricate the young man if he could. He did not know exactly what was afoot. He was without allies. All he could do for the present was to remain as inconspicuous as possible, cultivate Philip Deltchev and check up on Aleko. But for a while he did not make much progress with either intention. Philip Deltchev did not like him. The best he had been able to do about Aleko was to remember what the gun-pointing gesture had reminded him of. The 'K. Fischer' note which I had found was the result. It was Pazar who finally supplied the essential information.

When Aleko had taken over the conspiracy, Pazar had been in a pitiable state of exhaustion and terror. The arrest of Rila had cut off his drug supplies. He was without money or lodging and hunted by the police. Philip, who then had (in the name of Valmo) the room in the Patriarch Dimo, had taken him in and for nearly a week the two had remained there, hungry, because they feared to go out to buy food, and in constant fear of discovery. The night Aleko arrived on the scene Pazar had collapsed and was in a state almost of coma. It took him several days of ready access to the supplies of heroin, which Aleko had miraculously procured, to bring him back to anything like normality; and when he did come back it was to find that he had been superseded.

Pazar was not unintelligent. Quite soon he perceived what Pashik already knew – that Aleko was not of the Brotherhood – but, unlike Pashik, he drew a wrong conclusion. His drug-twisted mind linked his discovery with his own fall from power and also with the memory of the traitor who had never been unmasked. All the paranoid projections of his mind focused suddenly upon a single object – Aleko. From that moment, he began to plot against Aleko and to spy on him. Philip had moved into Aleko's apartment and Pazar had the Patriarch Dimo room to himself. It was easy, therefore, for him to keep track of Aleko's movements outside the apartment. One night he followed Aleko to a house in the suburbs. It was a big house and there was a car outside of the kind that usually has a chauffeur. Aleko was there an hour. When he came out Pazar did not follow him but stayed to watch the house and the car. Ten minutes after Aleko had gone, a man came out, got into the car and drove off. As he passed by, Pazar recognised him. It was Brankovitch. Two days later, seething with malice and excitement, he told Pashik of his discovery.

It took Pashik ten seconds to make up his mind what he had to do. The first thing was to control Pazar and urge discretion. The second thing was to make him tell the story to Philip Deltchev in Pashik's presence so that while the boy would at last realize what was really happening, his desire for revenge could be usefully canalised. Obviously, Brankovitch's idea was to destroy his rival with the Party and to put the guilt for the crime on the Deltchev family. In other words he would manipulate the original conspiracy so as to convict the father and use the second conspiracy, his own, to dispose of Vukashin and have in his hands the perfect scapegoat, Philip. Pashik's idea was to remove the scapegoat when it was too late to change the assassination plan and let the whole affair recoil on Brankovitch. What was more, Pashik knew just how the idea could be put into practice. But everything depended on Philip.

It was a ticklish business. When Philip's first neurotic outbursts were spent, he lapsed into a hopeless depression which persisted for some days and which was noticed by Aleko. Fortunately, Pashik had managed to make his proposals understood and Philip Deltchev had presence of mind enough to play the part he had been given. It was not

211

too difficult. All he had to do was to continue to appear fanatically devoted to the task of killing Vukashin; and fanatics do not have to make much sense. The problem was Pazar. His hatred of Aleko soon wore so thin a disguise that an outburst of some sort was inevitable. All Pashik could do was to remind him constantly of the need for absolute secrecy and hope that when the explosion came, Pazar the drug addict would be more in evidence than Pazar the conspirator. And so it turned out. The occasion was one of the bi-weekly meetings at which Aleko insisted on going over the entire plan of campaign afresh and justifying each part of it. The plan itself was simple enough and clearly the object of the meetings was to keep the conspirators in hand; but that night Pazar chose to put a different interpretation on the meeting. Quite suddenly and fantastically he accused Aleko of having police hidden in an adjoining room to listen to the conversation. Without a word, Aleko rose and showed the next room to be empty. Pazar replied that there were microphones hidden and began to tear up the carpet to prove it. Philip Deltchev sat as if he had not heard. Pashik sat sweating for what was to come. Aleko watched with a smile but listened attentively to Pazar's babbling. There was just enough sense in it for him to guess what Pazar had discovered. When, in the end, Pazar collapsed, sobbing, Aleko gave him a big injection of heroin. When Pazar was quiet Aleko looked at the others and shook his head. 'We cannot rely upon him,' he said. 'He will compromise us all.'

The other two nodded quickly. They were in heartfelt agreement.

Aleko smiled. 'Leave everything to me,' he said.

At the next meeting, Pazar did not appear and Aleko announced briefly that he had committed suicide in his room, that the body would be left for the police to find and that, as his services had never really been necessary, no Brother would be sought to replace him.

It was on the day after that meeting that I arrived.

I presented a serious problem to the harassed Pashik. To have someone in and about his office, poking and prying, hampering his movements, possibly endangering his neutral relations with the Propaganda Ministry; that was bad enough. To have someone directly concerned with him in contact with Petlarov was alarming, for who knew what that might not suggest to Brankovitch? He had already recognized and been recognized by Sibley whom he remembered as one of the intelligence officers who could know his story.

Sibley knew me. Another potential danger. Especially as I was inquisitive. My interview with Madame Deltchev threw him into a panic. The night he learned of it he faced Aleko with his gun in his pocket instead of in his brief case. But nothing unusual happened at that meeting. It was after it that Aleko took him aside, gave him a wad of papers and asked him to put them in Pazar's room to 'mislead' the police who found them. Pashik guessed that Brankovitch wished to take the opportunity afforded by Pazar's death of planting further incriminating evidence against Deltchev. When he got to Pazar's room, he found me there.

His dilemma was awful. It could be explained in several ways. I was telling him the truth or I was lying. But even if I was telling the truth I might still be an unwitting agent of Brankovitch's and this might be a trap to catch him out. On the other hand I was doing work for one of the American clients and was therefore under the protection of the Pan-Eurasian Press Service. If this was a trap, then the only safe thing to do was to take me to Aleko for questioning. If it was not a trap, however, he might be taking the representative of an American client to his death.

'What made you decide to take me?' I asked.

Pashik blinked at me sheepishly. 'I did not quite decide, Mr Foster,' he said; 'I compromised. I left part of the decision to you.'

'What do you mean?'

'While I hid the papers Aleko had given me in the room, you were walking to my car at the end of the street. I thought you might take the opportunity to escape. If you did not . . .' He shrugged.

'Do you know why I didn't run?'

'Because you were not alarmed?'

'No. Because I wanted to ask you questions.'

He sighed. 'You have been very lucky, Mr Foster,' he said. 'It was difficult to persuade Aleko that you were harmless and very embarrassing when he found that you were not. I certainly did not expect to find you alive this morning. And when you tell me of Katerina's foolishness, I marvel.'

'I suppose she got back all right.'

'If she had not done so you would not be here. The check on the Deltchev house is carried out at eight every morning.'

'Does Madame Deltchev know what's happened?'

'I have been able to send her brief messages.'

'By that old friend of the family who drops in for tea?'

'You are too well-informed, Mr Foster.'

I finished my fourth cup of coffee. 'When you begin to make flattering remarks, I am suspicious,' I said. 'You really mean that I still don't know at all what's going on.'

His brown eyes contemplated me through his rimless glasses. He was smelling strongly that morning. The seersucker suit was horribly dirty. He shrugged. 'As for instance, Mr Foster?'

'As for instance – why are you here at all at this moment? Why aren't you in Athens with Philip?'

We were in my hotel room. He opened his brief case, took out a battered meat sandwich and began eating it. He had his mouth full before he answered. 'You forget, Mr Foster, that there is to be an assassination here to-day.'

'I hadn't forgotten it. What I was wondering was why you've been so cagey about it. What exactly is going to happen? What's the plan? When did Philip come into it? What happens now he isn't here?'

214

'They do not know he is not here. He did not leave until after the final meeting last night.'

'But what's going to happen?'

'I will tell you. Pazar's original plan was simple and stupid. The celebration march takes place in the St Mihail Square. The parade marches in along the Boulevard and out along the Prospect. The saluting base is the stone platform half-way down the great steps that lead up to the portico in front of the Ministry of the Interior. It was the main state entrance to the old palace. From the bronze statues at the bottom up to the platform there are forty steps. On these occasions the steps are flanked with troops, forty each side. They are a bodyguard and they are armed with machine-pistols. It was Pazar's idea to kidnap four of these men and replace them with his men. They would shoot Vukashin as he stood on the platform and hope to escape in the confusion because it would seem to be the real troops who had fired. This I may tell you was the plan which the Prosecutor at the trial did not wish to explain.'

'Why not?'

'Because the absurdity of it would make people laugh. Does it not make you laugh, Mr Foster?'

'It might have worked.'

He shook his head mournfully. 'I can see, Mr Foster, that you would not be a good conspirator. One has only to think for a moment of the kidnapping . . .'

'What were all those messages about?'

'The uniforms, naturally. They could not buy them. Instead they stole them from the soldiers' brothels. It was all very childish. When Aleko took over he made a new plan. Uniforms were wanted, but those of ordinary line troops, not those of the bodyguard. Three men only would be needed. It was a good plan. You know, when there is a parade great care is taken to guard against assassins. The occupants of rooms overlooking the Square are carefully checked by the police and the flat roofs of the buildings round it are guarded by troops from outside the city. The first part of the plan was to conceal a machine-gun and ammunition on one of the flat roofs. Then, just before the parade, men in uniform would go up to the roof and tell the troops already there that the guards were being doubled, as trouble was expected. As the real troops were from outside, these would not expect to recognize men who said they were from a city battalion. The false men would have bottles of brandy and things to eat in their haversacks. After a while they would offer to share it. The brandy would be heavily dosed with morphine. The soldiers would go to sleep, the gun would be produced and set up and trained on the platform. All would be in readiness for the appearance of Vukashin. And when the thing was done, escape would be possible. It would be difficult in the surprise and confusion to say exactly where the shots had come from. The troops on nearby roofs might think they were from a window below. But there would be doubt, there would be time for us to descend to the street and mingle with the crowd. Who is going to suspect three soldiers? Until the real ones wake up, hours later, nobody will know how it was done and by then it will be too late.'

'Philip Deltchev will have escaped?'

'Exactly, Mr Foster. That was why the plan seemed so good at first to Philip and Pazar and so strange to me. Until I knew that Brankovitch was deeply involved and saw that it would be quite easy for him to arrange for the police to be warned that, say, thieves disguised as soldiers would be raiding such-and-such a building during the parade and that a patrol waiting at the exits could catch them red-handed.'

'So as there will be no Philip, there will be no assassination. Is that it?'

'No, Mr Foster, that is not it. There were to be three on the gun – Philip, myself and one of Aleko's men.'

'One of those who tried to kill me?'

'That is so. But there is another man and Aleko himself.

216

What, I asked myself, would they be doing while Vukashin was being assassinated?'

'Leaving the country, I should think.'

'Yes, I thought that. But three days ago, there was a serious complication. Aleko told us that there would be a second gun on another roof and that he and the other man would man it. Philip would have the honour of firing first but Aleko would be there in case of an emergency. What would that suggest to you, Mr Foster?'

'That he was suspicious? That he didn't trust Philip?'

'Yes, I considered those possibilities. But then another thought occurred to me, a very interesting idea. Luckily I was able to check it. The following night the guns were hidden on the roofs we had selected . . .'

'Which are they?'

He smiled. 'That I think I will not tell you, Mr Foster. You will discover.'

There was something very disturbing about that smile. I suddenly became uneasy.

'Go on,' I said.

'The guns were wrapped in sacking and hung by wires inside the brick chimneys. Very early in the morning, I returned by myself and examined them.' He paused, smiling again.

'And?'

'The gun on Philip's roof had no firing pin. It had been taken out.'

I looked blank. 'I'm sorry. I don't see . . .'

'Don't you, Mr Foster?' His eyes gleaming through the spectacles were no longer sad. 'Power is a great thing, you know. To be able to move and control great affairs – not the characters and situations on a stage, Mr Foster; but the real – that is the greatest of all pleasures. You feel it in the stomach.' He patted his own. 'Here. I feel it now.'

'Yes?' I wondered suddenly if he were mad.

'Consider.' He stood up and strode over to the window. 'A man in Aleko's profession is always in a difficult position.

217

He must always be sure that his master has the power to protect him. He must always be sure that the master wishes to protect him. And he must consider the future. It is dangerous for him to serve one powerful person at the expense of another who may later do him harm. Aleko is clever. He would not have survived if he had not been. He is used to weighing advantages. And so I ask myself questions. Why are there two guns? Why is there no firing pin in a gun that Aleko expects to pour bullets into Vukashin. I answer, because it is Vukashin who is Aleko's best master and has been so perhaps from the first. What ultimate chance has Brankovitch in a struggle for power over Vukashin's dead body? None! He would go down in the end. His own intelligence would trip him. The sort of brutal cunning that lets him dig his own grave will always win. That is Vukashin's strength and Aleko knows it. Philip would have pressed the trigger of a gun aimed at Vukashin and nothing would have happened. Aleko would have pressed the trigger of the second gun, aimed at Brankovitch, and the gun would have fired. Philip and I and Aleko's man would have been arrested and hanged. The gun which would be used in evidence would be the one Aleko left on the other roof. The two murderous Deltchevs would hang together. The murderous Agrarian Socialists would be punished. Vukashin would be secure both from the opposition and from the plots and ambitions of Brankovitch. Aleko, who loves ski-ing would be waiting, rich and happy, for the snow at St Moritz. A pretty picture, Mr Foster!'

'Yes.' There seemed nothing else to say.

'But a picture that will not be seen.'

'Because Philip is in Athens.'

He held up a finger. 'And because I am here.'

'I don't understand.'

'You will see now why I wish you to understand. The one obstacle is Aleko's man – one of those who tried to kill you – the one who was to have been with Philip and me. In one hour's time he will go to a rendezvous to meet us. If we do not arrive he will go to Aleko to warn him, and when Aleko knows that Philip is not there he will not fire. Brankovitch's life will be saved.'

'I see.'

'But if I stop this man, Aleko will fire. Brankovitch will die and because there is no Philip to arrest, Vukashin will have to take Aleko. And when Philip has told his story to you and it is ringing round the world, Vukashin's day will begin to end. That is, if I stop this man.'

I said nothing.

For a moment he continued to stare out of the window; then he turned to face me, his self-assurance gone, his face working grotesquely. 'Do I stop him, Mr Foster?' he demanded. '*You* tell me!'

I stared at him, and he read my thoughts.

He shook his head. 'No, Mr Foster, it is not in your hands. There is nobody here for you to tell this story to. That is if you yourself wish to live. Warn Brankovitch, and you will be rewarded by him with a bullet. Warn Vukashin, and it will be the same. You know too much for either's safety.'

'There's our Legation. They could warn Brankovitch.'

'Then you would be killing me instead. I do not think you will choose that alternative. No. You have no moral dilemma, Mr Foster. It is my own I put to you.'

I was silent.

He sat down and gazed sullenly into space for a moment. 'Do you know America well?' he asked suddenly.

'Not very well.'

'No,' he said slowly, 'neither do I.'

He was silent again. I did not speak. I knew, as if he were thinking aloud, that he was submitting his problem to the judgment of Passaic, New Jersey, Oakland, California, and Hagerstown, Maryland. It was perhaps as good a way of resolving it as any other.

When at last he stood up he was as calm and businesslike

as the day we had met. He took an envelope out of his pocket and handed it to me.

'Your ticket for the press box at the Anniversary Parade, Mr Foster. I should have given it to you before. Even after what has happened, I do not see that there can be any objection to your using it. Your train, I would remind you, is at five. Have you money?'

'Yes, thanks.'

He held out his hand. 'I will try to get to the station to look after you, but there will be the cables and so on to attend to. You will forgive me if I cannot make it.'

I shook hands with him. 'Yes, of course. Thank you very much for all your help.'

He put up a protesting hand. 'A pleasure, Mr Foster.'

He turned away briskly, picking up his brief case and walked to the door. Then he paused.

'You're welcome,' he added, and went.

Chapter 20

The parade began at two o'clock.

It was only a quarter of a mile or so from the hotel to the Square, but the crowds along the route of the parade and in the streets approaching the Square were dense. It took me a long time to get through. The day was very warm and I felt tired and ill and frightened. I had not eaten any lunch. My legs were like paper and I kept thinking that I had lost something valuable. The sensation was curiously familiar. I had felt like that once before. And then I remembered; it had been when I was walking back to an hotel in Seville after seeing my first and only bull fight.

The press box was in a wooden stand built over the cathedral steps and at right-angles to the front of the palace. The parade would pass below it, then bear left to march past the saluting base half way up the palace steps. There, a waist-high balustrade had been erected. It was draped with flags and on the step below flowers were banked to give an appearance of depth to the structure. Behind and above it were the crowded boxes of the lesser dignitaries. The whole Square was a mass of flags and brilliantly coloured flowers. The façades of the buildings that formed the Square were mostly of a honey-coloured stone but the paving had been spread with white sand and in the bright hot sunshine the effect was dazzling.

It was five minutes to the hour when I got there and all but a few seats in the box were already filled. I could see the back of Sibley's head near the front. Nearly everyone had sun glasses, but I had forgotten mine and the glare from the sand was painful. Somewhere a military band was playing and every now and then a section of the crowd would raise a cheer. Heads would turn at the sound but the

221

cheer would die away. I looked at the rooftops. There was a canopy over the stand I was in and I could see only a small section of them. From there to the saluting base was a little over two hundred yards. At that range even a recruit could hit a man with one burst from an automatic gun. Perhaps, even now an eye was peering through sights at the palace steps.

I wiped my face and neck with my handkerchief and looked at the official programme. A duplicated translation had been slipped into it for the benefit of us foreigners. The parade would symbolize the plough and the sword in harmony together. First would come the floats carrying the tableaux of the various industries and crafts. Then the massed representatives of sport and culture. Finally, the parade of military and air power. The whole parade would be led by a special tableau depicting the victory of the People's Party. This tableau would halt before the Ministry of the Interior to summon the Party leaders to witness the parade, the visible demonstration of the triumph of their work for the Motherland.

I had seen this float lurking in a side street just off the Square. It was a huge affair, mounted on a platform carried by an aircraft transportation truck. Art, Science, Industry, Agriculture and Armed Might, each with its subsidiary tableaux were grouped round a white flag-decked plinth supporting a huge Winged Victory in wood and plaster. The subsidiary tableaux had the usual props: for Industry there was an anvil, for Science, a retort on a bench, for Agriculture a plough, and so on. There were brackets and ledges jutting out from the sides of the plinth obviously for the use of the girls in voluminous white robes who would presently drape themselves round the feet of the Victory.

At eight minutes past two, another band entered into the Square and formed up round the statue in the centre. Then the bodyguards marched in with machine-pistols at the ready, and, to the accompaniment of excited cheers, took up their positions on the steps below the saluting base. The stage was being set. At two eleven a squadron of cavalry clattered round from the far side and halted in line beneath the stand I was in. An order was shouted. The cavalry drew their sabres and a single note on a bugle sounded. With a crash the bands began to play the national anthem. All those who had seats rose to their feet. Then, with a roar of cheering, a waving of flags and hats and another crash of music, the Winged Victory float began to move into the Square.

My heart was beating so quickly and the blood was thudding so violently in my head that the din of brass bands and cheering was like a continuous rushing sound. I sat down; but it was no better. I stood up again. A man's voice came through the loudspeakers. He was talking very quickly – giving a description of the tableaux I suppose. The Victory, preceded by a small detachment of troops on foot, turned jerkily and passed our stand. The statue was wobbling as it moved along and the girls posing on the plinth wobbled with it; but I had no desire to laugh. I found myself staring at the tableau of Industry on one corner of the platform. A man in a leather apron had a sledge-hammer raised above the anvil as if to strike. His arms were already feeling the strain and I watched the head of the hammer gradually getting lower. Then the float began to turn again and he was out of sight. On the far side of the Square troops presented arms as the Victory came into view. It crawled on until it was nearly level with the centre statue, then swung across to the foot of the steps exactly facing the saluting base, and stopped. The girls on the plinth took up a new pose so that they all faced the palace.

Suddenly there was a tremendous roll of drums and over the entire Square the crowd fell silent. The drums ceased abruptly. Then the bands began to play the People's Party marching song. All heads were turned towards the palace portico and the aisle of steps that ran down between the upper boxes to the saluting base. Through the loudspeakers

223

came the sound of a choir singing the song. The crowd joined in. The air seemed to quiver with the sound. Then, as the song reached its climax – the great shout of affirmation that came on the final note – Vukashin appeared at the top of the steps, and the cheering began.

He was wearing a black suit and had a cloth cap in his hand. For a moment he stood there motionless. Then he raised a hand in salute and began to walk down the steps towards the saluting base while the cheering swelled up. When he was about two steps down, a man in the uniform of a marshal stepped from the group behind him and began to follow. The Minister of the Interior came next. And then Brankovitch started down.

He, too, was dressed in black, but very neatly, and he wore a grey Homburg. He walked down slowly and deliberately as if he were unaware of what was going on in the Square below. As he passed the upper boxes, the occupants of which were clapping, he nodded casually to someone he knew there.

Vukashin had reached the base. Now he walked forward to the balustrade and looked down. A fresh storm of cheering greeted him. The marshal and the Minister of the Interior moved to left and right of him. Brankovitch moved to the balustrade beside the Minister of the Interior and said something to him. The latter smiled and pointed to the Victory. By this time the whole length of the balustrade was occupied. There were two or three uniforms but most wore dark suits with grey Homburgs. There was only one cloth cap – Vukashin's. On the other side of Brankovitch was a stout man who held himself as if he had a boil on his neck. They were about a foot apart. Brankovitch turned sideways to say something to him.

Vukashin raised his hand in acknowledgement to the Victory tableaux, and with a jerk it set off again. At the same moment the band struck up and the main procession began to move in.

It was headed by a detachment of men in white dungarees

marching eight abreast. But I barely noticed them. My eyes were on Brankovitch. He was still talking to the man at his side.

As clapping and cheering broke out again, I began desperately to try to reassure myself. It just could not be! I had been listening to the babblings of a lunatic. Or – better, far better – the verdict of Passaic and Oakland and Hagerstown had been that those things that were God's should be rendered unto God, that – Article-something-or-other-of-the-Constitution-of-The-United-States-of-America – nobody can do anything that affects the life, liberty or person of anybody, without the aforesaid democratic procedure is properly and faithfully observed, and that the best thing Georghi Pashik could do would be to get his fat arse the hell out of it and send that suit to the cleaners.

I was suddenly sure that it was going to be all right. At any moment now, Pashik would appear beside me, business-like, courteous and all for playing ball with the regime. I almost laughed with relief. The time was two-nineteen.

And then it happened.

The head of the parade had curved into the straight in front of the saluting base and Brankovitch turned to look at them. For a second or two, he stopped talking and was absolutely still. The next moment, the toneless, tearing rattle of a burst of Spandau fire echoed round the Square. And, almost, it seemed, before the echo of the first had done one leg of its journey, a second burst came.

I had my eyes on Brankovitch. There must have been some sort of stool or bench behind each of them to rest against during the parade, for he lurched back as if he were falling and then stopped for a moment. I saw the second burst hit him in the neck. Then, he turned slightly sideways as if he were going to talk to the Minister of the Interior again and crumpled out of sight behind the balustrade.

The man with the boil was the quickest witted. He took cover behind the balustrade a second after Brankovitch fell. There might, after all, have been other bullets on the way.

The Minister of the Interior just stood staring. Vukashin gave one quick look round, then went as if to help Brankovitch. I think that for about ten seconds only a very few of the spectators realized that there was anything amiss at the saluting base. Most of them had just shifted their attention to the parade. But someone screamed. At the same moment, men began shouting above the noise of the bands and the bodyguard closed in defensively round the saluting base with their guns pointed at the crowd. Then a wave of panic came. All at once everyone seemed to be shouting and screaming. The bands stopped and the parade slowed uncertainly. The Winged Victory, now on the far side of the Square, jerked to a standstill. I saw one of the girls fall off the plinth as a great mass of people trying to get out of the Square surged forward round the thing. A man near me in the press box was shouting like a maniac. I was very near the exit. I stumbled to it and got down the steps. An official coming up shouted something and tried to stop me but I pushed past him and made for the narrow street which ran between the cathedral and the adjoining building in the Square. This street had been closed by the police and made to serve as a main entrance for box ticket holders. I thought that if I could get behind the cathedral before the crowds in the Square were completely out of control and the surrounding streets impassable, I might reach the hotel in time to finish what I had to do.

Others in the boxes had had the same idea. The street was filling rapidly and most of the people were running. I began to run too. By the time I reached it, the police barrier at the end had been swept away and people were clambering over the remains of it to join the frantic stream pouring out of the Square. It would have been difficult to walk then even if I had wished to, for to the shouting and screaming in the Square behind us was now added the sound of shooting as the bodyguard fired over the heads of the panic-stricken crowd. Everybody ran. I must have run about a quarter of a mile before it seemed safe to walk. People had begun to sink down exhausted on to the pavements. Many of them were crying. I walked on and found myself in a street of small shops. I had no idea whereabouts I was. The shopkeepers had put their shutters up for the day and I did not want to try asking anyone who knew what had happened for directions. It was not a good moment to reveal oneself as a foreigner.

I walked on aimlessly looking for a familiar landmark. What I felt I had to do was to see Madame Deltchev and tell her about Pashik before I went. In the confusion I had had the absurd idea that I might get my bag and typewriter from the hotel, be driven to the Deltchev house in an hotel car and go straight on to the station from there. I knew now that that was out of the question. Even if I managed to find my way to the hotel and hire a car, the chance of getting anyone that day who was willing to drive to Yordan Deltchev's house was small. And that made me realize something else. Unless I could get to the house before news of the assassination reached the sentries on the door, the chances were that I would not be allowed in. It was twenty to three now. Almost certainly the radio had shut down the moment the thing had happened. It would be at least an hour before any official statement was issued; but meanwhile the news and wild distortions of it would be spreading all over the city by word of mouth. I would have to be quick.

I hurried on. The sun was in my eyes. If I kept on walking west I must eventually come to the wall of the Presidential Park. Then, if I followed the wall round, I must come eventually to the quarter in which the house was.

I got there; but it took me well over half an hour and towards the end I began to think that I must be too late. The atmosphere of the city was extraordinary. Just by looking along a street you could see that something serious had happened. People stood about in small groups on the pavements outside their houses, talking very quietly. I had guessed right about the radio being off. Not a sound came from the open windows of the apartment houses. There were armoured cars about, too, parked at road junctions or slowly cruising. Vukashin must have been ready to put a standard emergency control plan into operation the instant he got back into the Ministry. As I walked along in the hot sun I began to see that I might have difficulty in leaving the city that night.

To my dismay there were several groups of people standing about outside the Deltchev house and, as I drew nearer, I saw that there were extra guards on the door. I wondered if Vukashin yet knew that there was no Philip Deltchev to be arrested. The chances were that, with Vukashin unable to admit to any precise understanding of the situation, things at the palace were still confused. The people waiting here in the street must have heard fantastic rumours and gravitated to the Deltchev house simply because it was the nearest place with important political associations. I could even reflect brutally that with Brankovitch dead the worst thing that could happen to me here now was that I would be refused admittance. The same Corporal was there. He was looking more sullen than usual and anxious. That probably meant that he knew nothing. I went up to him and he recognized me with a nod. I produced my papers. He glanced at them doubtfully and handed them back but made no signal to let me through.

'I don't know, *mein Herr*,' he said in German. 'I must await orders.'

'What orders?'

'Something has happened.'

'What?'

He shook his head uneasily. 'There are many rumours.'

'You mean the riot?'

He looked at me keenly. 'You know what it is?'

'There was a riot in the Square during the parade. The troops had to fire.'

'A riot? You are sure it is nothing more?'

'It was very serious I heard. Many were killed.'

228

'But a riot?' he insisted.

'But of course. I was told by an officer ten minutes ago.'

'An officer told you?'

'Yes. I have said . . .'

He sighed impatiently. 'These sheep!' he exclaimed, nodding towards the waiting people. 'These silly sheep, with their gossip! They tell me the Agrarian Socialists have attempted a *coup* and that a revolution has broken out. Sheep!' He spat and then grinned. 'A riot you say. I know a way with rioters.'

I grinned back. He nodded to one of the sentries. The bell pealed and after a bit came the familiar sound of Rana's sandals in the courtyard. I felt the eyes of the street upon me as I went in.

There was the same smell of furniture polish and the same slippery floors. There was the same room and she rose from the same chair to greet me. There were the same gentle, intelligent eyes below the same broad forehead and there was the same polite smile. And yet for me nothing was the same; I saw her now in a different context.

The smile went out. 'Herr Foster,' she said quickly, 'I am so glad you have come. What has happened? Something has. Rana says that there are people waiting outside in front of the house and additional guards. I don't understand it.'

I did not answer for a moment. Then I said: 'If you are asking me whether Aleko has succeeded, the answer is yes.'

'Aleko?'

'I have a train to catch, Madame. Perhaps it will save time if I tell you that Pashik and I have talked very frankly to one another and that at this moment, and because it has been difficult for Pashik to keep you fully informed, I know a great deal more about the affair than you do. I came to tell you what you don't already know.'

She stared at me and then very calmly sat down. 'I see. You are a messenger from Pashik.'

'No. Pashik doesn't know I'm here.'

'Where is he? With my son?'

'Your son is in Athens. Pashik is in the city somewhere.'

'You tell me Vukashin is dead. You saw it happen?'

'I did not say Vukashin was dead, Madame. I said that Aleko had succeeded. Brankovitch was assassinated just about an hour ago.'

'Brankovitch?' Her hands came down on the wooden arms of the chair with a violence that would have been painful if she had been able to feel pain at that moment.

'Yes, Brankovitch.'

'You saw it yourself?'

'Yes.'

'Well? Go on.'

I went on. It was difficult, for she kept interrupting with questions to not all of which I knew the answers. I said nothing of Katerina's visit. There was no reason to do so. She probably knew of it, anyway. When I had finished, she sat back slowly and shut her eyes. Her face was very smooth and beautiful.

'I am leaving for Athens on the five o'clock train. That's if they'll let me out, of course. I'll see Philip to-morrow. His signed statement and mine will be in New York, Paris and London by Tuesday at the latest. That will give Vukashin two days to make a fool of himself. After that he hasn't got a chance.'

Slowly she opened her eyes. 'My dear Herr Foster,' she said wearily, 'do you suppose that you can defeat men like Vukashin with external propaganda? The conception is naïve.'

'I rather thought it was yours.'

'Mine?' She stood up angrily. 'Pashik's, perhaps. Not mine. Don't you understand? They have defeated us.'

'Then you were defeated anyway.'

She shook her head. 'No. You see, Herr Foster, we could have come to terms with Brankovitch. He would have needed the Agrarian Socialists. He would have thought he was using them.'

'And your husband?'

She looked vague. 'Agreement could have been reached about that. An acquittal and then temporary retirement.'

In a very short space of time a lot of things went through my mind. Above them all, however, was the memory of my own voice asking if it were not dangerous to deny the street, and of the reply, the beautiful, saintly reply: *'For my children, yes. For me, no, for I shall not try to impose my private world upon the real.'*

I was aware then of a profound dislike of her and did not trouble to keep it out of my voice.

'Do you really believe that?' I asked.

She turned away to the window. 'Herr Foster,' she said thoughtfully, 'do you think you are safe here?'

It was very unexpected. My wretched stomach jerked unpleasantly. 'Safe?' I said.

'Aleko must realize by now what has been done by Pashik. You say he has already tried to kill you once. He might guess you were here.'

I saw then. I was being punished. I laughed. 'If Aleko realizes what has been done, he will be far too busy getting out of the country to trouble about me. I can't hurt him. If he doesn't know what's happened then he is most probably under arrest by now. In that case I don't think he would talk until he knew whether Vukashin was going to save him or not.'

'You are very confident,' she said coldly. 'I think you are unwise to stay here.'

'Then I shall go. I would like to say good-bye to your daughter if I may.'

'I will give her your message.'

'Is there any message you would like me to give your son?'

'Yes, Herr Foster. You may tell him if you will that he did well and that it is not our fault, his and mine, that we are defeated. If it is possible, Katerina and I will join him soon in Athens.'

'I'll tell him. There's one thing I would like to know.'

'Yes?'

'What induced your husband to make that election speech? What had gone wrong?'

'Nothing that would make a newspaper story, Herr Foster.'

'It is for my own information that I ask.'

She shrugged. 'As you please. It is no longer important, I suppose, what sort of a man my husband was.'

When she had told me, I left.

I did not go back to the hotel. I reached the station with half an hour to spare. My passport got me on to the train. The delay was at the frontier. It took me thirty-six hours to get to Athens and by that time the Vukashin account of the Brankovitch assassination was out. The assassin was a man named Alexander Gatin, and he, together with an accomplice named Pashik, had been shot and killed while resisting arrest.

Philip Deltchev was a pompous but amiable young man and very grateful for his mother's message. He said that it made him feel much better about everything. He was quite sure that she would contrive to join him. He did not mention his father.

Chapter 21

I saw the end of the Deltchev trial in the projection room of a newsreel company in London.

In the hard blacks and whites of the Propaganda Ministry's cameramen the scene looked more real than the one I remembered. Perhaps the film gave it an authority the original lacked. Or it may have been the sound track that produced the effect; there was no interpreter to divide one's attention. With the six reels of film which Brankovitch's successor had selected for foreign consumption a translation of the proceedings had been sent; but for the moment I wanted just to look at it; and to look at Deltchev.

There was not a great deal of footage which included him. Only one of the three cameras had covered the dock, and the film had been received in an edited form which favoured the judges and Dr Prochaska; but during one evident denunciation of the prisoner there was a shot that showed him frowning anxiously and shifting his position in a way that made him look guilty. Most likely the shot had some other true explanation – boredom or some physical discomfort – but for me, as for the Propaganda Ministry, it had another significance. The Propaganda Ministry saw a scheming villain brought to book. I saw a pre-war Minister of Posts and Telegraphs struggling to be a statesman. But then, I had listened to his wife.

It was the word 'Papa' that defeated him.

The first time Deltchev saw the word printed in front of his name it pleased him; for, knowing his countrymen, he recognized the note of wry affection in it. It meant that they trusted him and that, although they might grumble, they would accept hardship at his hands and would not hate him too intensely. With amused pride he showed the newspaper

233

to his wife and son. The small pang of anxiety he experienced he found unaccountable and ignored.

The nickname soon gained currency and its use was no longer an occasion for comment; but he did not, for some reason, get used to it. On the contrary; as time went by, he began to experience discomfort whenever he saw it or heard it used. It had begun to feel to him like an accusation.

'Yordan always invites criticism,' his wife had said; 'and always fears it.'

Deltchev was aware of the jokes about his motives and had hitherto thought himself a better and not more prejudiced judge of them. Shrewd he might be; yet in nineteen forty he had opposed the Nazis, not for any personal advantage – unless internment and oblivion were advantages – but because he had thought it right to do so. Ambitious he might be; yet he had organized the Committee of National Unity, not for the risk of dying a martyr's death at the hands of the Gestapo, but because he thought it right to do so. But now, with his power increasing daily and that word 'Papa' fastened to his name, he was no longer sure of himself. The whole climate of his thought and feeling seemed to be changing. If he were held in affection, trusted, he must be worthy. His conscience told him that he was not.

'Yordan is a self-torturer,' his wife had said.

A terrible conflict now began within him; and the battle ground chosen was the question of the election promise.

Reason and experience told him that the Provisional Government was the best that could be devised for the country in the present situation and that elections might well mean the accession of the People's Party to power. He believed that would be a disaster for the country. Reasoning, a lawyer's reasoning, told him, too, that the promise had been one of *free* elections and that the essential condition of freedom was not at present obtainable.

Yet the other voice, the cruel, accusing, contemptuous, punishing voice that haunted him, offered arguments of a different kind. 'Why are you so anxious?' it inquired. 'Why do you hesitate? Is it because you know in your heart that you have become corrupt and that these reasons you invent for keeping the power in your hands are mere devices to conceal the fact? Is it? You dictators are all the same! You whine that what you do is for the people's good and that they love and trust you. But when there is a chance that you may have to put that love and trust to the test, you find reasons – oh, excellent reasons! – why you should not do so. And the reasons are always to the same tune. It is for the people's good, you cry. That, my friend, is the spiral of corruption you are ascending. Government by consent of the governed! You know the phrase? Who are you to determine what government they shall consent to? Your power and their trust in you gives you a responsibility above your party interests. You see now the distinction between a statesman and a politician. The statesman has courage. Did you speak? Ah no! . . . not the courage of his convictions. (How you twist and turn, my friend, to avoid the truth!) The statesman has the courage to be impartial – even at the risk of his own destruction.'

He told no one until after it was over; and then he told his wife.

'My hands are clean,' he said. It was as though by violating all his own beliefs and interests, as well as those of other honest men, he had performed an act of absolution for some unnameable sin.

'Last reel,' said the cutter who was supervising the running. 'Judge's summing up and sentence.'

I looked at the screen again. I looked at the tired shell of a man who had been Yordan Deltchev and at the Presiding Judge delivering the sentence of death by hanging which had since been carried out.

There was silence in the courtroom after the sentence. Probably the spectators were expecting him to say something. But there was nothing. He nodded his head slightly and turned to go. The guards stepped forward. Then he climbed down from the dock and walked slowly away between them.

I recalled another departure he had made from the courtroom and the parallel I had attempted to draw from the trial of Socrates. My memory of it was better now. There were words more apt than the others I had chosen.

'*But, Sirs, it may be that the difficulty is not to flee from death, but from guilt. Guilt is swifter than death.*'

'That's the lot,' said the cutter. 'Would you like to see the assassination of Brankovitch? I've got it here.'

'No, thanks,' I said, 'I've seen it.'

Patrick O'Brian

Writing recently in the *London Review of Books*, John Bayley compared Patrick O'Brian's writing with that of his compatriot, J. G. Farrell:

'O'Brian, a similar and at least as great a talent [as Farrell] has to have a ship and the sea for his marvellously delicate and humorous fantasies set in Napoleon's day. They are emphatically not the kind of mechanical marine thrillers which sprang up in the wake of C. S. Forester. Smollett and Marryat are here being rewritten less for the excitement than for the feeling, as Dr Johnson said of Richardson: both O'Brian and Farrell share the wholly civilised, entirely good-humoured champagne Irishness of Laurence Sterne. . . .

'Like Farrell, O'Brian has solved in his own individual way the problem of getting history – in terms of habits, assumptions and ideas – into the texture of the novel . . . [Jack Aubrey] is a Lord Jim without the author's philosophic pretension, and in his context far more convincingly contrived. [In him] O'Brian's combination of sagacity and magic is at its best.'

Master and Commander	Treason's Harbour
Post Captain	Desolation Island
HMS *Surprise*	The Far Side of the World
The Mauritius Command	The Reverse of the Medal
The Fortune of War	
The Surgeon's Mate	*and in July 1989*
The Ionian Mission	The Letter of Marque

FONTANA PAPERBACKS

Dudley Pope

'Takes over the helm from Hornblower . . . Dudley Pope knows all about the sea and can get the surge of it into his writing.' *Daily Mirror*

'An author who really knows the ropes of Nelson's navy.' *Observer*

'The best of the Hornblower successors.'
Sunday Times

RAMAGE
RAMAGE AND THE DRUMBEAT
RAMAGE AND THE FREEBOOTERS
GOVERNOR RAMAGE R.N.
RAMAGE'S PRIZE
RAMAGE AND THE GUILLOTINE
RAMAGE'S DIAMOND
RAMAGE'S MUTINY
RAMAGE AND THE REBELS
THE RAMAGE TOUCH
RAMAGE'S SIGNAL
RAMAGE AND THE RENEGADES
RAMAGE'S DEVIL
RAMAGE'S TRIAL
RAMAGE'S CHALLENGE
RAMAGE AT TRAFALGAR

FONTANA PAPERBACKS

Fontana Paperbacks
Fiction

Fontana is a leading paperback publisher of both non-fiction, popular and academic, and fiction. Below are some recent fiction titles.

☐ FIRST LADY Erin Pizzey £3.95
☐ A WOMAN INVOLVED John Gordon Davis £3.95
☐ COLD NEW DAWN Ian St James £3.95
☐ A CLASS APART Susan Lewis £3.95
☐ WEEP NO MORE, MY LADY Mary Higgins Clark £2.95
☐ COP OUT R.W. Jones £2.95
☐ WOLF'S HEAD J.K. Mayo £2.95
☐ GARDEN OF SHADOWS Virginia Andrews £3.50
☐ WINGS OF THE WIND Ronald Hardy £3.50
☐ SWEET SONGBIRD Teresa Crane £3.95
☐ EMMERDALE FARM BOOK 23 James Ferguson £2.95
☐ ARMADA Charles Gidley £3.95

You can buy Fontana paperbacks at your local bookshop or newsagent. Or you can order them from Fontana Paperbacks, Cash Sales Department, Box 29, Douglas, Isle of Man. Please send a cheque, postal or money order (not currency) worth the purchase price plus 22p per book for postage (maximum postage required is £3.00 for orders within the UK).

NAME (Block letters) _____

ADDRESS _____

_____

_____